A Room in Blake's Folly

by

J. Arlene Culiner

A Room in Blake's Folly

Cover Art by *Jennifer Greeff*

The Wild Rose Press, Inc.
PO Box 708
Adams Basin, NY 14410-0708
Visit us at www.thewildrosepress.com

Publishing History
First Edition, 2022
Trade Paperback ISBN 978-1-5092-4202-3
Digital ISBN 978-1-5092-4203-0

Published in the United States of America

"Luck was on my side...finally. The night was very dark. There was no moon, and no clouds. I heard them leave the house, I saw them, and I knew where they were, where they went. When I sensed the time was right, I crawled out from my hiding space, slid along the ground on my belly, just like a snake. Headed out to those hills in the far distance. Running away from all I'd ever known was terrifying, but I knew I wouldn't survive otherwise."

"We're very far from Blake's Folly."

Her smile was slightly mocking. "My luck held. I saw a campfire. I didn't know who was out there, but I headed for it. Three men were passing through the area—oh, I knew they were probably up to no good, cattle rustlers or bandits keeping to the shadows—but what choice did I have? They fed me, kept me with them as they traveled north. Then, a few weeks later, they left me in Blake's Folly."

She had used the work "luck" twice, and he admired her spirit, the optimism and strength that had kept her alive, but he also knew what she was leaving out of the story.

Praise for J. Arlene Culiner

"Culiner has a knack for intertwining believable characters, plot, and setting, but her voice makes her book stand out."

~*The Book Breeze*

~*~

"Culiner's use of contemporary language and laissez-faire attitude is refreshing, yet endearing. Vivid details bring the reader up close with the town watering hole, the Mizpah Hotel. Locals are realistic in their time-gone-by colorful entertainment."

~*Lisa McCombs, Readers' Favorite*

~*~

"*BLAKE'S FOLLY* has seen better days, as have most of its residents—a rag-tag assembly of loners, misfits, and ne'er-do-wells. But looks can deceive, and the citizens blossom."

~*Deborah O'Neill Cordes, Writer*

~*~

"A must-read book unlike any other. There was an air of 'truth.' At the end is 'About the Author' and it made sense. She has lived a fascinating life."

~*Long and Short Reviews*

Acknowledgments

I am grateful to those who have helped bring this book to fruition.

Both the reviewer Christine L. and romance writer Deborah O'Neill Cordes wanted to read more about Blake's Folly, and their enthusiasm encouraged me to dig into the dusty town's past, learn about its earliest residents, and uncover their secrets. It was Deborah's old family photos that put faces on my characters.

Thanks to musician Jean Livingston and romance writer Dee S. Knight, who read through the first versions and gave me excellent suggestions, to Cheryl Pierson of Fire Star Press, who let me use extracts from a much earlier short story, and to artist Jennifer Greeff who has captured this book's essence with her intriguing cover.

Most sincere thanks to Eilidh MacKenzie, my wonderful editor at the Wild Rose Press. Her suggestions are invaluable, and it is always a treat to work with her.

And thanks to proofreader Les Tucker whose eagle eye missed nothing.

I

The Boomtown: 1889

If music be the food of love, play on,
Give me excess of it...
> ~William Shakespeare, *Twelfth Night*

"You trust Big Jim?" Resentment rippled down Westley Cranston's spine, meshed with scorn. "A lousy cad who jilted you when you were carrying his child? Who knew your bigoted family would kill you?"

Seemingly unperturbed, Sookie Lacey dipped her forefinger into the oily pot of carmine on her dressing table, spread the rosy salve over her lips. Turned, met Westley's eyes squarely. "Jim didn't have a choice. He was on the lam. He had to keep moving."

"Because he was wanted for a violent robbery! Why the hell are you making excuses for an unscrupulous criminal who forced himself on an impoverished family?"

"You weren't out in this part of the world back then. You can't even imagine that winter when cattle froze to death on the prairie. How could anyone, good or bad, have survived in the open?"

"And while hiding out with your family, he seduced you."

"Seduced!" Her nostrils flared. "Being with Jim

1

protected me from my vicious brother, my depraved father, I told you that. They both tried to have their way with me."

It was an old argument, one they'd had many times. Why couldn't Sookie see that Big Jim's perfidy could have ruined her life—would have ruined her life if she'd been a weaker woman? A pregnant fifteen-year-old runaway when she arrived in Blake's Folly, Sassy Sookie had gone to work as a prostitute in the Red Nag Saloon. It wasn't the lowest sort of brothel, but it wasn't a classy parlor house either. Yet, clever, lighthearted, and a favorite with the men, she soon realized her own worth. Never succumbing to the temptations of alcohol or laudanum, she'd left the Red Nag, come to the Mizpah, and as a saloon girl, made such excellent money selling dance tickets, encouraging men to buy alcohol, and to gamble, she no longer needed to sell herself.

"So, four years after jilting you, Jim walks into the Mizpah, sees you've become successful, and decides to stake his claim. That makes him a decent man?"

"He's changed. Jim has become a respectable businessman, and he wants to marry me. He's building us a big fine house where we can live together with our little son."

"Where? Where will this wonderful fine house be?"

"In Virginia City."

"Have you ever been there? Seen what he's building?"

"You know I haven't. Jim's been on the road for the last five months. He sends me letters from Denver, San Francisco, New Orleans, and Phoenix."

How can she be so blind? Westley took a deep breath, forced himself to sound steady and reasonable, not like a man hopelessly in love with the woman he would soon lose. "And what about us? What about what we shared? The nights you spent in my arms?" Nights when she had given herself without reticence but with warmth, tenderness.

Sookie stood, shook out the short, ruffled skirt and colorful petticoats floating just below her shapely calves. Her golden beauty, caught in the lamp's uneven flicker, made his heart ache. How desirable she was in the low-cut sequined bodice that barely hid the sweetness of her breasts.

"Westley, what you and I shared is our secret. A delicious secret that no one else can know about or even suspect, particularly since Jim has sent Doug Lazy here to protect me."

"To spy on you, you mean."

Sookie's chin tilted defiantly. "Think what you'd like. Just don't forget I'm marrying Jim in September."

Pushing past him, she swept out of her boudoir and into the long dark corridor. The tapping of her tasseled kid boots on the stair held a note of finality.

****

Leaning on the mahogany, the Mizpah's long bar, Westley watched Sookie dance in the arms of cowboys, trappers, and miners with the price of a ticket; also with the town's "respectable" citizens: politicians, businessmen, the silver barons and their sons, the judge, the sheriff, all of them righteous moralists who left their prudish sour-faced wives at home.

In Ned Hardy's establishment, the so-called soiled doves, nymphs of the prairie, scarlet ladies, fallen angels, or painted cats didn't entertain men in upstairs bedrooms—not unless the price and the situation were unusual. This was a respectable saloon, unlike the town's lesser houses. In those other taverns, cheating three-card monte scams were the rule; women picked drunken men's pockets or sold sham room keys to doors that never unlocked; and bloody sport—animal baiting, dog, cock, and badger fights—took place in back courtyards. Here, Neddy's saloon girls were his profitable commodities, and he protected them valiantly, catering to their whims, allowing romance, although that usually ended in a woman's marriage and financial loss to himself.

Westley wondered if Neddy had known of his own liaison with Sookie. Had he realized that, when the dancing was over and the ladies had retired upstairs, Sookie slipped down the passageway leading to his room? That theirs had been a love story, one rich with discovery and promise? He wanted nothing more than to marry her, take her far away from this life, this town. He would be leaving soon, heading north to the Yukon, taking up the offer to run a new newspaper. If she accepted his proposal, they could go on together to adventure.

Their relationship had started as friendship, when he'd opened his library to her, for he appreciated her quick mind, her thirst for the knowledge that had always been denied her. He'd known she was betrothed to the absent Big Jim, but fascinated by her intelligence and beauty, Westley had fallen in love. And one early spring night, when the soft air held a new season's promise, they had passed each other in the dark, stopped, turned, and then come closer.

Their nights of lovemaking had continued over months, and each new day without Big Jim's reappearance had given Westley hope that Sookie would decide in his favor, would accept their love story was the right one. He'd held her tight, loving her touch, the sweet scent of her skin, and the warmth of her heavy golden hair. Burying himself deep inside her, he had imprinted his body on hers, showing her they were one, and that their love was eternal.

But if Jim hadn't returned, his henchman, Doug Lazy, had. And Sookie's visits to his room ceased. Only temporarily, he decided. He would do his best to ensure they began again.

****

Hattie smelled the town long before they arrived. What a stink: she hadn't been prepared for it. Despite the morning's unusual heat, she pressed her shawl tightly to her nose. Terrible odors, a mixture of rotting garbage, dung heaps with human and animal waste, of blood and offal left to rot beside butcher shops, all booty for snuffling pigs and stray dogs. She saw decomposing corpses, too, those of animals lying where they'd fallen, and some had obviously been there for weeks, magnets for clouds of flies. More gruesome still were the hanged men swinging from gibbets at the town's entry, a warning to horse thieves and cattle rustlers. Justice was swift out here: arrest and punishment took place within hours.

Yet, she couldn't help feeling a little thrill as they rumbled down the uneven, rutted town streets, passing busy shops, wooden sidewalks, and crowds of people. She'd been away from the hustle and bustle of the world for so long, yet here she was. Finally. She had escaped. *And now that you're here, what exactly are you planning to do?* She silenced the niggling voice, quashed her fear. *Just concentrate on this lively panorama. You haven't seen anything like it for years, not since you left Baltimore.*

Axel's cart came to a halt in front of the Mizpah Saloon. The peddler looked over at her but didn't say a word. He'd hardly said a word for some seventy-two hours—not to her, anyway—and this was the end of the line. He wouldn't take her one step farther, for Axel had little charity left in him. A frail old man with a rattling wagon full of buttons, needles, shell boxes, cigarette cases, combs, and brooches, he was doomed to wander over the prairie with his wares until too old to move. Then what? Cut his sad shambling nag free of her bridle, lie down where he was, and wait for death.

Still, he'd done her a favor, one she had paid for with the last of her riches—a few silver spoons, a shawl of old-fashioned lace, a gilt mirror, a few books— things from her girlhood, that she had brought from the East. Precious things she'd hated to give away. But they had bought her freedom. In exchange, she'd had three days of travel under a relentless sun alongside roads so rutted no vehicle could use them, forging rivers where one false step could land you in quicksand or carry you to your death. But every mile they'd traveled took her away from the bleak place she'd called home, and far from her husband, Sam Graham. Too far for him to come looking for her, if that's what he ever intended to do.

Along the way, they had stopped at one austere homestead farm after another, where Axel plied wares to folk who might never see a town or a shop. To exhausted women who watched her suspiciously, showed no warmth, and certainly no mercy. Not to women like her, the outcasts. She couldn't blame them: their lives consisted of raising numerous children, endless washing, cooking, fighting vermin, bugs, weather, illness, and hopelessness. Were their men as brutal as her own husband had been? Some were, certainly. Others must be worse still. Western men thought their role was to dominate women, and domestic violence was widespread out here. Yet, most abused wives stuck it out, believing their married status and a promised place in God's heaven were worth beatings, black eyes, split lips, and broken bones.

Humanity leached out of them by hardship, those women took out their frustration on those even lower down: divorcees, concubines, rejected wives, barren women, widows whose husbands had been killed in warfare or brawls, saloon girls, and prostitutes. Yet divorce was easily available. Women could get one on grounds of alcoholism, abandonment, or extreme violence; men could divorce women who refused to wash clothes, cook, or have children. It was after divorce that things became tricky. Men married again, but women? Some became laundresses, or seamstresses, or they ran boarding houses. Those with no home base had little option other than prostitution.

Hattie almost laughed at the thought. Surely, she would never be considered a lady of pleasure. She was too worn out, too tired. What man would want a woman ground down by the prairie's hard life and a man's brutality? She might even have to depend on Salvation Army soup kitchens or begging, for fate was a two-faced proposition, granting some an easy life, beauty, riches, and talent, but throwing scraps to the rest.

Axel was still waiting. No, it couldn't be put off any longer. Squaring her shoulders, Hattie grabbed her round bundle of belongings, stepped out of the cart, and stared up at the solid two-story building. This was where her fate lay—perhaps. Taking a deep breath, head high, she marched up the steps, crossed the wooden plank sidewalk to the high twin wood-and-glass doors of the Mizpah Saloon. Opened them. Stepped into her future.

****

"I'm looking for work."

One elbow propped casually on the mahogany, one foot on the brass rail, Westley observed the woman who had just addressed Neddy. Work, she wanted? What sort of work did she think she would get here? She was your typical schoolmarm, strict, dried-up, and unrelenting-looking. Did she think she could join the saloon's dancing girls, audacious ladies like Sookie, who waltzed men to pleasure, had them eager to spend hard-earned cash? If so, she was sadly mistaken. Sure, men might want that schoolmarm rectitude in their stay-at-home wives, but it was the sensual world in here that attracted them.

This woman, well…he could guess her story before hearing it: a widow, rejected wife, or runaway, she had surely been a sweet-looking wide-eyed girl once upon a time, but life had since taken its toll, and he felt sorry for her. Her skin was tired, her eyes had no sparkle, and her shabby frock was grimy from travel. Still, she held herself tall, her head high. Yes, she obviously still had pride. But hope? Probably not.

"The peddler Axel dropped me off here. He said

8

you'd know who's looking for hired help in town."

Westley saw Ned's slow nod, could see the sympathy on his friend's face. Out here, only the toughies did well. This woman, she didn't look brash or tough. She didn't even look like a candidate for a new husband.

Once upon a time, some twenty, thirty years ago, women had been scarce in the West, and husband-hunters, whether ugly or good-looking, mean-tempered, sharp-tongued, or sugar sweet had easily found partners. Nowadays, things were different. Women were arriving in abundance, fleeing domestic service, poor farms, mill work, or factory toil, and men could take their pick. They went for the young, fresh ones, women to replace wives who had died in childbed or from exhaustion. Strong women to raise children, attend to harvests, garden work, and laundry, to scrounge for firewood, and cook. Older women? The luckiest had grown children who could take them in, but not everyone wanted a mother or mother-in-law in residence, especially if she were no longer capable of helping out with the drudgery.

"I can cook, clean." The woman's voice was clear, steady. As steady as those hazel eyes. No, she had no illusions about her appeal. Cook and clean? She didn't look as if she had the strength for jobs like that. She was too thin, too frail. Ned must be thinking the same.

"Don't need a cook. Don't need more hired help here in the saloon." He continued wiping a glass with undue assiduity.

"I suppose I'm not the only woman who's come asking for work this week, either."

It wasn't a question, just a statement made without

despair or bitterness, as if she had no illusions left. The woman surely had guts, you had to give her that.

"No, you aren't," Ned conceded before turning to him. "What have you heard, Westley? Anyone come into your newspaper office, looking to hire?"

Ned was buying time, Westley knew that. He didn't want to turn her away. That bundle by her feet must contain everything she owned in the world, yet there was something classy and educated about her. Something that told him she'd come a long way from her origins. *Just like you have.* Shoving the thought to the back of his mind, he mulled over possible occupations that might suit a woman like her. He couldn't think of a thing…with one dazzling exception…

"Not unless you know how to play the piano."

The woman turned those unwavering eyes to him. Finally. Sized him up, took in his fashionable clothes, his well-shined boots, his casual pose. Did she approve? Impossible to tell. She looked as though a million thoughts were running through her head. Then, she nodded. "I do."

"Well, how about that, Ned. Isn't that a lucky break?" Westley couldn't hide the laughing triumph in his voice. Pushing himself away from the counter, he came to stand beside her. Grinned over at his friend. "A piano player's exactly what you're looking for."

Ned blinked as if dazed. "I'm looking for a piano player, all right. But not a lady player."

"Man, woman—what difference does it make?" Now that his mind had grabbed the idea, Westley was going to fight for it. "You need a piano player, Ned. Fast. Men come here to dance with the girls. Sure, a banjo and a fiddle are fine, but they aren't noisy enough, and you'll lose custom. A couple of the men have already gone over to the Red Nag, and it might be hard to wean them back, especially since they're offering jugglers and a minstrel show over there."

Ned was looking at him as if he'd lost his mind. He probably had. Why the hell was he making such an effort to convince his friend to take the woman on, give her a chance? He knew nothing about her; she was nothing to him. This really was ridiculous.

"Westley," Ned said calmly, "this is a saloon. A lady player in a saloon?"

Westley looked down at the woman right beside him. Her calm eyes shifted between him and Ned. She wasn't in the least intimidated by these two men now deciding her fate.

"Waltzes, polkas, mazurkas, any dance tune, that's what I know how to play," she said, her voice even. "Sentimental songs too. And if anyone wants it, lots of classical music."

Ned was still wiping that same glass he'd been working on when she'd walked into the Mizpah, but Westley felt a smile growing on his own lips. *Good girl.* Tired, skinny, wearied out, she still knew how to defend herself.

"Look, lady, this is a saloon—" Ned began.

"Yes, I know perfectly well what sort of business this is," she said, effectively cutting him off. "And I understand what you're saying, too. But dance tunes are still dance tunes. A piano player is a piano player."

"And a saloon is a saloon. People come here to drink and gamble, and they do a lot of both. Both make men mean, and fist fights can get nasty, especially when knives and guns come into play. You know what happened to Mister Bob, the last piano player we had? Met a stray bullet. Right over there." Ned's head jerked in the direction of an upright piano, deep in the murky depths of the large room.

"I see." She didn't look as though the news fazed her. She even looked strangely amused. "But since both of you seem to be alive and breathing, stray bullets can't be an everyday feature."

Westley couldn't stop his own roar of laughter. Even Ned was smiling now. He put down that glass. "Look, lady, no matter what you think, this ain't no fancy ballroom. The girls who work here get paid by the dance. They also get paid to encourage men. And a few of them, if the price is right, might go off somewheres to make a man happy. You know what I'm talking about?"

"I do." Her voice was dry, and her chin went a notch higher. "But a piano player is here to get those men dancing with your girls, not to make men happy, so I don't see how it affects me."

Westley was still grinning. Any pity he'd felt a few minutes ago had vanished. He decided he liked her.

"Still," Ned continued, "you'd be better off looking for work as a piano teacher. This town needs a constant supply of school and music teachers, because there's a big turnover. Out here, before a lady can say jackrabbit, she's married."

Impossible to overlook the tightening of her lips, the slight narrowing of her eyes. "Well, I can guarantee that's not my ambition. And if I had a piano, a home, or even a room, being a music teacher might be a reasonable solution. But I've just arrived in this town from far away, and it's work I'm looking for. You seem to be in the position to offer me that."

Ned was silent for a minute, perhaps impressed by the woman's mettle. "Lady, if you think you can handle cussing, lousy behavior, and drunks, the job's yours."

"I can." Curt and definite. "So it's settled, then?"

His nod was a reluctant assent. "Okay, ma'am. Give it a try." He probably didn't think she would stick it out. Westley hoped she'd prove him wrong, that she wouldn't disappoint either of them—although why that was important, he didn't know.

"I'm Ned Hardy. This newspaper hack taking up floor space is Westley Cranston. And your name is?"

There was a second's hesitation. "Paumier. Hattie Paumier."

Westley caught the reluctance. Paumier? French background, if that was her real name. It might be, or it might have been...once. He had the feeling that her legitimate name, the one she wasn't giving them, was her husband's. Well, that wasn't unusual out here. He looked over at Ned and winked. "Room and board come with the job, right, Neddy?"

He couldn't miss the relief washing over Hattie Paumier's face. Couldn't miss Ned's surprise either.

****

"Room's clean," said Beatie, the sour-faced saloon cook who'd shown her up here. "Not like some places here in town. Nests for vermin, that's what they are."

This was it. The hoped-for miracle had happened. Hattie looked around this space that was now hers, perhaps for the rest of her life—who knew?—a tiny room near the landing of the first-floor corridor. It was no bigger than a closet, barely wide enough for a narrow cot, a chair, a rickety washstand with a porcelain basin and, on its bottom shelf, a chamber pot. The one tiny window was so high up, she couldn't see out. What was there to see anyway? Pushing the chair beneath it, she climbed up, peered onto a back courtyard with animal sheds, a water trough, and the public privy: at least that convenience was in a little hut to preserve the dignity of women and children.

So what if this was as basic as you could get? It was a sight more civilized than that poor shack she'd called home four days ago, half sunk into the ground, with a dirt floor, battered wooden table, straw-filled mattress, four chairs, three wooden boxes for household items and clothing. For decoration, she'd once cut a few pictures from old newspapers and pinned them on the lumpy walls.

These four hooks would be where Hattie could hang her clothes. They'd do perfectly. She had only two tired-out frocks in coarse material, mended over and over, turned back to front when the fabric had worn too thin, sewn, and re-sewn. She did have one good dress, thank goodness, the one she'd worn when she'd first come west with all her hopes intact. The same dress she'd been married in, when she'd allowed herself dreams.

Why think of that disastrous marriage now? That was in the past. She was here, in a safe haven. For how long? Perhaps she would hold down the job of piano player for merely one night, perhaps for a few days, but that would buy her time: thinking time, planning time. For the moment, luck was on her side. She wasn't sleeping in the street, and she hadn't been left to die of starvation. The saloon owner, Ned Hardy, seemed a good-hearted man, and without her asking, he had told Beatie to provide her with hot bean soup and fresh bread—the first decent things she'd had to eat in days. Now it was up to her. Starting tomorrow evening at eight o'clock, she had to prove her worth. Make people dance. What a joke!

Play piano? Oh yes, she'd been able to do just that, but that was long ago. She looked down at her dry, wrinkled, work-worn hands. What sprightly reels could they thrum up these days? Years had passed since she'd lived in the pretty red brick house in Baltimore with Aunt Agatha, taking lessons with the churlish widow Wilson. She had worked her way through endless scales, Kulau sonatinas, and Strauss waltzes, suffered a wooden ruler's cruel smack at every false note. And once she was able to play with ease, Aunt Agatha had forced her to sit for hours, churn out the elegant dances from her own youth, when engaged to a handsome army captain. But that brave soldier had died at Antietam alongside twenty thousand others on a mild September day in 1862, and Agatha, bitter, half mad, lived on in a world of illusion.

How often had Hattie dreamt of escaping her aunt's despotism? She pictured marriage to a handsome man with a fine black moustache, one who would watch adoringly while she, in flowing white muslin, played entrancing concertos. Or perhaps she would give concerts in palm courts. To make certain she would succeed, she'd taught herself to replicate the songs of passing marching bands and street players as well as the better music heard in church. But before her fantasies could be realized, Aunt Agatha died, and life projected her into quite another world.

Hattie smiled wryly. Never could she have imagined that a piano, once an instrument of tyranny, would one day save her. What would her severe and prim aunt have said if she'd known that her shy little niece would end up playing bouncy tunes in a bawdy house in the Far West? She closed her eyes. Yes, the melodies were still here, in her head. Would they be adequate? Would they be enough to get men and women dancing? She didn't know. Perhaps early tomorrow morning, when the saloon was closed and everyone slept, she could sneak down, practice. She had to do well. She couldn't lose face. Especially after that other man, the newspaper person, had come to her defense. What had Ned Hardy said his name was? Westley Cranston.

Involuntarily, she shivered. She'd noticed him as soon as she'd entered the saloon, had seen him leaning, one elbow on the mahogany. A dangerous man? She hadn't been afraid of him, not exactly. It had been something else. Dark-haired, a dark moustache, his black hat underlined the tawny, sun-honed skin. He had obviously done well for himself, was beautifully dressed in a white shirt with starched collar—she hadn't seen one of those in a long time—and a ribbon cravat with its shiny stone, a striped vest, and dark frock coat. He was so much like the imaginary prince of her youthful dreams, the one who should have come to rescue her.

But those daydreams had nothing to do with reality, and she was not the sort of woman a man like that would choose. How he'd watched her with those dark, clever eyes of his, as if reading her soul. A man who knew women well. And, gut instinct told her, a man to avoid thinking about.

****

Making as little noise as possible, Hattie crept down to the saloon's main room where the smell of alcohol, tobacco smoke, and perfume still hung on the early morning air. As she'd hoped, there was no one about—the "ladies" were probably all sound asleep after the night's activities. What were they like? Would they jeer at her raggedy clothes, her inexperience, or, would she be invisible, just the woman who tapped out notes on the piano? There was so much she didn't know. After life out on that prairie homestead, she felt as naïve as a child, and anxiety had kept her tossing sleeplessly in her narrow bed.

By the gentle light, she took in everything she'd been too nervous to see yesterday: the main room with its long mahogany, the back bar with its shelves of long-necked bottles and cigar display case, the door with a sign reading Water Closet, the steadily ticking wall clock, the gold-framed paintings, the large mirrors. A long runner rug protected glossy wooden floors; brass spittoons and foot rails gleamed; and high above was a finely patterned tin ceiling. Yes, this sure was a classy-looking place, notwithstanding the many salacious photos of half-clad women on the papered walls. And right over there, past a row of tables, was the piano.

She moved over to it, lifted its lid, let her fingers stroke the keyboard. Then, pulling out the stool, she sat, put her left foot on the damper pedal before pressing down a key. The piano's soft tinkle was strangely reassuring, as if it had been waiting for her touch, for someone who could make lovely sounds. It was a friendly instrument. It would be on her side.

A friendly instrument? Nonsense! Scornfully, she chased away fanciful thoughts and tried to remember polkas, schottisches, and Virginia reels. What had she heard when she'd first arrived in the West, that one time Sam had taken her to the Shaw's farm for an evening of cribbage and cards? Alf Shaw had played the fiddle, his wife Nelly, the melodeon, and two of the pieces had been "Old Zip Coon" and "Leather Breeches." Slowly, Hattie picked out the jumpy melodies. Funny how things you thought you'd forgotten years ago came back when you really needed them—although this stiffness in her fingers would have to be overcome, and that would take long weeks of work. She moved on to other numbers with more confidence, and much relief. Until a faint noise startled her.

Turning, she saw a man sitting at a table at the far end of the room. She half rose, embarrassed at having been caught out. And by Westley Cranston of all people. The very man she'd sworn to avoid. She could see his smile, all the way over here.

"Didn't mean to startle you," he drawled. "But I couldn't help stopping, listening to you play."

She settled back onto the stool. "Oh." Certainly not a clever remark. How long had he been there? How long had she played? Early light had slipped away, given way to golden sunbeams dancing across the wooden floor. "I hope I haven't woken everyone up…"

He laughed. "If you have, that's a very pleasant way to have done it. You have a nice touch. But why are you starting so early in the morning? The girls won't slide into their dancing shoes until this evening."

His tone teased. She wasn't used to teasing, and not knowing how to react, she defended herself. "I woke up early to do some practicing...I'm...I haven't played in a long time." Even she heard the slightly panicked note in her voice. Had he caught it too?

"And that worries you?"

"It does."

"Then you don't know what cowboys call music. Out on the ranches, when they're really lucky, someone can play a one-stringed fiddle, a mouth harp, or a harmonica. But mostly, the boys do what they call singing: onomatopoeic noises, mixed with Indian cries and yodels."

Hattie's laughter could only join his, despite her terrible doubts. Then she sobered. "You're trying to make me feel better."

"Not at all. I've spent time out on the plain and over in the mines. Believe me, the very best anyone gets out in those places are off-key old Irish or German songs. What you're doing on that piano will be magic to their ears."

"Magic?" Her lips quirked. "Well, perhaps not magic, but I want to do a decent job. And this piano does have a nice sound."

"She sure does, even if she's a girl with a lot of experience behind her. Came west on a wagon, way back when, and made it to here. She was one of the lucky ones. Most pianos got dumped along the way because they were far too heavy. This one got covered in a lot of river mud during her travels, but the boys in town cleaned her up nicely. Now she's as pretty as you please." He paused for a minute. "I guess you've been stuck out on the prairie for some time."

There was a little silence, as if he were waiting for her to say more. How had he known? And what business was it of his? Then again, what did she have to hide? When people wanted to know about you, they snooped and dug until they gleaned all they could, then slapped together a mighty skewed version of the truth. She took a deep breath. "Yes, you're right. I've been trapped out on a homestead farm for years. Not much chance of piano playing out there."

He nodded, but she hadn't satisfied his curiosity she could tell. "You a widow?"

"No." She could hear the tightness in her voice and feel the tension in her shoulders.

His eyes glinted. "A runaway wife."

"Not that either." Did she have to say more? She didn't. But since people were bound to be asking that same question over and over, she might as well get used to it, even though the answer was only partially true. Even though it could never express what her life had been like up until now. "I left of my own accord, but with my husband's full agreement. He'll be looking into getting a divorce."

"And your children?"

Ah, there it was. The big question, the one thing everyone would be curious about. "No children. I've never had any."

He said nothing. Had he heard the note of anger in her voice? She'd done her best to sound neutral, but neutrality wasn't an easy note to hit. How vividly she remembered the first time she'd caught sight of her future husband, Sam Graham, waiting with a little knot of men by a shanty train station in the middle of nowhere. He and the others had been eager to grab a sight of their brides-to-be, women lured west by the promise of marriage, land, and a home. How had the other women fared? Had they been as discouraged as she at the sight of the vast lonely wasteland, the emptiness, the bleached-out colors, and the coarse men who would be their lifetime partners? Men honed by the elements, a hard life. And rough alcohol.

Westley Cranston stood, walked in her direction—no, walk wasn't the word she could use. He sauntered, a slow, elegant saunter. A man sure of himself, of his power to seduce. Yes, that was why she'd felt so wary yesterday. He stopped when he was standing beside her. Smiled. No, there was nothing seductive in his smile. She'd been wrong. What had she been imagining? That she was still the young attractive woman she'd been years ago? What a fool she was.

He touched the top of the piano with a gesture that was almost a caress. "Don't worry. You'll do well. The boys you'll be playing with are good musicians, nice guys, too. They play at all the dances in town, and they'll teach you the sort of pieces folks out here are used to hearing."

"Thank you."

His eyebrows rose. "For what?"

"For being so kind."

"Kind?" He guffawed. "It's not kindness. I'm fighting for survival. High time we got a good piano player in this place. Bob, before he let that stray bullet hit him, knew how to slap at the keys, all right, but he didn't know the first thing about keeping time. I'll bet pretty well all the customers were happy to see him taken out of the running." Grinning, he moved away in that casual easy way of his, headed toward the front door. Then stopped, looked back, his eyes twinkling. "But they couldn't do that, not legally, anyway. One of the rules here in town forbids shooting pistols in a barroom."

She grinned back at him. "Sounds like a pretty good rule to me. And what are the other rules, if you don't mind me asking. If there are any others, that is…"

"Sure there are. Need plenty of rules in boomtowns, especially after payday. The other ones are, you can't insult a woman, you can't ride a pony or horse on the wooden sidewalks, and you can't ride them inside this establishment or any other business in town." He was chuckling again when he turned the lock, stepped out into the street, and disappeared.

Hattie remained seated at the piano. Her anguish had totally vanished. Amazing, how he had put her at ease. He hadn't judged her, hadn't looked at her with disgust when she'd told him some of her story, hadn't condemned her for feeling unsure about her piano playing. She wondered why she'd felt so mistrustful. He had behaved like a perfect gentleman—and a friend.

Then another thought struck her. What had he been doing here in the Mizpah so early in the morning? Had he slept here? Obviously he had. Hadn't he just let himself out? And that meant he had probably spent the night with one of the ladies upstairs. That he was a client.

Disappointment washed over her. She couldn't condemn him—men had needs, desires. Why was she so saddened by the thought?

****

In the palatial dining room of the Emerald Hotel, it was easy to forget that Blake's Folly was a rough boomtown of mud streets where violence reigned. In here, there were no drunken cowboys, no rough miners, and no farmhands. Over in one corner, a full orchestra played, and instead of the pancakes and beans that were the staple of every other town eatery, there were oysters on the menu, lobster, salad, fresh vegetables, and fresh salmon.

Westley's eyes feasted on Sookie, seated opposite him, her golden hair glowing, her candid blue eyes steady. How he loved her, her desire for knowledge, and her passion for books. At least she'd been taught to read out on that isolated farm where she'd grown up, even though the reading material had been narrowed down to religious tracts.

These days she savored everything, from John Rollin Ridge's biography of the West's Robin Hood-like bandit, Murietta, to Westley's newest acquisition, McCook's *American Spiders and Their Spinning Work.* She even shared his fascination for those useful but unloved creatures; and together they had searched window ledges and corners, found the blobbed matting of *Ciniflo*, the funnel-shaped lairs of *Agelena*, and the exquisite webs of *Aranea.* What a superior mind she had, one that would be wasted on a brutish oaf like Big Jim Bally.

"Doug Lazy is beginning to frighten me," she said, her fingers toying with a heavy silver spoon. "He is always there. I've even seen him late at night, lurking in the upstairs corridor of the Mizpah. I know Jim sent him to Blake's Folly to keep an eye on me, make sure I'm safe, but I hate the way Doug looks at me…the way he follows me…"

Tamping down his ire, Westley bit back the spicier

words in his vocabulary. "What the hell was he doing upstairs in the Mizpah?"

"Sometimes, he…well…it's Laney-Mae. She's…" Sookie swallowed.

"Does Neddy know?"

"No, he doesn't. Please, Westley. Don't tell him."

He leaned forward, still managing to keep his voice under control. "Don't tell him? Why?"

"Because you can't play the knight in shining armor, not in a situation like this. I'll tell Jim when I write to him, but you keep out of it. I don't want anyone to know about us. It could be too dangerous for you."

"And for you?"

"No, I don't think so."

"Think? But you don't know, do you." He felt his exasperation build. "Sookie, look at me, please. Keep looking at me. Tell me why you put up with this? Try to imagine what life with Big Jim Bally will be like. Don't you see what will happen?"

"No. I don't," she said, her voice calm. "I can't see into the future, not any more than you can."

"But you believe in Jim's promises of a big house, an easy life."

She raised her hands, a gesture of submission. "He loves me."

"I love you. Very much. And you love me. It's that simple."

"Westley. Please. We're so different. I need security, a peaceful life, everything I didn't have when I was younger. I want to live in that big house Jim is building in Virginia City. I want a comfortable, secure nest. I want my little son Clarence to have a stable home, to go to school and become somebody one day. I don't want him raised in a tent, or out in some empty cold wilderness. You, me…we'd only be unhappy together when things got rough. When being on the road wore me down, or when enforced immobility ate at your soul."

Was she right? Possibly. A doctor's son, he had come from a stable background, one he'd rejected. Like many men who'd ended up out here, he had a gambler's mentality: he needed to take chances, feel risk. He couldn't give up his dreams for her, but she wouldn't abandon hers for him. Checkmate.

She touched his hand. "Let's talk of more pleasant things. Savor this time together."

He caught her fingers in his. Brought them to his mouth, kissed them. How he wanted her. Why ruin the moment? He couldn't win this round, but the fight wasn't over, not yet. "All right," he said. "What sort of pleasant things?"

She smiled with grateful relief. "Neddy told me he's hired a lady piano player."

"That's certainly true."

She cocked an amused eyebrow. "You've met her?"

"I was there when she came in yesterday, asking for work. And I spoke with her this morning."

"Really? What's she like?"

"An interesting woman, I think. She certainly plays the piano well enough, but I think she's had a hard time with a bad husband."

"Another runaway wife?"

"A rejected wife. She could do with a little kindness."

Sookie smiled. "I'll make sure she gets some of

that."

"I know you will. I've never known you to do otherwise." Wasn't generosity her most endearing trait? Hadn't it placed her firmly in Big Jim's hands?

****

The women—the painted dance ladies—standing near the stairwell stopped their bright chatter to gawp at Hattie as she approached. She would have circumvented them if she could, avoided running the gauntlet of their bold scrutiny, but how else could she get to the stairs? Their unfriendly eyes sized her up, came to heaven-only-knew what conclusion. Just look at her, in her one good dress, dark and sober; look at them, in various stages of undress, with their loose diaphanous peignoirs, their lacy underclothes, their embroidered colorful stockings—Hattie hadn't even known those existed, stockings that weren't black and modest. Thank heaven, they couldn't see her own sewn-together undergarments, the stock of prairie women with no money for town finery, made out of flour and sugar sacks, whatever you could get your hands on.

"Who might you be?" The hostile-sounding question came from the rouged lips of a large woman, fleshy and opulent.

Hattie wouldn't allow herself to be intimidated. She met the woman's stare evenly. "I'm the new piano player."

"Is that so?" The plump mouth curled. Behind her, another girl, smaller, hard-faced, tittered.

"Yes, that's so." Hattie kept her voice dry, controlled. "I'm the one who will be playing the music that gets men dancing and keeps money coming into your pockets. So you see, we're to be partners, in a way."

"Last piano player met a bullet. Shot straight in the heart. Didn't stand a chance."

"Which is why I now have a job."

"Betty, why are you making the woman miserable?" said a new voice.

Hattie turned. A smiling blonde woman had appeared, a lovely creature, despite the heavy paint. She approached, linked her arm through Hattie's, and led her down the hallway. "Come on, everybody, let's go into the sitting room, get to know each other better before we all go downstairs." She smiled at Hattie. "What's your name, sweet lady?"

"Hattie."

The blonde woman laughed. "Just plain Hattie? All of us are something more. I'm Sassy Sookie." She jabbed her chin in the direction of the women who had followed them. "There's Snaggle-tooth Sally, Big Betty, Rodeo Liz, Rosie Ready, Lift-em Em, and Laney-Mae. So you'll just have to do the same, choose a colorful moniker. How about Harmony Hattie?"

The room was filled with an odd assortment of chairs and couches. It was much like a conventional middle-class sitting room anywhere, and there was a large selection of books in a cabinet near the window. She caught a glimpse of *Godey's Magazine*, the familiar covers of *Beadle's Dime Novels*—the story on the top was *Lights and Shadows of Orphan Life*. Hattie planned to peruse them all. Books had been impossible to come by in the years with Sam.

Sookie turned to the large woman who had followed them. "Betty was just trying to see if you scare easily, weren't you, Betty? We all know Neddy hired you on as a lady piano player." Settling into a comfortable settee, she pulled Hattie down beside her. "Westley Cranston gave me the information, and I passed the news around."

Hattie hoped her face was utterly expressionless, but she now knew with whom Westley Cranston had spent the night. She couldn't blame him. Sassy Sookie was every man's fantasy. She couldn't help wishing she could conjure up some of the same loveliness and freshness, but those qualities had vanished, victims to a scorching sun and endless wind. "Westley seems like a very nice man," she ventured.

"Oh, he is. He's a wonderful man." Sookie's eyes softened, and a secret smile tilted her lips. "But you never know how long he'll be sticking around. He's a drifter, moves from one place to the next, never settles down permanently."

"He's a reporter for the local paper at the moment," said dark-haired Rodeo Liz. "But two nights ago, he told me he's feeling restless again, that he's been offered a job up north, in the Yukon."

Hattie stared. Rodeo Liz wasn't as eye-catching as Sookie, but she did have a rough charm. So, Westley was the sort of man who went from one to the other? Well, why not? Why expect him to be different? He wasn't. He was a man, and all men were the same.

****

The bar was very different at night. Hot, noisy with men's loud voices, thick with smoke, and heavy with the reek of whiskey. At tables, men played poker, keno, blackjack, and faro, encouraged by the painted ladies. There was wild laughter, also barely controlled violence, a strained, unstable atmosphere, and the feeling that anything could happen. Too much alcohol, a card game gone wrong, jealousy, missing money, and the consequences would be dire.

Hattie, her eyes lowered, her heart thumping, made her way toward the piano. She felt the men's unflinching stares on her as they sized her up, took in her sober dress, her tightly pinned hair. She'd done all she could to make sure no one would think she was competition for the colorful saloon girls who arched their backs provocatively, filled the room with gay laughter, tapped their toes, and waited for the music to start.

To her sincere relief, she saw two men near the piano. One was tuning a violin; the other, a banjo in his arms, was sprawled in a nearby chair. "Good evening." She smiled at both as she sat.

They smiled back. "Ma'am," and waited for her to begin.

"You're the ones with experience here," she said. "You both know what people like to hear. I'll just follow along, if I can. I'm new at this, so please be patient with me."

The fiddler picked up his bow. "Why not start with a polka? Gets them on their feet."

"Okay. Do you know the 'Cincinnati Polka'?"

"Good choice."

Hattie raised her hands. *Please make this work.* And as her first notes sounded, the banjo's bright pluck, and violin's jaunty swell joined in. Relief washed through her, and fear trickled away. Yes, everything would be all right. They were making music, bright, cheery music. She saw a few men stand, begin drifting toward the ladies. The atmosphere changed. Tension dissipated, became bright anticipation with its dark undertones of seduction, sexual desire.

On and on they played, until her fingers ached. Talk became louder; the stink of rancid perfume and sweat filled the air. She barely looked up, but once, she caught a glimpse of Westley Cranston. Yes, there he was, leaning against the bar, just the way he had been when she'd first caught sight of him. His eyes, encouraging, warm, caught hers over the distance, and he nodded his approval. Why did that make her feel so good? Why did that tell her she had an ally?

****

He stood in the arched entry of the empty room, listening. There she was again, like yesterday morning. Sitting in dawn's early light, her fingers barely touching the piano's keys, playing softly. Mellow, rippling sounds, quite different from the rowdy dances of last night. He was proud of her, proud that she'd done so well, especially since she wasn't sure of herself. Yet, she'd been so quick to follow the violin's lead, to sense when it was the banjo's turn to take over and carry everyone away on its nervy pulse. She was also good at picking up themes.

Yes, she'd do fine, and no one would tease her about being a lady piano player in a saloon.

Why? Because, despite her fears, she was a cool-headed woman, and he appreciated that. Prissy and refined as she seemed to be, she wasn't shocked by improper behavior. Sookie had told him that she'd passed yesterday afternoon with the ladies and had shown no condescension. She took people as she found them, condemned no one. She might even hate hypocrisy as much as he did, and that thought was mighty satisfying.

A few soft, dreamy chords, and the piece ended. She sat there, motionless, gazing at nothing in particular. He wondered what she was thinking about, then wondered why he was wondering. Shaking his head, he stepped into the room.

Catching the movement, she looked over. What did her expression tell him? That she was pleased to see him? Then her eyes shifted to the two big mugs he was holding. He moved toward her, held one out. "Coffee?"

"Coffee?" She blinked.

"You do drink coffee?"

"I do. When—and if—I can get real coffee to drink." Her appreciative warm smile reached her eyes, lit up her whole face. She reached for the mug, curved her elegant fingers around it. Long musician's fingers with short, oval-shaped nails.

"When you can get real coffee? Meaning what?"

"Out on the prairie, the real thing wasn't available." Her mouth was a rueful moue. "I had to make do by roasting corn, bran, or okra seeds. Coffee was just too expensive to buy."

He pulled a chair close to the piano, settled onto it. "Well, this is the best you can get. No corn, no seeds. Pure Arbuckle's. Since cowboys are undoubtedly the most devoted coffee drinkers in the world, they won't settle for anything less." He chuckled. "Of course, I didn't make it the way they like it."

"Which is?"

"Well…out in ranch kitchens, cooks never do take the grounds out of the pot. They just add new grounds to each brew until the pot's too full to hold more."

"Sounds awful."

"Cowboys have a word for weak coffee—brown gargle. They think if a spoon won't stand in it, then it's sissy women's brew." He couldn't miss the suspicious look she gave the dark liquid. "Don't worry. Cowboy coffee isn't to my taste either."

"Thank goodness for that." Raising her mug, she sipped. Smiled again. "Tastes just like good coffee should. I like a man who's true to his word."

"That, I am," he said quietly. "I can assure you of it."

Her brow furrowed. Was she surprised at the seriousness of his answer? Perhaps. So was he. Her calm, appraising eyes searched his. "I hope you won't think I'm being too impertinent, but I am curious about you. You have the accent of a man from somewhere in the East. What brought you out here, to a silver boomtown like Blake's Folly?"

"A taste for adventure. A desire to experience it all, see it all. I grew up in Paterson, New Jersey, a doctor's son. I went to medical school in Philadelphia, was expected to carry on in my father's shoes. But I couldn't do it."

"Why not?"

"Because medicine is a calling, not a job. You take up a calling because your heart won't let you do anything else. Me? I didn't have it. It would have meant sacrificing who I was, what I wanted." He paused, thought briefly about the life he might have led if he'd followed all the rules, stayed put, proposed to the well-born Elizabeth Lowry. "I was supposed to marry someone from a good family, have children, live in a good solid brick house, and be a respectable citizen. Instead, I simply walked out. Ever since, there hasn't been one morning when I don't wake up thanking my lucky stars I didn't succumb to the lure of a tidy life."

"What have you done instead?"

He told her about trudging through the snows of Canada and working on steamboats on the Colorado River. How, as a journalist, he'd headed for mining communities that became towns in a matter of months, then died out just as quickly. "Most were terrible places, no more than open cesspits. After the covering of trees is ripped out, mud slides down the hills in torrents, covers tents and smothers the men inside. Miners live a rough life, worse than anyone imagines."

"Tell me more."

"Are you sure you want to hear?"

She smiled. "Please, I'm sure. Your words might be the closest I'll ever get to seeing more of the world."

No, she was no faint-hearted woman, and he didn't have to spare her. He talked about the filth, the lack of good water, the dirty boots used as pillows, and the clots of lice combed away with bowie knives. "Sometimes there are so many rats waiting to gnaw human flesh at night, the men keep wild cats and snakes inside the tents during the day. People die like flies out in those places, and the unburied bodies are left out in the open air for scavengers to eat. As for the mine owners, they don't waste time worrying about the men who make them rich. In writing about it all, exposing what is happening, I feel like I'm doing a little something to help."

"You enjoy being a journalist?"

"I certainly do. Besides, it's a handy niche. Out here, newspapers bring new towns into existence, advertising and propagandizing them, roping in settlers as well as big investors. And that results in a bit of class alongside all the roughness."

"How so?"

"Excursions are arranged back East to encourage the wealthy to come out, take a look. You can't put them up in the usual hotels—those are lice-infested with one towel, one sheet for all comers, and wall separations made out of strips of old paper—so towns have to build hotels like the Blake's Folly Emerald. It's a grand place, too, with authentic cast-iron pilasters, a paneled dining room, and a raised stage for an orchestra."

She quirked a quizzical eyebrow. "Surely a journalist's main duty isn't to propagandize, but to present what's happening elsewhere in the world."

He grinned. "We do manage to print real news, too. Winter's a slack time out in the mines and on ranches, and that's when the men catch up on things. You might not believe it, but many are educated, and they do like reading. They fight to get their hands on papers that are months old, and they certainly love books, especially romantic stories about the West. *The Trapper's Bride* is a particular favorite. I heard of one bar where the boys pooled their money, sent to San Francisco for enough books to make up a library that included geography books, and an encyclopedia."

"I definitely know how dull life can be without books." She shook her head as if pushing away unpleasant memories. "But I've been told you won't be staying on here for long."

"Darn!" He chuckled. "In this town, gossip travels faster than any bullet. But no, you're right. I won't be. Being a journalist gives me a ticket to travel, and

Blake's Folly is just a stop along the way. There's a big wide world out there, and I'm aching to see as much of it as I can."

Her expression was—what? Wistful? As if she would also like to taste adventure. But women weren't like that, not really. Women made nests, settled in. That's what made them so different from men.

****

Relishing the early morning's breeze, Westley Cranston strolled down the plank sidewalk toward Martha's little establishment, right next to the general store. He pushed open the wooden door. Even at this early hour, it was doing a roaring breakfast trade: the air was as hot as a Chinese laundry, and the windows were moisture-streaked.

"The usual?" Martha called. She was a plump, soft-looking woman, but that was just a lure. Underneath, she was tougher than old boots. A widow who'd been left nothing but gambling debts by a worthless husband, she worked this thriving business single-handed, churning out the simple food the men needed to fill their bellies.

Westley took a seat by the window, let his thoughts drift back to Miss Hattie, her fine eyes, and soft mouth. Damned if he knew why, but she brought out his protective male instinct, although, fine eyes and soft mouth aside, she didn't look like a woman who needed any help from him. No, he'd changed his mind about her: she was a toughie, all right. Whatever her background, life had turned her into a real pioneer woman, as resilient as the well-padded Martha standing behind her counter, ladling out smoky-tasting breakfast beans, and flipping her special pancakes.

Then again, Westley loved women. He loved being around them, loved their chatter, loved getting their take on things—whether or not he agreed with their conclusions. Most he kept company with weren't the decent ladies of polite society. They were the ones who gathered where whiskey flowed and men's pockets were filled with money. Who, pretty or not, wanted to be noticed; who provoked, dressing themselves in gaudy frocks costing up to seven or eight dollars. Who had no hesitation about giving a man a few minutes of gratification, and they earned more in a few days than any well-educated girl in the East did in a month.

Sure, a few were rough, but they'd been born into hard circumstances, had had to fight their way through life. Others were educated women running from tyrannical or violent husbands, or those who'd made one false step and given birth to a baby whose father refused to marry them, or who was already married. It was always women who paid the price for a misstep, not men. Life went on as usual for men.

"Respectability," Westley muttered. He'd seen how thin its veneer was, and that most "upright" folk were hypocrites. The town's "righteous" females with cozy homes on neatly laid out streets, those who sat smug in church pews, laying down moral law and dividing folks into good or bad, were right now mounting a campaign to run the good-time girls out of town. For them, a woman's role should be limited to educating children, doing housework, being a model wife, and going to temperance meetings; and the sexual act's sole purpose was to conceive children. Was it any surprise their men were more comfortable with the painted ladies? And how many times had he heard of wives letting their daughters take on the sordid duty of satisfying a sexually demanding husband?

Those good women didn't consider for one moment that fate could turn, that security might be transient. It wasn't rare for a good husband to run off with a lady like Rodeo Liz and her raucous laughter, or luscious Big Betty. As for Hattie Paumier, once town women discovered she worked in the Mizpah, she too would be branded a soiled dove. He almost laughed out loud. How would the prissy Hattie react to that? Prissy? Was she? No. Just tired. And pale.

Then he shook himself. Damn! Why was he so concerned about the woman? Why was he even thinking about her again? He got to his feet. Time to head for the station, leap on the next train to Virginia City. There were things he had to do, pressing things. And if he failed in his mission to get at the truth, what then? What if he lost Sookie? Well, if that happened, he'd do exactly what he planned: move on without her. No matter how much that hurt. Besides, hadn't he always been a loner? Why was he suddenly craving a woman's permanent company? "Be careful," he muttered to himself. "Age is softening you up."

****

Every day, Hattie wandered through town, basking in the liveliness of civilization—or what passed for it out here: wooden sidewalks running all down Main Street, prosperous-looking shops that were two stories high, or with false fronts, phony windows, and massive cornices to make them appear larger. Most had overhanging eaves to protect clients from the blazing summer sun, others had crudely painted pictures to help both the illiterate and the immigrants who could read no

English: a rotten-looking tooth decorated the dentist's storefront; a large cow designated the butcher shop. Cigars, Bert Freedman, Proprietor, was next to a tiny bakery; then came J.W. Chrisman, Drugs and Patent Medicines, Luigi's Barber Shop, the Red Nag Saloon. Opposite, L. Szymansky, Wines, Liquors, was right between Lucas, General Merchandise, and a corner bank. Farther along was a police station with its adjacent jail, and beyond, a stone-built courthouse—those last were signs of prosperity, all right. Not every new town could pay a sheriff and a judge. Only where silver was king could luxury be counted on.

Looking closer, though, not everything was so polished. Main Street was no more than a dirt road, one that would become a sea of mud when the rains came. Turn a corner, and here were back lanes with the poverty endemic to boomtowns: filthy, lined with poor huts, tent homes, tent restaurants, and tent saloons. Here women, surrounded by passels of dirty children, knelt in front of tubs filled with rags, or they chopped wood, or carried slops to the ubiquitous dung heaps. They eyed her with curiosity mixed with hatred: how could they know her lot had been similar until recently? They simply saw a tidy lady in a decent dress picking her way around foul puddles and witnessing their misery.

Who were they? What had their dreams been? Had they also come as mail-order brides, hoping for freedom and fresh air? Then found themselves shackled to a poor miner who drank to make life tolerable. Or had they, like so many others, abandoned the wagon trails. At this very moment, caught in a tourbillion of swirling dust, one tired line of covered wagons was passing through Blake's Folly: pioneers plodding on to an uncertain future, managing to hope it would be a good one. She knew how false that hope could be. She'd been the same, thinking wide open spaces brought freedom from drudgery and exploitation. Then, had found herself trapped on a motionless prairie with only the wind for conversation and the prickly scrub to hear her sighs.

Dreams of open spaces? Right over there, sitting in the dust were Indians, long rows of them, Paiute, Shoshone, Washoe. All had been evicted from their lands; all were waiting for government food handouts. They didn't resemble the fearsome savages of legend. They were just people, impassive, silent, without hope. She'd heard talk of white men's vengeance, of Indian shoots for thrill, of rape, and slave taking. Where was right? Justice? Who was civilized? Where did the truth lie?

Here in Blake's Folly, there were several grand houses, too, those belonging to mine owners, silver barons. Just beyond town limits, the yellow-painted Treemont mansion was as high, filigreed, and complicated as any fine residence back East. She knew the sort of life those people lived. She also knew that, behind pretty façades, there was another world altogether.

And this afternoon, turning back, regaining Main Street, she caught sight of Westley Cranston standing in front of the office of the *Morning Sun*, smoking his cigar. So he was back in town. Her steps slowed, and she watched him. How handsome he was!

Before she could look away, he turned, saw her staring. How humiliating. She felt the sudden red flush rise to her cheeks. He must have seen it, too. Eyes amused, he lifted one hand, tipped his hat to her. Giving a brief nod in return, she forced herself to look away, continue on down the road. How foolish she felt. A mere alley cat gazing at a king.

****

He was here again, caught in frail early sunlight. A fantasy figure? No. He was real enough, a flesh and blood man holding two mugs of fragrant coffee and coming her way. Heart beating swiftly, she took the one he handed her and smiled her thanks.

"Still keeping up the morning practice?" he asked as he settled in a nearby chair.

"Doesn't practice make perfect?" She laughed at herself. "Well…probably not perfect, if such a thing exists. But there is something special about coming down here while everyone is still sleeping, getting to play the songs I love. I've even sent away for some sheet music. I hadn't realized how much I missed playing the piano."

"I can tell." His eyes were sober, intense, eyes that could read secrets. "Just by listening to you."

Yes, there might be many things he would know. Had he also sensed how much he fascinated her? She searched for a neutral subject of conversation. "You've been out of town. Where did you go? Anywhere interesting?"

"Just as far as Virginia City. Doing a little investigating on my own."

"What sort of investigating?" Although she had no business asking. She'd seen his frown, one that told her the subject wasn't a pleasant one.

He was silent for a long moment. Then, shifting in his chair, he crossed one leg over the other. "Getting the lowdown on a conman who passes himself off as a respectable businessman. But his particular business is owning cribs all across the West."

"Cribs? You mean houses where…"

He nodded. "A line of shacks on a back street where women sell themselves for the lowest price—older, worn-out women who can't be employed in the better brothels, and Chinese girls sold as slaves. Most die from consumption or syphilis. Or when they're no longer useful, they're encouraged to take an overdose of laudanum. If they won't, they're murdered."

"How horrible. Can't anything be done to help them?"

"Aside from a few rescue missions, no one cares about the fate of fallen women."

"So why were you investigating this…this scoundrel? Will you expose him in your newspaper?"

"What good would that do?" His tone was bitter. "No, I did it on behalf of a lady who believes this louse will marry her, who doesn't know he already has at least one wife who helps him run his filthy businesses."

"Have you told that lady what you discovered?"

"I have." His expression was hard, his eyes angry. "She didn't believe me. Told me I was stepping in where I wasn't wanted, that I was lying." He scowled. "But the truth will sink in eventually. For the moment, she needs time to let her faith in the man die."

"I've heard so many similar stories," Hattie said. She sensed his pain, wondered what he wasn't telling her, but didn't dare ask. "I've seen some of the men the saloon girls love. Men who take their money, then treat them badly, or ignore them."

"There are many cads of that ilk."

"Some are well-disguised," Hattie agreed. "Like my former guardian, Mr. O'Hare. Back in Baltimore, he took me in after my Aunt Agatha's death, told me I was lucky to find a safe haven with a good family."

"It wasn't?"

"It was anything but a haven. My aunt had left debts behind her, or so O'Hare told me—I never did find out if that was the truth. He claimed he'd paid off her creditors, and to compensate, I was to be a governess to his three unruly children. And since I was just another of his servants, I saw what really takes place under bourgeois respectability. The imperious, condescending Mrs. O'Hare with her posh friends, coffee afternoons, and well-dressed children must have known that her husband climbed the stairs to the servant's quarters every night."

"It freed her from her wifely obligation."

"Yes, it probably did. And no one ever complained, either. Ellie, the parlor maid, took it all in her stride. She was a happy-go-lucky character, and she said all men were like that in all the houses where she'd worked. That such goings-on were considered normal. I asked her what she'd do if she found herself with child, and she said she'd have to disappear, just like Victoria did, the maid who'd worked there before her."

"Did she get caught?"

"No." Hattie put down her coffee cup. "Ellie was the one who told me about Mr. Sassy and the marriages he arranged for women willing to come out west. That's how my correspondence with my future husband started. I never realized that Sam Graham's story of homesteading and success was a lie; that his letters were written by a public scribe who churned out the proper sentiments on a Remington Standard; that Sam was illiterate."

"Even though you didn't know him, you were willing to take a chance."

"I didn't have a choice. Mr. O'Hare decided to change concubines. One night, I saw the curtain to my cubicle opening. It was O'Hare in his dressing gown. He came to my bed, pulled back the covers, said, 'Be quiet, I'll finished in a minute.' But I wasn't a servant, not really, and I didn't have to submit. Even though the aunt who raised me was half mad, she had given me romantic dreams and a sense of self. So, instead of keeping quiet, I told him, quite loudly, I'd scream the house down. He covered my mouth, pushed my head down into the pillow." She hesitated, momentarily embarrassed by her own frankness. "I was so frightened."

"Of course, you were."

"But I was angry, too. And I bit him, sank my teeth into that repulsive flesh, hung on, ripped at it, even as he punched me. Squeaking with pain, he finally skittered off."

Westley's shout of laughter rang out. "You won!"

She grinned. Then sobered. "That particular battle, yes. But I saw the look O'Hare gave me the next day. I'd only fired his lust, so I went to Mrs. O'Hare, told her everything. That spoilt, arrogant woman accused me of lying and sent me away. I ended up coming west with Ellie."

"Where is Ellie now?"

"Who knows? She left the train to meet her intended hundreds of miles before I did." Had gone off into her future with a jaunty step and no backward glance. "I never heard from her again. Perhaps her marriage is happy. Perhaps she found a partner in life. Perhaps she's one of the lucky ones."

****

Teddy Grimes put down that precious banjo of his and headed for the bar: time to wet his whistle. Rake Luna settled his fiddle on the top of the piano and followed. Hattie stayed right where she was, resting her tired hands, and looking with satisfaction around the room. I could get to like this, she thought, but knew she was only fooling herself. She already did like this life. This was the closest she had ever come to comfort, to earning a decent salary, to being independent. Little over a month had passed since she'd arrived, and it was already home.

A few ladies, dressed in their provocative finery, sat laughing amongst themselves, ignoring the heat in male eyes. Others concentrated their charms on those who still had money to spend. Thank goodness, most men washed themselves for a night in town, but they were rough, nonetheless. Yet, Rosie, now clutching a shaggy cowboy's arm, didn't look as though she minded in the least; and near the bar, Laney-Mae was laughing shrilly at the mayor's very doubtful jokes. They thoroughly enjoyed what they were doing. What had Rosie said to her a few days ago? "Why do most women want to work themselves to death, have one baby after another, tend to animals, bring in crops, and cater to ungrateful husbands who prefer our company?"

What about Westley? Was he here tonight? She peered through the cigar smoke, saw him over there by the dark window, talking with the divine Sookie. Wasn't she his sweetheart? Perhaps. Although Hattie had never seen him dancing with any of the girls, not even with Sookie. However, he did sleep here every night. Where? She thought of Sookie's room with its large gilt mirror, soft bed, and pretty trinkets on little side tables. There was an elegant porcelain washbasin and jug, and they stood on a marble-topped washstand with delicate rosewood legs. Yes, everything was luxurious, sensuous, like Sookie herself. A woman who gave men something to dream about.

She couldn't help wondering what might have happened if she had met Westley years ago, when she'd been attractive and youthful. She allowed herself to imagine how his broad shoulders would feel under her fingertips, how his warmth would envelope her if he took her in his arms. He was as seductive as any hero in a romantic novel and just as unattainable. He was the dream man, the one who provoked the secret passions in poems. Secret passion. Through all the years she had never known what that meant. Now she did.

Strange thoughts, and she didn't understand them: the reality of the sexual act was so different. She had known Sam's roughness, the hatred she'd felt whenever he, grunting, stinking of the dirty long johns he'd sweated into for months but refused to take off, lay on her, forcing her to do her duty. Yes, that was the difference between desire and reality. One had you wanting, dreaming; the other showed how false those dreams were.

****

The meetings with Westley continued. There was no longer any reason for her to go downstairs to the main room of the saloon so early, or to practice. Her fingers now tripped over the piano's keys with confidence, and the tunes she played were merry. She could have stayed in bed after the night's hard work of making music, but these early mornings were magical. She wouldn't have missed them for the world.

She loved sitting in this large silent room where sunbeams caught floating dust motes, turned them into stars. The big mug of coffee Westley always prepared for her was ambrosia; the air was always cool, not hot, not oppressive like it would be later in the day. And no one ever interrupted these secret moments they shared, just sitting, just talking.

He regaled her with stories of riverboats, high stakes poker, roulette, the gamblers who sought fortune, their bold women. He added colors to a world she had only read about. And she watched him as he talked, delighting in the tawny skin, the thick wild curl of his hair, his laughter. He was an exceptional man, and she envied Sookie.

What would it be like to lead a life of adventure? To never know where you'd be waking up tomorrow? It sounded exciting, she thought wistfully. Ideal. But it was out of reach for her, she knew that. She didn't have the courage to do those things, strike out on her own. Certainly there were women who were brave enough, but she wasn't.

"It's easier being a man," she told him.

In exchange, she talked freely about her life out on the prairie, the years of isolation, Sam's bouts of drinking to prove his manliness, and his subsequent violence. How she'd learned to avoid him, hiding in the scrub throughout the night, waiting long frozen hours, listening to the unseen animals around her, fighting back fear until she knew sleep had overtaken him, and the danger was over.

"Why didn't you leave him?"

"I had no money and nowhere to go," she said simply. "We were so far from the next farm. Too far to walk. And because Sam only took me to see other people twice in all those years, I didn't know how to get anywhere. Even if I could have reached the neighbors, what would they have done? They wouldn't have let me stay on. They wouldn't have protected me. I was Sam's wife, and a wife's duty is to stick by her man, despite the violence. I remember hearing about one woman who had tried to run away. Her husband found her again, just wandering around in the middle of nowhere, starving and thirsty. After he brought her back home, he chained her to the doorpost, chained her up like a dog. That's what Sam would have done if I'd left and he'd caught up with me. He told me he would."

"He isn't coming after you now."

"No, because this time he forced me to leave. I can't conceive children, you see. Sam said it was my fault. He wants a big family, so I'm no good to him." She laughed shortly. "That's what saved me."

****

Sitting at the desk in his office at the *Morning Sun*, he'd sometimes see Hattie when she passed on her daily walks, crossing over the road, entering the dry goods shop. He imagined her going through the fabrics, looking at pearl buttons and lace. Clearly, the ladies were having an effect on her. A woman like Hattie Paumier would never allow herself to be overtly provocative, but she dressed differently now, with a touch of color and always something frivolous, a flounce, a frill. She was letting her femininity show, her hair wave. Her eyes often glowed with the humor he had seen the first time he'd caught sight of her, standing there in front of the mahogany, asking Neddy for work. That, and a new confidence, added a languorous softness to her movements, something only a man might notice. He saw how she caressed the piano's keys, and he couldn't miss the happiness in her eyes when she took the mug he handed her each morning, the faint blush on her cheek. She liked him, and that made him feel very good...because he also enjoyed their meetings.

He liked the soft timbre of her voice, he liked hearing her stories, and he appreciated her openness and her honesty. How ready she was to discuss any subject with candor, how unflappable and unflinching. And because of that, he told her things he'd never talked about before—his reluctance to become a doctor, how difficult the task was of stopping cholera, smallpox, flu, and bronchitis when whole families drank from the same glass, bathed in the same water, and used the same towel. How helpless he'd felt when called in to save young women dying from abortions gone wrong: their families, knowing that almost half of these terminations ended in hemorrhage and infection, didn't hesitate to sacrifice wayward daughters. At least out here, mixed-descent men and women with their native knowledge of medicine carried out abortions, and chances of survival were greater in their hands.

He'd watched out for Hattie at first, keeping his eye on her in the evenings, waiting to step in if some drunk thought she could be had for the asking. But no one had. Everyone seemed to respect her position as the lady piano player—perhaps it was the dignified way she carried herself, the feeling she gave of being able to take care of herself, no matter what wallops fate threw her way. He knew she'd be okay when he left town, because any day now he'd be on his way. The world was calling to him; he couldn't stay here in Blake's Folly. If he did, he'd spend the rest of his life thinking of missed chances.

He had come to accept that he would be going alone; his one-sided love for Sookie wasn't enough to bring her back. He was sick of dark sleepless nights, of hoping she would appear, slip into his arms, warm his skin with her soft breath. Yes, she had forgiven him for delving into Big Jim's life, but he, Westley, was now a friend, a former lover. His fingers would never again curl into the rich tangle of her hair; he would no longer hear her sighs of pleasure.

And Hattie? She was a real ally. No…more than that. A woman. A steady woman with loyalty and honesty. And a hidden, subtle beauty that would appeal to the right man.

****

"Take this telegram up to Westley." It was Beatie, the housekeeper, her voice as harsh as usual.

Hattie turned, blinked. What did the woman want from her? Yes, she saw the envelope Beatie was holding out. Still…"Take it to Westley? I don't know what you mean."

"I can't leave here." Beatie's chin jerked toward the kitchen, the bubbling pots, then to the men sitting at long tables in the back room, waiting to be fed.

Hattie stood there, still confused. She'd just seen Sookie a few minutes ago, sitting at the gilt-framed mirror in her room, powdering and rouging her face, preparing for the evening. Westley hadn't been in there with her. In fact, she'd never seen him in that part of the house.

"I'm sorry…I don't know where he is."

"In his room. Saw him go up there not an hour ago."

"What room?"

Beatie glowered, obviously exasperated by Hattie's obtuseness. "Go up the stairs, turn to the left on the landing. Walk until you see the dark green door. After that, go to the end of the corridor. Westley's room is just down the hall, close to Ned's."

"Westley's room?"

But Beatie, caught by the complications of a hearty stew, had already disappeared into her steamy kitchen.

Hattie climbed the stairs. Funny…she'd seen this other turning off the landing every single day, but had never once thought it could lead to another wing of the building. She hadn't been the least bit curious. After the green door, the long hallway was dark, but she could see a sliver of light at the very end. Slowly, she approached. Hesitated, just for a second, before raising her hand and knocking.

"Yes?"

"Westley? It's Hattie. I have something for you. Beatie sent me. I…"

The door swung open. He stood there in his shirtsleeves, the crisp white fabric emphasizing his solid-looking shoulders and a chest as broad as she had imagined it to be.

"Hattie?" His eyes were surprised. Amused, too. Had he noticed her discomfiture? He probably had. He noticed everything.

"It's a telegram. For you," she added inanely as she held out the envelope.

He opened the door wider. "Come, come in."

She stepped into the softly lit room, and her astonished eyes took in a heavy wooden desk, shelves of books, and the large rug. There were two comfortable leather armchairs, and a newspaper was flung across a low table. It was very much a man's room, intimate, deeply masculine. The smell of good cigars hung on the air, and something else—something deep, intoxicating. An enticing male musk.

She watched his fingers as they tore open the envelope, pulled out the telegram. He read it, his face expressionless.

"Bad news?"

He looked up. "On the contrary. The new journalist is arriving from Oklahoma City."

"Journalist?"

"The one who will replace me on the paper here. Which means I'll be free to move on."

So, it really was about to happen. Hattie's heart sank. Westley was leaving. The early morning coffees, the friendship, everything was coming to an end. Why did the thought make her feel so dreary? She was nothing to him. He was simply her make-believe man, the one she wished she had met all those years ago. The man she wished she had the right to love.

He was staring at her, his eyes probing. Surely he couldn't read her mind. Surely not. She had to cover her chagrin, hide the way she felt. "What a beautiful room. I never imagined...I mean...I thought..." Goodness! What had she been about to admit now? That she'd thought he lived with Sookie? That he was her man, that…

"What did you think?" he prompted.

She bit her lip. She couldn't tell him, although the relief she felt was almost overwhelming.

"Hattie?" He was smiling, watching her curiously. "You're holding back. That's not like you."

It wasn't. She'd always been open with him, had always been so honest. Why? Because he'd been as open, as honest as she. A deep trust had grown between them.

Well, why not tell him? What did she have to lose? "I didn't know you had your own room. I thought, each morning, when you came downstairs, that you and Sookie…" She stopped, caught by the sudden flash in his eyes. "That she is your woman. That you stayed with her."

"Did you?" He put the telegram down on the desk.

She raised her hands, palms forward, a gesture of apology. "I never knew about this separate wing. I suppose I should have opened my eyes, but I didn't. I often see you and Sookie together in the saloon, and…"

"Yes," he said, his voice still low. "Yes, I often sit and talk with Sookie. She's a highly intelligent woman. She makes me laugh, she's warm, and she's kindly."

"She's all of those things, I know," Hattie said quickly. "She's lovely too."

"That, she is." He nodded his agreement. "And she touches me deeply. I care about her—very, very much. But she's not *my* woman."

"Oh."

"Listen…what I…" He stepped in closer, reached out, took her hands in his, but didn't complete the sentence. Only stared at her. What was he thinking?

It was the first time he had ever touched her, and the feel of his skin against hers affected her more deeply than she ever could have imagined. No, that wasn't true either. She had imagined his touch, how wonderful it would feel in her secret thoughts, but that hadn't prepared her for the warmth now reaching into her heart.

His unwavering gaze didn't leave hers for a moment, and there was something else in the air, something intense. As if being here, in his room, had opened a secret passageway, dark, intimate. Something closer to her fantasies. *You shouldn't be in a man's private rooms.* But this was exactly where she wanted to be. Right in here, with Westley.

The air seemed to thicken, buzz with a strange intensity. Her body felt soft, languid, and uncontrollable. She felt his nearness surround her, take hold of her. She wanted to feel his mouth on hers. She wanted to feel the heat of his body touching hers.

"Hattie," he said, his voice low, thrilling, then his head descended with excruciating slowness, and her heart stood still. He brushed his lips across hers, sliding to one soft corner, then the other, as if testing her reaction. Her lashes fluttered, her eyes closed, and she stepped in closer still, filling the gap between them. Releasing her hands, he reached for her waist, angled her against him.

Of their own accord, her hands curled over his shoulders, loving the feel of knotted muscle and hard bone. With a soft moan she gave herself up to the overwhelming sensation of being held with a tenderness she had never known. Again he took her mouth in a kiss that was caring and sweet, also knowing and masterful.

Confirming he was a man who knew women. Many women… The thought chilled her, let the real world burst into the room.

She pulled back slightly. "Westley…I can't stay. I have to go downstairs…I have to play…" But she didn't sound convincing.

"I wondered what it would be like to kiss you," he said, his voice gritty.

She stared up at him, astounded by his words. Surely he couldn't mean them. Surely not. "Impossible! Me?"

In answer, he laughed, a rich, secretive sound. Then pulled her tighter still, one hand circling her waist, the other moving down her back, cupping her. Again, his mouth claimed hers in another kiss, one more demanding, penetrating, one that told her he had spoken the truth.

When the kiss ended, he loosened his embrace slightly, and they stood there, catching their breath, staring at each other with amazement. "I want you, Hattie. I want you in my bed."

The words seared through her, and her heart thrilled. Never in her wildest dreams had she imagined she would ever hear them from Westley. He wanted her. He wanted her as much as she wanted him, his touch, the feel of his body, his taste, the natural scent of him. But what was the point? He was leaving. He was an adventurer, she'd always known that. He'd been truthful from the start. The telegram sitting over there on the desk was proof of that, and her heart would be ripped into tiny shreds.

He was watching her, his eyes scanning her mouth, reading her soul. "Go," he said quietly.

"Westley...I..." She what? What did she want to tell him? That it didn't matter if he were leaving? That she wanted him, too?

"Just go. Now."

****

Her breath caught in her throat, and her heart pounded in fear. Why had she left her room to come out here in the middle of the night? Why was she so eager to make a fool of herself, give herself so willingly? And now, standing here in the shadows, she realized how unwise her decision had been, because she wasn't alone. There was someone else out here, too, someone moving slowly at the other end of the dark corridor. A man who had just left one of the girl's rooms? No, that wasn't possible. If a woman's word wasn't strong enough for a drunken cowboy, there was plenty of muscle down in the saloon, ready to make things clear.

Then, suddenly, she knew that the shadowy figure was Westley. She couldn't see him, but she could sense him in the dark. Instinctively, she pulled the frothy peignoir around her—a gift from Sookie—but even she knew the absurdity of the gesture. Diaphanous, revealing, it was a garment meant to entice. As was her hair, finally let loose from its pins, tumbling over her shoulders and down her back.

"Hattie?" His voice was quiet, but she could hear the surprise. "Why are you in the hallway? Is something wrong?"

He was right in front of her now, a hair's breadth away, his white shirt gleaming in the dark, but unbuttoned, sending out an invitation to touch. She could smell the deep masculine fragrance of his skin, feel his heat. Then he reached out, caught her arms in both hands, and logical thought spun through the air, evaporated into the sultry dark. His touch. She hadn't been able to forget how it had felt being in his arms earlier this evening. Being kissed by him. She wanted more, even if they never met again.

"Hattie."

How she loved the warm tones of his voice, hearing her name on his lips. She fought to keep her reason. Failed. "I wanted to see you," she said softly. "I was coming to your room. I…" She swallowed. Then heard his soft laughter. Her heart sank, and she stepped back.

Deftly he caught her. "No, Hattie, don't go. Please. Stay. Stay with me."

"You're laughing at me."

"Hardly. I'm laughing at this situation. I was coming to your room to see you. I wanted to apologize. I couldn't sleep. I tossed and turned, thinking I had offended you. Knowing…" He stopped suddenly, as if a new thought had struck him. "What are you…"

She didn't let him finish. Reaching up, she caressed his mouth. "I want you, too," she said simply.

He laughed again, a low soft sound that sent shivers throughout her body. Then his laughter ended in a groan as he folded her tightly against him, bent his lips to hers. The kisses they had shared earlier were enticing and tender, but there was nothing tender about the way he now plundered her mouth. This was raw desire, and she pushed in closer to him, wanting to feel his body over every inch of her. Needing his skin, the tightness of his muscles under her fingers.

Then, as if she weighed less than the soft dark air around them, he picked her up and carried her down the passageway, through his dark sitting room. Farther still. To a bed caught in moonbeams. Letting her down gently, he stood, just watching her. Now what?

She felt shy, suddenly. Would he allow for her modesty? Would they undress? What was the correct procedure? This was new to her, despite her age. With her husband, sex had been a half-clothed and dreaded duty, and that experience hadn't prepared her for desire or seduction.

But already his fingers, gentle but determined, were sliding the peignoir back down over her arms, were already lifting her soft nightdress over her head. "I want to see you naked, Hattie. I want to feel every inch of you. Touch you."

His words captivated her, and something deep within her blossomed. How she needed Westley. Now.

"Oh, yes, it's what I want, too. I want the feel of you inside me." Her words shocked her, but she knew how true they were.

Stripping off his clothes, he lowered her down onto the bed, then knelt beside her, let his fingers graze her skin, her ribs, her soft belly, rise to her breasts, trace soft circles. Bending, he took one tender nipple, then the other, into his mouth, circling, ever circling, his tongue an instrument of torture and delight, before raising his head again, gazing at her in the silvery light.

"Westley," she whispered achingly. "I...I didn't know I could feel this way about a man. I didn't know..." But she did know that desire like this might never come into her life again. That she was willing to brave its loss when it was gone.

Words no longer mattered when she felt his heat over her and his hardness against her belly, and knew how much he wanted her. She opened her legs to him, aching for him to fill her, and she heard his soft groan. Then his hands moved lower, down to her wet warmth, his fingers seeking her core, slipping inside of her until, her breath ragged, she bucked against him.

"Please... Please, Westley..."

"Please?" His word teased, but her heart thrilled at the sharp need in his voice. As if he, too, had no will to resist. Settling between the cradle of her thighs, he parted the soft lips of her warmth, slid deep inside her...stealing her heart, scattering her senses, spinning them both toward the edge.

****

She wouldn't be here, Westley thought with a feeling of discontent as he made the coffee: Two mugs, just like every other morning...just in case. In case what? How could he expect her to keep their rendezvous? They had loved each other until early light had touched the dark sky, and he had escorted her back to her tiny room in the other wing of the rambling building. Now he was prepared to be disappointed, to see the stool before the piano empty, to hear the silence of the room.

Last night, he had known complete oneness. She had felt the same, he knew that, had sensed it in the trusting way she had given herself, touched and tasted him, and in the abandon of her lovemaking. Now what? How would she feel in the day's brash light? Would she regret what had happened? No, that wasn't possible. She loved him, he was certain of it. As certain as he was of his own feelings, of what he wanted, of what the possibilities were. Sookie? She was the unattainable dream woman, the fantasy he would never possess. He loved her deeply, possibly he always would, but Hattie was a real partner. An equal. It was another sort of love altogether.

Then he heard it. The soft sound, a tranquil music, soothing rippling notes. He stepped into the saloon, saw her sitting there, just as he'd hoped. She raised her head, looked over at him, and met his eyes with such gentleness. Crossing to her, he carefully put the mugs on a table, then lowered his mouth to hers and felt the joyful answering passion in her lips.

"Good morning, charming lady," he murmured.

She laughed softly. "Very good morning to you, kind sir."

Grabbing a chair, he pulled it up beside the piano, just as he did every morning. Reached for the coffees and handed one to her. Watched her long fingers curve around the mug, raise it to her mouth. He couldn't believe the tenderness he felt, the closeness.

"No regrets?" He hated the unsteadiness in his own voice.

"Regrets?" Her hazel eyes were as calm as ever, but the sudden flush on her cheeks gave her away. Was she remembering her own abandon? "I'll never regret what happened last night. How could I? Last night happened because I love you, Westley."

His heart turned over. Yes, it was true. She loved him. But how much?

"Enough to make it permanent?" To his own ears, he sounded weak, unsure. He was letting hope ruin clear thinking.

"Permanent?" Her eyebrows rose; she looked confused. Then confusion subsided into sadness. "How could it be permanent? You'll be leaving for the Yukon.

That's what you said."

He leaned in closer, as if by his nearness he could make her understand what he wanted from her. "I'll be going up there to run a newspaper. It's an opportunity to be more than just a journalist, to have a say in how a paper is run. I don't want to pass it up, Hattie."

"No, you don't." Her voice was steady now.

"And all of this…" One arm waved, taking in the big room filled with early light. "All of this has come to mean something to you. The piano playing. The money you earn. You've found a home here, I know that, but…" His gaze held hers. "But Hattie, would you consider giving it up? Coming with me?"

"What do you mean?"

"Come with me. As my partner. My woman. And when you get a divorce, as my wife. As the person you'll spend the rest of your life with."

She stared at him wordlessly, her face pale. Carefully, she put her mug down. What was she thinking? "How can I?"

He fought his deep disappointment. "Hattie, just hear me out. I know I can't offer you stability and a settled life, but I can promise I'll always be faithful to you, take care of you. I'll never betray or abandon you." He saw something else now. Warmth, serene, and compassionate. And it gave him hope. "What do you think?"

"I wish I could go with you. With all my heart, I wish I could."

"But?" He wanted to keep that soft warmth in her eyes. If only he could make her smile. "I'll always make sure there will be a piano and place where you can play it. How's that for a deal?"

The smile came. Dazzling him. Then it faded again. "But it's impossible. Don't you see why?"

"No, I don't. But I want to understand." He knew her answer would be truthful because that's the way she was. Always honest, open, truthful.

She looked away, biting her lip, as if trying not to cry. "Because what if you want children one day? What if you want to start a family?"

That was what worried her? That was all? "Is that the reason you can't come with me?"

She nodded slowly, her eyes downcast.

"Hattie, look at me."

She did, and he saw the deep sorrow he had to vanquish.

Reaching out, he cupped her chin, and his voice was soft. "Do I look like a young buck just starting out in life? Don't you think that if I'd wanted children, I'd have had some by now? I never did want to settle down in one place, go for family life. I told you that once, and I meant it. I didn't want that years ago, and I certainly don't want it now. Please, believe me."

She watched him steadily, but said nothing.

His thumb caressed her lips. "Until now, I've been a loner, traveling on my own, relying on myself only. But I'm at the point where I want a partner, a real partner who is my closest friend. A woman who will stick by me through thick and thin. Who will be willing to cross over mountains with me, take chances, risk danger, see what life can bring. Someone who won't balk at adventure." He paused. "I'd like that woman to be you, Hattie. Very much. But I don't want to force your hand. Make you give up your life here for me. Do what only I want."

Had he gone too far, asked for too much?

Silently, she watched him, as if wanting to believe, but fearing she couldn't. Then she raised her own hand, covered his. "Westley? It would be an honor to be your partner. I'm not a nervous person, and adventure sounds exciting to me. That's all I've ever really wanted, too."

"We'll never be rich."

"Who cares?" She laughed softly. "As long as there's a piano and a saloon in the area, I can always keep us in bean stew."

He stood, pulled her up into his arms, took her mouth in a long drugging kiss, then nuzzled the sensitive warm skin below her ear.

"So here's where it all begins, Miss Hattie. Right now. With the two of us. And the whole world at our fingertips."

"The whole wide world," she murmured. "How wonderful."

And gleaming sun filled the room, touching up the dark wood, dancing across the wooden floor, dragging in the day's heat. And hope.

****

"You're finally leaving." Sookie stood in the main room's shadow.

Westley watched her, taking in her golden loveliness, perhaps for the last time in his life. "Yes, finally."

"You see?" Her smile was faint. "Everything has worked out for the best."

"Has it?" He caught the jaunty positive note in her voice, but it sounded forced. There was something else, too, something hidden. Regret? A terrible knowledge of irrevocable loss? Possibly. Or was he just projecting his own turbulent feelings onto her.

"It has. You have the perfect partner in Hattie. She dreams of adventure, just like you do. She's a good, strong, and reliable woman, just what you need. And thanks to the information you gave me about Big Jim, I've made my own enquiries and discovered you were right. I didn't want to accept the truth at first, but you stopped me making a terrible mistake and putting myself in a very bad situation."

"I see. And how is Big Jim taking it?"

"He won't be bothering me again. I've made use of my best contacts to make certain of that." She smiled faintly. "Even that horrible spy, Doug Lazy, has dropped out of sight."

"What will you do now?"

"Do?" She cocked her head to one side. "I'll carry on as usual. Continue my life here in Blake's Folly, put money aside, perhaps buy a plot of ground and open a business one day. And I'll take care of my children. Provide them with a good education, give them a chance." She held out her hand. "So I suppose this is goodbye."

"Sookie…" He caught the hand, brought it to his mouth, kissed it with longing, sadness, also resignation.

With her other hand, she reached up, caressed his cheek lovingly. Then, turning, she went to the front door. Opened it. Stepped into the blazing day.

He followed her out, watched as, without a backward glance, she strode down the wooden sidewalk, passed the waiting cart with his and Hattie's baggage, crossed the dusty street, continued on through town, and disappeared from sight.

His heart heavy, he stood there, unable to move.

Until, slowly, her words came back to him. Her children? She only had one child. Why had she mentioned children? Was it possible that... His mind reeled. Yes, it was.

The wave of that passion he'd fought so hard to tamp down welled up again, uncontrollable, almost overwhelming. Sookie! She might be having his child! He leapt onto the dirt road staring wildly. He had to find her, know for certain. It was of the utmost importance.

But she was gone. Where?

"Westley?"

He turned. Saw Hattie standing in the doorway of the Mizpah, smiling, her eyes filled with love. Waiting for him. Waiting to begin their adventure together. Trusting him implicitly.

He looked at the soft hair, the slender fragile figure of this woman he had sworn never to betray.

Then went to her, pulled her into his arms. Held her tightly. Let her love and joy wash over him, fill him completely.

II

Evenings at Madam Lacey's: 1926

"Will you walk into my parlor?" said a spider to a fly...
~Mary Howitt, (1799-1888), *The Spider and the Fly*

Susanna Victoria Lacey, professionally known as Madam Lacey, entered the main room of her brothel. Yes, Alexander Treemont was here, sitting in that deep armchair near the window, and she couldn't deny the warm feeling of satisfaction his presence gave her. He was a fine man, remarkably handsome, always elegantly dressed, and she relished his polish, his excellent manners, and his steadiness during the most virulent debates; for when fueled by lust and alcohol, men often forgot themselves.

In some strange way, she had come to depend on Alexander, to revel in the way she felt in his presence— feminine, intelligent, and interesting—yet she knew enough to keep her feelings in check. Too much separated them. He came from a wealthy mine-owning family; she, a former prostitute and dance girl, was now madam of the state's most lavish bawdy-house.

Like the others, Alexander came here for the relaxed atmosphere, the pungent, albeit illegal, moonshine whiskey, and the regular company of professors, writers, lawyers, wealthy businessmen, also politicians and sheriffs who, sidestepping prohibition, enjoyed social drinking. Why, even President Harding in far off Washington kept the White House well stocked in liquor!

Most men, however, indulged in intimate moments with the house's luscious ladies who catered to their personal preferences in exotic theme rooms—the Persian Room, the Japanese Room, the Turkish Room—or in upstairs boudoirs with elaborate draperies, large beds, and exuberant ornaments. Alexander, although he participated in the discussions of books, politics, or the consequences of the Great War, did not seek carnal gratification. Susanna couldn't help but wonder at his indifference.

She knew some had left desire behind years ago; others, jaded by repeated failure, had lost their sexual appetite; several had penchants not catered to on her premises; and a few needed to talk of their financial troubles, sad marriages, or unfaithful wives. But the saddest men were those traumatized by war, the proximity to violence and death: they came here for a few hours of forgetfulness and peace.

Whatever the reason, unlike the lesser establishments in other towns—brothels and cheap bar houses—Madam Lacey's was a haven, one that aimed to soothe the male soul out here on the bleak flatland.

****

"The way things are going, Blake's Folly will be abandoned one day." To add an exclamation point to that well-worn phrase, Ben Trouverie jammed a thick cigar into his mouth.

"Damn right," added Dr. Lou Marton. "Why, back in the 1880s, Blake's Folly had a population of 10,000.

Today, how many of us are left? Five hundred and twenty-three poor grubbers. And any remaining mining activities are so small-scale, people can barely feed themselves."

Alexander frowned with the obligatory regret, but the well-worn lament bored him. If the U.S. government had once purchased millions of ounces of silver each year, the market had collapsed way back in 1893. Thirty-three years had passed; time enough to accept things would never be the same.

"So many silver boomtowns—Rhyolite, Austin, and Aurora, to name just a few—have disappeared."

Covertly, he watched Susanna Lacey as she moved around the large room, skirting large potted plants, rococo side chairs, and damask-covered sofas. What a captivating woman she was, sleek and elegant in that long-sleeved silky tea dress. Unlike many, she had refused to bob her silvery hair, and the heavy old-fashioned style set off her features beautifully. She had to be somewhere close to his age, sixty-three, and she held herself straight, defying local scorn and high-minded hypocrisy.

As he watched, she turned in his direction. Impossible to miss the warmth in her clear gaze. Was it for him? He wished it were, but wasn't naïve enough to believe so: there was no reason to think she valued him more highly than she did the other men who frequented this establishment. No, she was simply a gracious and efficient hostess, a madam with a good judge of character, for any customer might act differently when alone in a prostitute's bedroom. She also knew how to parlay with—or bribe—those in power, and negotiate with bootleggers.

As Susanna approached, Alexander rose to his feet, as did the other men.

"Good evening, Miss Susanna," Ben Trouverie boomed.

"Good evening, Senator." She nodded to all in the little gathering. "Gentlemen."

"Do come and sit with us for a minute. We need to get an intelligent woman's opinion on things. We men take things too seriously."

"Is that so." Eyes twinkling, she settled on the edge of a very contemporary Louis Majorelle armchair. "What are you clever men taking seriously this evening?"

"We're complaining about how nothing ever seems permanent here in Nevada. It's not like California. Why, that raggedy little San Francisco created its whole financial district on silver from Virginia City."

"San Francisco! What a snooty self-important city it's become, too." Dr. Lou Marton's tone was sour.

Another moth-eaten argument. Sighing inwardly, Alexander caught Susanna's amused glance before she turned to the others.

"The world has changed," she said gently. "Even Virginia City saw its heyday end thirty years ago. Now, that town is struggling, just like Blake's Folly is."

"So it is," conceded Al Blate, cattleman, before trotting into the conversation on his preferred hobby-horse: how to bring back the past.

Alexander blocked out the pedantic flow of words. Yes, it was hard watching the community crumble a little more each passing day, but Susanna was right: the world had changed radically. If, with prohibition and the closing of the mines, the town's old dash and glamour had gone, so had more abhorrent features: violent gunslingers, drunken cowboys, barroom brawlers, vile purveyors of animal fights, and those sordid back-street cribs where each woman serviced up to sixty men a night. Only this plush parlor house brothel remained, harkening back to earlier days.

But how could Al Blate's dull monologue hold the comely Susanna's attention? Alexander struggled to find another, more scintillating topic, one that might detain her. He found none. Was it shyness? Or was it because he wanted to know too much, far more than banal public chitchat could reveal. What did life look like from her perspective? What were her interests? What did they have in common? Impossible to broach such personal subjects here. Equally impossible to extend an invitation to meet elsewhere. Made in a brothel, that would be a proposition, a terrible breach of etiquette: a true gentleman never made advances to a madam.

He could only watch with regret as Susanna stood, excused herself, moved on to greet other men. The opportunity to snag her interest had passed, and Alexander wondered, not for the first time, how many men sitting in this softly lit perfumed room shared his feelings…and his doubts. He almost laughed out loud. He, a mature man, had led a highly unconventional life in France, had once been married. Yet here he was, rendered helpless by timidity. Ridiculous! Knowing that didn't make his plight any easier.

****

The large shaggy mongrel at his feet, Alexander sat at the broad desk in his library, lost in memories. This morning's post had brought sad news: His close friend, the sculptor Aymé Tisserand, had died. How had he even managed to survive for so long? No one had been prepared for the poison gas attacks at Ypres, and soldiers had never recovered: their scarred lungs were useless against tuberculosis.

Alexander hadn't seen Aymé in many years, but he vividly remembered their walking tours, the two of them tramping along Picardie's dirt roads, passing deep forests, verdant pastures, and villages of low red brick, spending nights in simple inns where rancid soup bubbled over smoky fires and people were artless. That had been a bucolic time, and they had thought it would go on forever. Yet in the blinking of an eye, all had been churned up by war, slaughtered, burnt in a bloody inferno.

Folding the letter back into its envelope, he forced the ugly images out of his mind. The war had been over for eight years. He had left France before it started, returning to Blake's Folly at his father's behest, to this yellow house, built in 1864 with silver-boom money. This library had once been the hub of family success. Both his grandfather and his father had sat in this chair, at this same desk, and he could almost smell the expensive cigars they had favored, as if their smoky essence had worked its way into the dark wood paneling, the leather-bound books, and the heavy Turkey carpet.

Hating boomtown violence, greed, and desperation, Alexander had left before his twentieth birthday. By the time he'd returned, the boom was over. After the economic depression of 1910, people had headed away from Nevada in a reverse stampede. The narrow-gauge railway line, carrying silver-lead ore out of town, had been dismantled; formerly busy streets were again rutted and weedy lanes; once-prosperous businesses were boarded up; and wooden house doors slapped uselessly in the eternally gusting wind.

Only the quaintest or the toughest could survive here now. Who else would take root in this bleak countryside? He felt affection for all, the losers, the would-be millionaires who tramped over the hills hoping to get lucky, and those who propped up failing shops. One crazy coot had just opened a furniture workshop, right in the town center, and he contentedly carved rococo table legs no modern householder would ever want. Optimistic housewives planted rosebushes in an area so arid, only dirty dishwater kept them alive. He knew that Lucky Grimes did well with his illegal still behind those half-abandoned buildings on Main Street, but his moonshine was a respectable brew: unlike many, Lucky added no lead toxins, no embalming fluid for kick, and no creosote for color.

There were still a few saloons, too. The rowdy Mizpah had become a conventional roadside inn, and the Red Nag was a coffee house run by Smithson Hardy; illegal alcohol could be found in both. Blake's Folly was well off the beaten track, and when prohibition officers came snooping, they couldn't hope for sympathy. Last winter, one, shot by bootleggers, had been left to die in the snow. If prohibition had effectively cut off this state's much-needed tax revenue, it hadn't reduced social drinking: in one year alone, the 90,000 Nevada residents managed to wangle 10,000 prescriptions for medicinal alcohol.

Alexander often thought of returning to Europe, to the places that once had meaning for him. He longed to stroll along the boulevards in Paris, paint on the banks of the Seine at Issy-les-Moulineaux, and he could do both, for he had enough money to live very comfortably. But he would miss Blake's Folly. There were things that mattered here.

Susanna Lacey. Yes, he acknowledged his deep attraction to her: wasn't that why he frequented her establishment so assiduously? He knew she'd been born on a prairie farm, that she had arrived here when this town had been a wild unruly place, that, as Sassy Sookie, she'd been a prostitute in the Red Nag, and a dance girl at the Mizpah. He also knew she had never married but was the mother of two children. Nothing about that past troubled him.

He was no moralist, no puritan. He had known many women in his Parisian days, those who had been part of the coterie of artists he'd frequented, and with whom he had passed nights in cafés, drinking, singing, arguing. Some had been ladies of easy virtue, some were actresses, or artists' models, mistresses, and muses. There had also been society women attracted by the exhilarating intellectual scene. In that rebellious world, sexual encounters were relaxed, and what was adjudged promiscuity elsewhere was accepted as natural.

He knew Susanna was warm-hearted, that she sincerely enjoyed the company of men, and treated fairly the women who worked for her. If the town's decent, church-going ladies had always excluded her from their company, they'd regarded her with a grudging admiration. And he, fascinated, charmed, wanted more from her.

What would she say if he proposed an outing? A

dinner? Perhaps a jaunt in his pride and joy, the perfectly maintained Oldsmobile. That classy Limited Touring had been a luxury car back in 1910 and quite ahead of its time, with its speedometer, dashboard clock, and full glass windshield. More modern vehicles had since appeared—road travel had become quite the thing after the creation of the low-priced, mass-produced Model T Ford—but keeping the Oldsmobile was a personal pleasure. Would Susanna accept? He didn't know, but all he could lose was his pride.

Perhaps, though, he should begin overtures in another way, one that would catch her attention, set him apart from all the other men.

****

Afternoon sunlight slipped past gauzy curtains, waltzed across the room. Susanna sat at the dressing table in her bedroom high at the top of the house, up where no outsider would dare enter. Here were no frills, only essentials: simple wood furniture, a good bed with thick linen sheets, and a feather comforter. She had never hankered after luxury, although she provided it for those who did.

Downstairs in her establishment, were silk curtains, gilt mirrors, oriental rugs, mahogany tables, and gold-framed paintings of lascivious nudes. In one corner, a small orchestra—a pianist, a violinist, a harpist, and a cellist—played soft swaying notes; the library's salacious illustrated collections were guaranteed to whet appetites; and dishes from the back kitchen were sumptuous. Yet she was a simple woman at heart, preferring basic foods, unpretentious conversation, and honest men. She never let herself forget that life could be unfair, and luck temporal.

Susanna's eyes slid to the round table, to the crystal vase holding the delicate blooms of two-dozen orange-tipped yellow roses. Yellow roses: the symbol of platonic love. How clever of Alexander, and how touched she was by his gesture. She had never misjudged that man's delicacy, yet she knew how wrong it would be to let her imagination run wild.

What was he offering? Deeper friendship? The position of mistress? How should she react? She would soon be sixty, no longer young, but that didn't bother her. She was fit and strong, and she knew that men still found her alluring. As a madam, she received proposals from clients, for some preferred an older woman's experience and wisdom to the sexy offerings of those younger: such men soon learned there were boundaries that wouldn't be overstepped. Surely Alexander Treemont knew that, too.

Was he a client? No, not like the others. And since that was the case, how was she to interpret the arrival of those roses? They weren't the first she had ever received, but Alexander's gesture had touched in a way none of the others had. Still…she was wary. She knew that, hidden under the suave demeanor of those with class, power, and money, lurked a very particular self-serving code of honor. The Treemonts were certainly no exception.

She'd known Alexander's father back in the days when she'd been Sassy Sookie. An arrogant, condescending man, he had left his uppity wife and imposing yellow mansion to come to the Red Nag for the tawdry glitter of an evening's self-indulgence in the arms of goodtime girls: Jolly Juney, buxom, shrill, and aggressive, had been his favorite. One night, he'd brought his eldest son Julius with him, a terrified and hesitant young man. Soon enough, like his father, he had become a greedy habitué of that establishment, craving the sexual release unavailable in cosseted society with "good" women from "decent" families.

She knew little about Alexander's life—they could hardly have belonged to the same social circles, and he had left town back in the early 1880s, gone to live in Europe. In 1913, he'd returned, accompanied by a fashionable French wife and two sons. The marriage hadn't lasted. His wife, shunning local society, had left Blake's Folly with their children. And Alexander had begun spending evenings at Madam Lacey's.

Still…however polite and engaging, Alexander was a Treemont. Why would his values be different from the others in his family? Had they given a thought to the men who had worked and died in their mines? They hadn't. Workers were ciphers, existing to make the life of the elite more pleasant. What about those whose salaries had been cut when the price of silver fell? Those with families to feed? The Treemonts in their grand house hadn't even noticed them. So what could she and Alexander possibly have in common? What beliefs, what values could they share? None.

****

The desert air was touched with spring's first gentle perfume, an essence so subtle it could easily be overlooked, so transient, its beauty had to be seized. Susanna crossed the rutted road, headed west, passing the abandoned houses of those who had given up. Over there, right on that corner, once—such a long time ago—there had been a hastily slapped together shantytown. And farther along, over there in the weedy field, was the rubble of a fancy new suburb that had burnt to the ground within a year of its construction. That had been back in 1893, and no one had bothered building another since.

She took a deep breath of the desert air, relishing its dry tang, and the hint of new vegetation. How many people could appreciate a landscape as bleak as this? She knew every inch of these rutted streets, every particle of dust, for she'd spent her entire adult life here, crisscrossing these roads on her daily walks. With its scattered streets, tent communities, and thrown-together shacks, Blake's Folly had never been a pretty town, yet there were still two handsome buildings in red brick and hewn stone—the schoolhouse and the courthouse. The once-splendid Emerald Hotel with its elegant dining room was now a flophouse for transients, and the old theater and opera house had burnt down years ago. Yet, she loved run-down Blake's Folly—not that she had ever seen much of anything else.

She knew she could retire, sell Madame Lacey's— it wouldn't be hard to find a buyer. What would she do then? Travel? Never having traveled, she didn't see its appeal. She had heard and read about hectic city life but never craved it, preferring the easy security of what she knew well. As the old adage went: better the devil you know, than the devil you don't.

Hearing the purr of a car's engine, something rare on these back streets, she turned. A large Oldsmobile, an old-fashioned car, elegant in its antiquated way, and obviously well cared for, was coming in her direction. She knew whose it was.

The car stopped when it reached her. Out stepped Alexander, smiling, dapper in fine leather driving gloves and a cream-colored suit, the sartorial choice of those with a well-nourished bank account. He removed his flat tweed cap, greeted her, and Susanna noted how his pomaded hair, glossy and silver, stayed perfectly in place. How easy it was for men with no combs or pins to battle with every day.

"I certainly didn't expect to run into you out here," she said, holding out her hand. "But it has given me the perfect opportunity to thank you for the roses. They are beautiful."

Briefly, he took her hand in his firm grip and bowed.

"Yellow. For friendship," she added.

He met her gaze evenly. "And joy."

Joy? "Ah. I didn't know."

His smile was warm. "I didn't expect to run into you out here either."

Susanna laughed. "I suppose most people do think I'm some strange night creature who never risks daylight."

A line of embarrassed confusion appeared between his brows. "I didn't…Excuse me if I…"

She couldn't let him finish. Reaching out again, her fingers touched the soft fabric of his elegant suit jacket. "I know you didn't mean anything offensive. You'll have to forgive my frivolity. This spring air does have that effect on me." With a strange reluctance, she let her hand drop. "However, I do come out walking every day."

"So do I." He cocked a curious eyebrow. "But I've never run into you before."

"Because I rarely head in this direction, southwest of the town."

"And what brings you here today?"

She was unprepared for the question, and the real answer would be too revealing. Why had she come out this way? Because she'd been curious. She'd wanted to catch a glimpse of that wooden mansion where he lived, that swanky building with its broad front porch and high balcony. Ever since the arrival of those yellow roses, she had thought about him constantly—although why pretty flowers had turned her head in such a way was beyond her comprehension.

"I wanted to see the desert blooms," she said simply, and that excuse did sound reasonable. "I've been told that there are far more of them out near the hills to the southwest."

"Correct." He nodded. "This year we're particularly lucky. Those late winter showers came at just the right time, not too late, or too early. This surprising early warmth is a boon, too."

"Although nights are still cool."

"Fortunately. That slows down the growth of grasses and mustards, but it doesn't destroy new flower buds."

Her curiosity had definitely been piqued. "I never knew you took an interest in botany."

His lips twitched. "It's a subject we've never managed to touch on in our conversations. Yes, I'm interested in all the phenomena the desert has to offer, and flowers are certainly included. But I'm an amateur botanist and not as knowledgeable as I'd wish to be."

Not arrogant or pedantic either, Susanna thought. But she'd always known that, too. "None of us are ever as knowledgeable as we'd wish to be."

He chuckled. "Too true." Then hesitated, but only

briefly. "And since it appears we share an appreciation of nature's lovelier gifts, would you care to join us for a drive out to the area just beyond the Spieler mine? That's where Russ and I are headed."

"Russ?"

He motioned toward the Oldsmobile. "An old friend."

For the first time, she noticed the large shaggy dog of indeterminate breed watching them from the back seat of the car. "I didn't know you had a dog." What a silly thing to say. He would never have brought that creature into her brothel.

"Unless you object to traveling with him."

"No, I don't. I've taken in many dogs over the years, mostly those abandoned by owners who left town."

"Russ and I came to know each other in exactly that way. Since he's a capable walking companion despite his age, we spend a lot of time exploring the countryside. I can guarantee the area around the old Spieler Mine is the best place to see wildflowers at the moment."

She was tempted to go with him, very much so, but would it be a good idea? She had nothing to fear from an excursion in the company of Alexander Treemont, but what about him? Wasn't he worried about his good reputation? She'd seen curtains twitching at a window just across the street and knew nosy Mary Mason was observing them. In a town this size, everyone made a point in knowing everyone else's business. Every person probably knew that Alexander Treemont regularly frequented her establishment, but what went on after dark was different from defying convention in broad daylight.

She tipped her head in the direction of the cabin. "Our tenacious local snoop is gathering information at this very moment. You'll be putting your good name at risk."

Alexander's eyes shifted toward the Mason abode, and he grinned with satisfaction. "How generous we are, providing the town busybody with grist for her gossip mill." Crooking his arm, he offered it to Susanna.

Surprised at the pleasure his words gave her, she snuggled her hand into the inviting crook, and they crossed to the waiting car. And she realized that, by accepting his invitation and riding out of town in full view of all, their relationship had gone to another level. She wasn't certain if that thought was entirely comforting.

****

The Spieler Mine, long ago worked out and abandoned, was nothing more than a heap of forgotten rubble on a distant hillside. Leaving the car behind, they followed a rutted track speckled with the spindly shrubs that thrive in bleak places—twiggy Mormon tea, bunchgrass, the inevitable sagebrush, resistant manzanita, and rabbit-brush—and the early afternoon was sweet with the scent of unseen blooms.

The path took them over a low hill and up onto a rocky outcrop, and there, quite suddenly, a startling sweep of color came into view: fiery red paintbrush, desert dandelion, pink phlox, and in the distance, a glory of purple penstemon. It was the most splendid desert flowering she had ever seen, and her murmured, "How breathtaking," seemed inadequate. Alexander appeared to be equally at a loss, and he gazed silently at the luxuriant natural carpet. She felt incredibly grateful that he had proposed such a sight: how many men would have considered a similar outing?

Making herself comfortable on a low stone, she cupped her chin in her hand and delighted in the near silence. Far overhead, a red-tailed hawk rode the wind, surveying all.

"Thank you for bringing me here," she said, finally. "I've never been out this way before, even though it's so close to where we live. Surely, this display is unusual. It doesn't happen every year, does it?"

"No, it doesn't. This is quite exceptional. Normally, winter and spring rains are much scantier than they were this year; and since flowering plants don't adapt to water shortage, they just wilt and die right after they appear, leaving behind their seeds."

"Although shrubs and grasses always do well."

He nodded. "Because some have long roots that reach down to the water table. Others spread their roots over large areas to catch moisture. They're a bit like kangaroo rats that squeeze every drop of liquid out of all they ingest and can go an entire lifetime without drinking water."

"You know that because you've been coming out here for a long time?"

"Yes," he said simply. "Being from a mine-owning family, I wanted to know about the land around me."

Russ came to where she was seated and settled at her feet. She caressed his large rough head and covertly observed Alexander, standing tall and straight, outlined by the vast sky. His profile was proud, his chin definite.

He had a natural elegance and all the manners good breeding could instill, but she also sensed he was a man who could be trusted, who was open-minded. Then she pulled herself up short: had mine owners ever been known for their scruples or charity? There was a breach between them, and it would never be overcome.

They were silent for a long moment, both staring out onto the glorious panoply of color. "I suppose I've just been lucky in my life," Alexander said, finally.

"Lucky?"

He turned, met her gaze. "My grandfather and father were unrelenting men. They raised us to be the same—domineering, without charity, and without pity. We were to focus on the two things that counted: power and money. But despite their hopes, I was never cut out for the role of mine owner. Unlike my older brother Julius, I lacked the ruthlessness, the greed. I wanted another life altogether. That's why I stayed in Europe for all those years. By the time I returned to Blake's Folly, the mines were played out."

"What did you do in Europe?"

"I dreamt of being a famous artist." His tone was mocking.

"An artist?" She was surprised. She had expected him to be involved in business. "What sort of artist?"

"A painter."

"And were you?"

"Was I a painter? Yes. Not a famous one, though. Sometimes dreams aren't enough. You need a certain amount of talent before fame strikes."

"Don't all decent artists question their talent? That's always been my impression from the few I've met. It's the mediocre people who think they are beyond criticism."

Amused, he laughed. "Possibly." But he didn't look convinced.

"You were gone for years. Where did you live?"

"I spent some time in London, also in Rome, but mostly, I lived in Paris." He waved one hand in the direction of the ruined mine. "That's what I mean about being lucky. I was independently wealthy and didn't need to support myself. I wouldn't have been able to do that, not with the sort of artwork I was doing. The artists I associated with were social protestors. We painted what we saw, not what clients wanted—not dreamy scenes with boats floating along the Seine, picnics in glades with provocative rosy women, or bucolic valleys. We were rebels, and we could see what a lie it was to paint pure loveliness."

She shook her head. "I've never heard anything about any of this."

He came over to where she was sitting, settled down on a flat rock near hers. "No surprise. Most people know of painters like Pissarro, Gauguin, and Cezanne. But that idyllic landscape they had been painting was changing radically, and the result is far less picturesque. The population was growing, new roads were being laid out, train lines and factories were appearing. At first, a few artists incorporated chimneystacks and industrial buildings into their work—you can see them peeking out from the greenery or reflected in the rippling water. But by 1890, it was clear that once-pristine scenery had been ruthlessly destroyed, disfigured by industry and rubble. That destruction is what we portrayed."

"Did any of you become well known?"

"Even the very best aren't famous. That's what happens when you don't please the comfortable bourgeoisie, when you don't vie for commercial success."

"What are their names?"

"Armand Guillaumin works with deep violet and grey. His rivers are dark, and deadly smoke belches out of his chimneys. Under Theophile-Alexandre Steinlen's terrible skies, streets are peopled by beggars, prostitutes, and skeletal children, all those whose lives have been sacrificed to profit."

"You also painted destruction?"

His grimace was wry, slightly bitter. "I did. Blackened skies and shriveled trees. Some of my friends were anarchists, and like them, I protested against all that was happening. Yet, I couldn't help feeling like a hypocrite, profiting from the money generated by mines thousands of miles away."

"Yes, there was that same destruction here. Now there's nothing left, aside from these scars on the hills, but back then the ugliness was just as complete."

He looked at her appraisingly. "That's what bothered me all those years ago."

This conversation was so unexpected, she hardly knew how to continue. "You were also an anarchist?"

"I sympathized with them. I was influenced by the philosopher Pierre-Joseph Proudhon who believed in the right of individuals to retain the product of their own labor." Abruptly, he stood offered her his hand. "Please forgive me. These are the words of a disillusioned witness to the times. I'm being a bore."

"No, you aren't," she said with sincerity. Taking the proffered hand, she rose from her perch. "I'd love to hear more." Although, again seeing the doubt in his eyes, she almost laughed.

"You would?"

"I know nothing of the world you're telling me about. My life has been here. Everything else—the things you mention, those glades and bucolic valleys—I've only seen in paintings and photographs."

He nodded. Then, again tucking her hand into the crook of his elbow, they began the descent.

"Do you still paint?"

"More rarely. And when I do, it's the local landscapes that I portray." His half smile was sardonic. "The urge to change the world has passed."

Yes, she knew about the wisdom born of experience. And acceptance.

When they reached the car, she looked up at him. "I'd be interested in seeing your work, what you do now, also the paintings you did back then. Do you have any of it left?"

He watched her, his expression unreadable. "Yes. Some. However, you might find the canvasses of my fellow artists more interesting. Being in a better financial situation than most allowed me to purchase what was rejected by others."

"And those are here? In Blake's Folly?"

"If you'll agree to dine with me at my home tomorrow evening, I'd be more than happy to show you what I have."

"Ah."

"And," he added, his eyes twinkling, "with Russ, as chaperone."

She smiled. The invitation was tempting, but she couldn't accept. "I'm afraid it's quite impossible."

"If you think the invitation is too compromising in this town where everyone knows everyone else, I'd be happy to invite other people to join us."

She laughed outright. "Please. Don't misunderstand my refusal. I've spent my life flouting convention. But I do have a business to run in the evenings."

"And no one can take your place?"

Why was she protesting? What was she afraid of? What was she risking? She knew Madam Lacey's would run perfectly without her, that Frisco, the doorman, and Cowboy Luke, the barman, would ensure order prevailed. "You're right. I can tell Lily to step in as hostess."

"I have the most excellent cook in Blake's Folly. I think Mrs. Peal's unusual talents even surpass those of the cooks in your own establishment."

If only he weren't smiling, if only she didn't want to hear what he had to say. She was fascinated by the world he had known. Too fascinated, perhaps? Too charmed? "Your arguments are most persuasive."

"Then you'll accept?"

"I can't possibly refuse."

How pleased he looked. As if it really did matter to him.

"What time would you like me to be there?"

"I'll come for you at eight, or is that too late for you? After almost thirty years in Europe, I'm used to the later dining hour."

"No, that's fine. But you needn't come for me, I can—"

He didn't let her finish. "Eight o'clock. I'll be there."

She settled into the seat of the Oldsmobile. Alexander Treemont coming to fetch her in this very recognizable car? Well, wouldn't that get tongues wagging with salacious imaginings!

****

Susanna turned the key in the lock, stepped into the upstairs back room of the Mizpah Saloon, the same room where, long ago, she and Westley Cranston had shared sweet nights of pleasure. The air was dusty, motionless, and in early evening's dusky light, old forgotten pieces of furniture were heavy shadows. Nothing had changed since Westley's departure back in 1889. The same books stood on the shelves along one wall, for knowing of her passion for literature, he had left them behind for her. And in this room's peaceful silence, she had read all: the classics, and the western novels, the few scientific works on spiders, ants, and snakes, and the histories so dated forty years later as to be laughable.

She had started coming to this room when the Mizpah was still owned by Ned Hardy. Poor Neddy. A non-combatant Quaker, he had volunteered as an ambulance driver during the Great War, then died in the icy wet mud of Flanders. What about Westley? Was he still alive? Where was he now? Did he ever think of her? Why would he? Why waste time remembering the superficial, flirtatious Sassy Sookie?

Westley had never known she had been deeply in love with him, a love that had come too late, after she'd realized how foolish it was to hanker after the worthless Big Jim Bally. What a silly girl she'd been back then, nurturing dreams of romance, building hope on a pile of dust, on a man with a string of terrified women who whored for him in Virginia City's cribs. Westley had warned her, but she'd turned against him. Until Rodeo Liz had confided that Big Jim had also promised her marriage and a big house. Until her instinct for survival had kicked in.

She knew her decision to stay in Blake's Folly had been the right one, but wondered what would have happened if she had allowed the relationship with Westley to flower? If he had discovered she was pregnant? If she had agreed to travel into the unknown with him? By the time she'd come to her senses, he was leaving for the Yukon with that scrawny prim Hattie, that piano player he'd met in this very saloon.

Westley had never known she had given birth to his daughter. What would he have done if he had? Come back? Impossible. She'd heard that he and Hattie had married; that, several years later, they'd gone to live in San Francisco where he'd settled, become the editor-in-chief of a respectable newspaper. And Hattie had finally given birth, to another girl.

Why waste time thinking of lost chances? The world was full of people who had suffered love's failure, why dwell on it? Was it because, this afternoon out on the prairie, Alexander had managed to touch her in some deep way? Because he might not be the unfeeling, ruthless man his background had groomed him to be? Because she knew she cared about him?

Well, what now? Even if she had judged him badly, what difference did it make? What did she want? Not a mate or marriage. That was something Alexander Treemont would never consider, certainly not with her. Why fret? She knew the truth behind the façade of domestic bliss, knew what life was really like behind the stiff curtains of gussied-up houses. Her information came first-hand, from the patrons of Madam Lacey's.

The faint tinkle of the piano filtered up through the wooden floor of the Mizpah. Downstairs, in that other real world, people were gathering for a drink, a meal. No longer a Wild West saloon, this had become a respectable roadside inn off the Reno road. The perfumed and painted dancing girls were long gone— most had married local lads or moved away—and the bedrooms were now used by modern tourists crossing America in cars.

Only this, Westley's room, was intemporal, a place of ghostly memory, and her secret refuge from the world. Sighing, Susanna stood, went to the door, closed and locked it behind her. Leaving the peace behind. Time to get back to Madam Lacey's. The night's activities were about to begin.

****

Closely observed by furry Russ, Alexander sat on the edge of his bed, staring across the large square room with its broad windows opening to the evening light. Susanna was coming to dine with him! He couldn't believe how easy it had been to get her here. It had been pure luck, seeing her out walking yesterday afternoon, and how pleased he'd been when she'd agreed to travel out to the old mine.

Now that she had accepted his invitation, he was as nervous as a young man in his first courtship, fretting about what he would wear for a dinner in his own home: a formal suit vest or a more casual pullover sweater vest? The orange silk tie, or the green? He was ridiculous, he knew that. He also knew he had to be careful, not make a false move.

His marriage to the small-boned dark-haired Laeticia had gone from agreeable to dull. She had once been a sculptor whose work he'd admired, but her artistic ambition had been swallowed up by motherhood, despite his encouragement. Although she hadn't openly objected to coming to America, she had never sought a place in local society; and bored with small town life, with the dullness of a dying boomtown, she'd soon left for livelier Reno.

He had taken their separation with equanimity and not a little relief; he had no desire to follow her to the city, and he surprised himself with the affection he felt toward Blake's Folly, a sentiment that had grown stronger since meeting Susanna. How he had savored their few brief seconds of contact, the delight of feeling her fine-boned hand in the crook of his arm. Yet, he knew that thoughts like those would have to remain hidden. For the moment.

****

The rooms he showed her were beautiful, deeply shadowed, and a faint perfume of fresh beeswax polish and flowers floated on the air.

"I always wanted to see what the interior of this house looked like, but never thought I would," Susanna admitted, then doubted the wisdom of such a confession. It slotted her firmly into the position of an outsider, pressing her nose against the glass, hoping to catch a glimpse of the town elite.

Neither surprised nor scathing, Alexander simply smiled. "I often feel the same way. Passing houses and wanting to sneak inside, see how people live, understand their choices."

She wondered if he were only putting her at her

ease.

The generations of Treemonts had certainly exercised good taste and restraint. The solid wood furniture and subtle embellishments contrasted sharply with the ostentatious luxury of her brothel. Inwardly, she cringed at the comparison...then reminded herself that clients seemed to prefer provocative vulgarity to their own refined homes.

"Everything is quite lovely."

The sardonic smile was back. "Of course, it is. The books, the fine furniture, this big house, the many servants—these were the trappings of success. My father wanted us to be envied by all."

"Your mother was happy here?"

"She was a wealthy man's perfect mate, as unrelenting as my father. She kept up appearances, ran this household with an iron fist and sharp tongue, instilled fear and submission into the servants. Yet, it was all show because our family's status was newly won."

"How so?"

"My grandparents were all born on Irish bog farms. My grandfather was dirt poor, but when he first came to this region, silver chloride was so plentiful, it could be pulled it off the rocks with bare hands. All his subsequent wealth was simply due to luck, to coming to the right place at an auspicious moment."

Susanna laughed outright, delighted by Alexander's iconoclasm.

The small, intimate room where they dined was more elegant than any fashionable eatery could have been, with its round oak table covered by a white damask tablecloth, the heavy gleaming silverware and crystal goblets. Even the wine they drank was pungent, divine. How had he managed to obtain it? Most wineries had closed with prohibition; their vines had been torn out and replaced with fruit trees.

"I stocked up seven years ago, before the law went into effect." He chuckled softly. "I also happen to know people who are still making decent wine with compacted grapes produced by the few remaining California growers."

On all the walls were framed paintings of the desert. "My more recent attempts," Alexander admitted.

To her eye, they were surprisingly good. He had chosen watercolor as his medium, and its clear transparency, when combined with his light hand and talent for subtle but deep coloring, had caught the desert's fleeting beauty.

Their meal of old-fashioned American dishes was equally surprising, and very different from what she knew: a smoky soup of herbed pecans, a main course of braised squash, carrots, fennel, and herbs, served with the finest Canada rice, and a dessert of home-preserved summer fruits. There was no meat, neither was there fish.

"A hangover from anarchist days in Paris," he explained. "We were influenced by writers like Henry Salt who protested against the appalling treatment of work horses and dogs in England, and Tolstoy, who thought it immoral to slaughter innocent animals that were themselves vegetarian—deer, rabbits, sheep, horses, and trusting cows."

"Yes, I can agree with that point of view," Susanna approved. "Do tell me more about those days. Were there also women artists?"

"There were. It was more difficult for them, because few academies accepted women. Many apprenticed themselves to male artists and received formal training in that way. Some became very well-known, like Berthe Morisot, Camille Claudel, Marie Braquemond, and Suzanne Valadon—Utrillo's mother." He frowned. "She did all she could to save her son. He's a brilliant artist, but alcoholic, violent, and mentally unstable."

After dinner, he took her to his library, showed her the art he had brought back from Europe. In the work of those other angry idealists, ugliness predominated and humanity was faceless. She did, however, note the evolution in Alexander's scenes, the slow change from dismal urban darkness to Nevada's abandoned mines, ruined houses, sparse vegetation, and the suggestion of constant dry wind. She was surprised he didn't take his talent more seriously.

"You never exhibit any of this now?"

"I can't see myself going out, hawking."

She smiled. "I understand. You're an artist with an artist's mentality. I see things differently because I have a crude businesswoman's mind. I always look for the financial viability of things."

"Even the viability in worked-out abandoned mine shafts?"

"Oh, yes." Her enthusiasm was sincere. "The protest is still there in your work. It's part of your style. Even if the themes have changed, there's always the ugly consequence of human interference in one corner."

"Now that most of the mines have closed in this area, we're spared the consequences. People think life will become easier with more motorcars, electricity, and paved roads. The war is over, and we hope there will never be another like it. But it's hard to believe in a perfect world."

She sat forward in her chair, observing him warily. "You have strange thoughts for the son of a mine owner, but you weren't here, in town, during the worst times. You were far away."

His brow furrowed. "For example, during the depression of 1893?"

She nodded, remembering the panic when railway companies failed, one after the other, falling like a house of cards: the Philadelphia and Reading, the Erie, the Northern Pacific, the Union Pacific, the Atchison, Topeka and Santa Fe. "The politicians lied, claimed the economy was prospering while 500 banks closed, and 16,000 businesses declared bankruptcy. When the price of silver dropped, the miners were desperate."

"I know. And the mine owners cut wages. If miners refused to accept working for so little, they were replaced." His solemn eyes met hers. "I wasn't here, but I knew what was happening. My grandfather, my father, my older brother were all hard men, and social justice meant nothing to them. I was the youngest, the one who had left the country. I had no say in matters."

"I did what I could to help people," she said. "Unemployed miners chopped wood and broke up rocks. Women sewed in exchange for food, and some became prostitutes, but because they weren't professionals, they couldn't handle the conditions, and they weren't protected. We arranged for medical attention to take charge of them and their children. We provided tents, and food. But there were too many needy people, and we couldn't keep up."

Alexander rose, went to a dark wood sideboard, poured brandy into two crystal snifters. "We'll never be able to keep up with need, or to eliminate poverty. Never."

"How true." Cupping the glass he handed her, Susanna sank back in the armchair and let the room's dark security surround her. What peace she felt in Alexander's presence, and in his territory. She could understand why he had come back to this house. No matter its history, it had become a haven, a graceful relic.

"What did your father think of your artistic dreams?"

"He didn't approve, but what could he do? He had my brother Julius to depend on. He'd already lost my brother Bradley, and he didn't want to risk losing me too."

"You had another brother who died?"

He laughed now, his teeth flashing in the dim light. "Far from it. There were three of us, three sons, and we were all raised in the same...unrelenting...way. We should all have become cold ambitious men, but life is unpredictable, and even the best plans often go awry. My brother Bradley was a light-hearted fellow. Instead of thinking of profits and gain, his passion was whittling, and he created tiny intricate pieces of sculpture using any bit of wood he could find. Then, to my father's horror, he fell in love with a cowboy. Since something like that was unthinkable, he was disowned; and Bradley, along with his handsome cowboy, left town, vanished without trace."

"What an amazing story. I never heard a word about it, although gossip spreads through this community faster than prairie fire."

"It was hushed up very quickly."

"It must have been."

"My father couldn't let something scandalous tarnish the family name."

She sipped her brandy, savoring its hint of oak. "And your brother Julius died of cholera, didn't he?"

"Yes. He contracted it out at a mining community inhabited by uneducated slum dwellers from the East, people who had always known deprivation and filth. Even out here, they were unwilling to adopt sanitary measures, preparing food out in the open but refusing to use privies, contaminating their own water sources. They created the perfect environment for cholera. By the time Julius managed to make it back to Blake's Folly, it was too late to save him."

"So you were summoned home, to step into his shoes."

"But by the time I arrived, there wasn't much silver left, and the mines had closed. Still, I stayed on. I had a family, so a certain amount of stability was called for, but my wife disliked the life out here. I briefly considered returning to Europe when the war was over—we all thought it would be a short, easy victory—but it raged on. I tried to enlist, but was considered too old for active duty."

"You remained in this house where you'd grown up."

"I relish the solitude and the silence. My sons, William and Edward, are attached to noisy city life. The last place that interests either of them is Blake's Folly." He chuckled. "Or having a father who paints pictures."

They returned to Madam Lacey's on foot, Russ

following sleepily. The night was pleasantly mild, and far out on the prairie, coyotes howled. Once again, she tucked her hand into the crook of his arm; it now seemed such a natural thing to do. She felt unusually close to him after this evening. What surprised her most was how similar their values seemed to be, and that deepened her feelings.

"I'm ashamed of myself," he said quietly.

Puzzled, she looked up at him, but his face was unreadable. "How so?"

"I've spent the entire day, both this afternoon and this evening, talking about myself. I know nothing about you. Where you were born, how you arrived here in town."

She laughed shortly. "My story hardly matches yours. There are no foreign destinations, and there are no hidden works of art. I was born on a prairie farm around a hundred miles southeast, down in the direction of Goldfield. I wasn't quite sixteen years old when I ran away from home."

"And you've never been back?"

"Never. Not that I'm opposed to doing that. I've often thought of returning, taking a look at what's left, but I haven't done it."

"The memories are painful?"

"No, I can't say that they are. Too many years have passed, and the anger and resentment are gone. I suppose that's one advantage of growing older."

"Your naturally light-hearted disposition does make life easier."

"Maybe…" Then she smiled, acknowledging the truth of his words. "Yes, you're right."

"Would you like me to drive you out there? I'd be

more than happy to do that."

She stared up at him in the dark. "It might be enlightening. Although not particularly agreeable…"

"Think about it."

She was silent for a long moment. "Why am I hesitating? How silly. Yes, I'll take you up on your offer."

His smile was enigmatic. "Confronting ghosts can be a liberating experience."

And with Alexander at her side, challenging the old specters might be less alarming.

They stopped in the quiet street outside her establishment.

"Thank you," he said, his voice soft.

She laughed. "I should be thanking you. What a stimulating evening this has been. Such glorious food and interesting conversation."

His answering smile was faint. Then taking her hand, he raised it to his lips, kissed it softly. Turned, disappeared into the night.

She stood there, not moving. That kiss, simple, soft…the warmth of it traveled up her arm, sped directly into her heart. It might be all the physical contact she would ever have with Alexander Treemont, but it was a simple intimacy she would never forget.

****

If this had once been a working prairie farm, those days were long over. Alexander noted the spiny green-grey shrub that had conquered all, its dull hue underlining the uniform bleakness. The road leading to the former ranch hadn't been used in years, the briny crust and clumped sagebrush indicated that clearly enough. How hopeless any attempt to survive in a place this desolate, where only greasewood and shadscale thrived in the salt-laden earth, where rainfall would never be anything but scanty.

He glanced at Susanna, sitting straight in her seat, her eyes fixed on a distant swell and a low cluster of buildings. She had been silent for the last part of the journey, as though aware that stepping into the past would be less easy than anticipated. He parked where the surface was still hard and brittle, not wanting to drive farther, risk sinking into soft ground: how unpleasant that would be in an area as lonely as this. "We'll have to continue on foot."

He helped her out of the car, and she smiled up at him. It was a fragile smile, soft, trusting, and it touched him deeply.

Buildings, once barns, had collapsed long ago. There wasn't much left of the small one-story house. Tipping dangerously to the left, its loose planks shuddered in the niggling wind, filled the air with a hopeless staccato. Part of the roof had caved in; the surrounding porch sagged; a front door had vanished, long ago carried off by intruders. In a few years, there would be nothing left.

Inside, there were still a few sticks of furniture: a table, smashed chairs, a sugar bowl, and a blackened forgotten spoon. The tatters of poor curtains hung at pane-less windows, but otherwise, the house had been picked clean.

"How strange it is to be back here again," she murmured. "What happened to everyone? Where did they all go?"

He took in the sad atmosphere, the floating smell of poverty that still invaded this space. The ugliness.

"How many of you lived here?"

"My mother, father, and my five brothers. I had two older sisters, but one died, and the other moved far away after she married. I never saw her again. I was the youngest, and by the time I was fifteen, two of my brothers were left." The bitterness in her voice was razor sharp.

He noted her tightened lips, her pallor. "It's a tiny space for so many people," he prompted.

She nodded once, her eyes traveling over every surface, seeking answers.

"Life must have been difficult," he continued. There was a lot more to the story, he realized. He wondered if she would confide in him.

Her eyes met his, finally. "Difficult? It was ugly." She began exploring the two remaining rooms, and he followed.

"My father was a short-tempered violent man with narrow religious ideas, a bigot of the worst kind. My mother was weak and submissive, willing to accept bad treatment. They were a pathetic couple. You can't imagine what it was like, all of us crowded together like filthy rats in a tiny cage. Outside, there was nothing as far as the eye could see, only that dry, hopeless plain, and the poor thirsty, starving cattle that never survived harsh winters and indifferent treatment. And my brother Ezekiel…"

He waited, unwilling to push her, but the air was filled with her scorn. She bent down, picked up a faded shred of fabric, perhaps once a bright ribbon, and toyed with it.

"Ezekiel pushed me into corners, tried to get his way with me. Threatened me, hit me when I protested.

My father knew, and he didn't stop him. Why? Because I could see the desire in his eyes, too. And then, one day Big Jim Bally showed up. He was my brother Zacharias' friend. Jim had been involved in a bank robbery and needed a place where he could lie low. When he told me he loved me, I fell hard. What choice did I have? I was in need of protection. But Jim disappeared when he suspected I was pregnant."

"And your father couldn't accept you were going to have an illegitimate child." Alexander knew he was right. How many similar stories had he heard? It was always the innocent victims who paid dearly when bigots and hypocrites meted out their merciless brand of justice.

She let the scrap of fabric drop. "I knew what would happen. I knew my father would kill me when he found out, he'd made his views clear over the years. For him, a Jezebel had no right to live. I knew Ezekiel felt that way, too. He was mean, and he'd been deadly jealous of Big Jim. When Jim disappeared, I used to think Ezekiel and my father had murdered him.

"And your mother?"

"My mother discovered my secret—after all the babies she'd had, she couldn't miss the first signs, the sickness, my loss of appetite. She'd once caught me in Big Jim's arms out on the veranda, and she knew what was going on. I begged her not to tell anyone although, goodness knows, I couldn't hide the pregnancy for forever. She knew what the consequences would be, too, but she betrayed me, called me a whore, a pariah."

Again, he waited as she looked around the room, her mouth grim.

"Come into the yard. I'll show you something."

Outside, she pointed to what was left of the roof. "You see that angle, right up there, where two sections of the house join? Whenever Ezekiel was feeling lusty and looking for me, I would sneak up there and hide. No one thought of looking for me in a crack on the roof, but I could hear everything that was said inside the house. That night, when my mother announced I was pregnant with Big Jim's baby, I heard them all raging. I was a miserable sinner; I had to die. I could hear them loading up their rifles."

"How long did you stay up there?"

Her eyes met his, clear, untroubled now. Even faintly amused. "Luck was on my side…finally. The night was very dark. There was no moon, and no clouds. I heard them leave the house, I saw them, and I knew where they were, where they went. When I sensed the time was right, I crawled out from my hiding space, slid along the ground on my belly, just like a snake. Headed out to those hills in the far distance. Running away from all I'd ever known was terrifying, but I knew I wouldn't survive otherwise."

"We're very far from Blake's Folly."

Her smile was slightly mocking. "My luck held. I saw a campfire. I didn't know who was out there, but I headed for it. Three men were passing through the area—oh, I knew they were probably up to no good, cattle rustlers or bandits keeping to the shadows—but what choice did I have? They fed me, kept me with them as they traveled north. Then, a few weeks later, they left me in Blake's Folly."

She had used the work "luck" twice, and he admired her spirit, the optimism and strength that had kept her alive, but he also knew what she was leaving out of the story: those men had probably taken care of her for their own titillation and selfish release, but they had at least brought her to the safety of the town—the encounter could have had a more drastic conclusion. Once in Blake's Folly, she'd known that prostitution was the way to survive, to have enough money to raise her baby.

Was she waiting for his shocked reaction? His rejection? Did she think her story had disgusted him? How far from the truth that was. He did the one thing that seemed appropriate. Reaching out for her, he pulled her into his arms and held her tightly, as if, just by contact, he could make ugly memories disappear. And felt a rush of tenderness deeper than any he had ever known.

****

A few miles down the road, a scattering of wooden houses still called itself a community. Rarely allowed to leave that place once called home, she had seen little of the world outside: even these few shambling dwellings had been unknown to her. In a rustic general store, the owner was a grizzled ancient man. How long had he been in the area? Even though she wanted to know more, she had no desire to see any of her family again.

"I once knew people who lived out this way," she began, unwilling to reveal her identity. "A rancher named Jeremiah Lacey."

The geezer reflected for a long while, poked at a bad tooth with the tip of his tongue, stared into the far distance, as if the right answer could be found out there.

"Name's sorta familiar."

"He had five sons and three daughters," she prompted.

103

"Plenny families like that out here in th' old days. Not many folk left."

"What happened to them all?"

"Gone, all of 'em. Beef prices unsteady, an' the railroad rates were too high. Then there was the bad winters that killed cattle by the thousands. Most ranchers went bankrupt in the late '80s, and they all headed out for somewheres else."

"There's no one named Lacey in the area now?"

"None I never heard of."

So she would never know more. Did it matter?

Night fell as they drove back to Blake's Folly. She glanced at Alexander from under her lashes. His expression was unreadable, and his face was the one he presented to the wide world, not the other Alexander that she glimpsed whenever his guard was down.

He must have sensed she was watching him, and his expression changed, softened. Reaching out, he folded her hand into his. "Are you hungry?"

"Hungry?" Caught in the simple but strangely heady pleasure of his skin touching hers, she could only stare.

She saw his amusement, even in the dark. "Hunger is the sort of thing that happens several times a day. There's a decent roadhouse a few miles away. We could stop for a meal. Blake's Folly is still some distance from here."

"I really should get back. There will be clients showing up. I should be there…"

He was still smiling. "Because your presence is essential?"

She couldn't help laughing. "I think we've had this conversation before. Yes, I know that things will run smoothly without me. No, I don't have to be there."

"So we'll stop for dinner?"

"Just this once."

"What a shame."

She raised her brows. "How so?"

"Because I was just about to propose an outing to Reno on Saturday. You've heard that the Empire Theatre opened last December? I haven't been there yet, but I've been told that the film, *The Crackerjack*, is very entertaining. There's also an *Out of the Inkwell* cartoon. Have you ever seen one?"

"I think I've been living in Blake's Folly for too long."

"The cartoons all begin with a drawing of Max Fleischer dipping his pen into an inkbottle. Fleischer finds the movements of animated cartoon characters too stiff and jerky, so he's invented a process called rotoscoping using a projector, an easel, and tracing paper. The result is highly interesting."

The thought of spending more time in Alexander's company was even more so. "It's a long drive to Reno."

"We can stay overnight. I'll book two rooms at the Palace Hotel." His eyes twinkled. "They have an excellent sprung wooden dance floor, and I promise you, it's a whole world away from Blake's Folly."

"A whole world?" She laughed. "I'm looking forward to it."

"So it's a date?"

"Definitely."

She couldn't miss the contentment in his eyes. Accepting his invitation was important to him. It was very important to her, too.

****

Susanna dressed for dinner in the room Alexander had booked for her. The Palace Hotel was a stylish stone and brick building, seven stories high, and designed in 1906 by the architect George E. Holesworth. From the lobby with its black leather upholstery, a new-fangled electric elevator had swept them up to their floor, and the luxurious bedrooms were equipped with telephones, electric lights, and heated steam.

Earlier, they had seen the very clever *Out of the Inkwell* cartoon feature, then had laughed at the antics of Johnny Hines in the role of a pickle salesman who becomes involved in a Latin-American revolution in *The Crackerjack*. And center stage, the organist seated before the new horseshoe-shaped Wurlitzer had provided all the music and sound effects necessary. It had been an enchanting afternoon.

Now, careful not to disturb her coiffure with its rhinestone combs, she slipped the creamy tiered evening dress with its beaded handkerchief hem over her head, and then examined herself in the room's large mirror. Her silky white stockings set off her sparkling-heeled golden dancing pumps to perfection. No, she couldn't have looked more elegant.

Did Alexander find her attractive? Why did that matter to her? He had never given the slightest hint that he wished for intimacy, and if that had been a relief before, it now saddened her. She had accepted, without any doubt, that she wanted him and was willing to become his mistress. She wanted to be in his arms, to share that big bed with him. As impressive as this room was, it would be a lonely place tonight.

He was waiting for her downstairs, and he stood at

her approach, taking her in from head to toe, his eyes shining. "You look absolutely ravishing."

"You're looking pretty delicious yourself." More than that. Ineluctably dignified in that single-breasted tuxedo with a white silk scarf tucked into the breast pocket, the brocaded waistcoat, crisp white shirt, and white silk bow tie. The man was pure joy for the eyes, and that joy hadn't dimmed, even after a day spent together.

Aware she was gaping at him, she pulled her scrambled wits together and settled into the seat the maître d' had pulled out for her. Forcing herself to look around the restaurant, she took in the shining silver utensils and glowing marble floor. A scent of flowers filled the air, and lilting melodies floated in from the nearby ballroom.

"As you promised, this is indeed another world away from Blake's Folly." It would be easy to get used to this atmosphere of warm luxury, too. She noted that everyone treated Alexander with a familiar but respectful cordiality: he was obviously well known.

"Do you come to this hotel often?"

"Whenever I need an escape from desert bleakness."

"I can understand that perfectly. Everyone needs a place they can escape to, even if that place is merely a room somewhere, or a field."

"And where do you escape to? Or do you only dream of it?"

She cocked her head to one side. "Yes, I have a secret place, one that is very unlike Madam Lacey's. A place where I can read, think, and be alone."

His eyes danced. "And are you about to divulge the

whereabouts of that secret place?"

She laughed. "Oh, it's not much of a secret. Brad Handy knows about it."

"Brad Handy? The owner of the Mizpah?"

"The very same. For years, I've been renting the back room upstairs at the Mizpah."

Evidently puzzled, his brow furrowed. "Why there?"

She understood his puzzlement. With her past, wouldn't that saloon be the one place she'd avoid? "Because it's a calm room where nothing, not even one stick of furniture, has changed since the late 1800s. I like the illusion of time standing still. There's another reason, too: I like showing myself how far I've come."

"Aren't there bad memories associated with the Mizpah?"

"Certainly not." She waved her hand, a dismissing gesture. "Those years, when we all worked there as dance girls, weren't bad, although most people would think so. We shared a certain solidarity and loyalty. We were very young, but we'd all been thrown out into the world to do the best we could with little preparation—or preparation of the worst kind. What possibilities did we have? A few of us had received only the poorest education, others, none at all. Some had been brutalized by family members, by employers, or were abandoned by lovers, and most of us had young children to support."

"And you all chose to be dance girls or prostitutes?"

"Prostitution can definitely be a choice for some. The women who work for me at Madam Lacey's have all done so. I made the same choice before coming to the Mizpah as a dance girl. The money is good, and pleasing men can be very satisfying. You see? It's all a question of attitude. Yet, we all shared the dream that, one day, we'd find true love, complete happiness, and have a home of our own. A dream like that can carry you a long way—especially since most of us often chose the worst sort of men to be in love with."

"Which is a mistake many of us make when young."

"True. I was particularly fortunate. I didn't become ill or die from an abortion gone wrong. I didn't marry the wrong man, and I was smart enough not to slide into the fake promises of drugs and alcohol. Instead, I saved my money and bought property."

"A woman with strength of character and determination."

She laughed. "You wouldn't have said that in my Sassy Sookie days. I was flighty, quite naïve."

"I doubt that. I'm certain you were as intelligent and kindly as you are now." He paused. "And just as lovely."

She couldn't miss the huskiness in his voice. Reaching across the table, she covered his hand with hers. "And since you're such a charming man, when we return to Blake's Folly, I'll let you be the first and only guest in my secret hideaway."

In the ballroom with its gold-leaf ceilings, crystal chandeliers, and potted palms, a most excellent orchestra played. Alexander took her in his arms and held her close, as though she were very dear. He was an accomplished dancer—she would have been surprised had it been otherwise—and she reveled in his male scent, in the heavenly sensation of being close to him.

Lightly, she rested her head on his shoulder, felt his breath on her hair. His arms tightened slightly, pulling her just that tiny bit closer, unless she were imagining that, letting wishes become reality. But why not dream for a while? Pretend this was a love story, and that it would go on forever.

****

This back room at the Mizpah was most unusual. Stepping through the doorway was entering a world that had ended years before. Much of the furniture was roughly made, the knocked-together practical necessities of early pioneers, but there were better pieces, too, created by craftsmen from the East who had brought patterns and styles with them. Alexander took in the awkwardly executed western-themed paintings and the shelves well stocked with old books.

"Have you read any of those?" he asked.

Susanna laughed. "Over the years, I've read every single one of them, even the bad ones."

They sat comfortably in two old leather armchairs, worn and cracked, and evening light filtered in from the one broad window above an empty courtyard.

"You've been renting this room for a long time?"

"Ever since Westley Cranston left it, almost forty years ago."

"Cranston? Wasn't he one of the journalists here in town?"

"He was. Back in the days when there was a local paper, and this saloon belonged to Ned Hardy, Westley's closest friend. Neddy always hoped Westley would return to Blake's Folly one day, so he kept this room intact for him. I think he was secretly in love with him, although, as you know, it was impossible to admit

110

something like that."

"Still, the condemnation and mockery was less drastic than today's so-called conversion therapies. It all comes down to the same thing, doesn't it? People refusing to accept what is natural."

"And condemning those who are different." Her solemn eyes met his. "Isn't it strange how often we agree on things, how similar our points of view are."

"Strange? Is it?" He took in the rich crown of silver hair, her soft features, and was filled with a deep longing.

"Yes. Because our backgrounds are very different, and our lives have been so disparate."

"But despite that, circumstance has brought us to the same conclusions." He leaned forward. "And those conclusions have separated us from society's mainstream."

"That's true, too. We've never fit into the normal schema of family life and conventional thinking."

"We don't want to."

She smiled, a joyous smile that lit her eyes. "You see? We really are similar."

He was deeply touched. He knew what he longed to say to her, where he wanted this conversation to go, but he had to make certain the bond between them was as clear to her as it was to him. "You have two children, don't you?"

"I do. They both live in Carson City. My son Clarence is married with his own family. He was always a good student, and I was able to send him back East, to study veterinary medicine at the University of Pennsylvania. I had hoped Margaret, my daughter, would continue her studies too, but she fell in love with

Thomas Potter, another veterinarian, my son's associate. She's now a conventional housewife and mother."

"Do you see them often?"

"Almost never." Her faint smile wasn't bitter. "A brothel madam isn't a respectable mother or mother-in-law. It's a profession that doesn't ride well with newly acquired middle class status."

"Do you mind?"

"No, I don't. There were a few tweaks in the beginning, but they didn't last long. I'm a practical woman, not a high-strung, emotional one. I did my best to raise my children properly, to send them away to school, far from local moralists who proudly condemn the illegitimate children born to 'bad' women. I know I made the right decision, because my son and daughter are secure, educated, polite, and self-confident adults. These days, I direct any stray maternal feelings toward those who work for me. They're some of the best-paid professionals in the business, but they're as sentimental, vulnerable, kind, or even as mean as other women. I'm a stabilizing influence, something quite necessary in the closed atmosphere of a brothel."

****

It seemed completely natural to return to his house for dinner. Standing on the broad wooden porch with Russ beside them, they watched the sun sink into a dusty rainbow horizon and relished early evening's windless peace.

He treasured the moment, loving the shine in her eyes, the lines of time and laughter along her face, the soft curve of her mouth. He knew how deeply he felt for her, how much he wanted her in his life, in his arms.

Was it too soon to speak up, reveal his feelings? How would she react? With surprise, certainly. With caution, too? Probably. But hadn't these days together shown them how well matched they were, how close they could be.

"Have you ever thought of selling up, leaving town, doing something else?"

"I have," she said. "I know it would be easy to find a buyer."

"Even if the success is due to Madam Lacey herself?"

Her smile was rueful. "I'm not irreplaceable. But what would I do? I've been so active over all the years, and I don't think an idle life would suit me."

"Does travel interest you?"

"It might. I never wanted to go anywhere else when I was younger, but I've become curious since then. The places you've told me about, Paris, London, Rome, all sound intriguing, but they're still distant." She laughed. "I wouldn't know where—or how—to begin."

"But I do." His heart was thudding. Taking a deep, calming breath, he turned to her. "Will you let me show you some of the world?"

She stared at him. His proposal was clearly the last thing she had expected.

Annoyed with his own abruptness, he frowned. "Forgive me. I've spent these last few days rushing you, taking you away from your life, keeping you in my company, but I couldn't see any other way of doing things. Now I'm going about this in the wrong way, leaping to the possible conclusion before admitting what I feel." Reaching out, he took her hands in his, turned her until she was facing him, could see how much she meant to him. "I want to marry you. I want you to be my wife, to live with me."

Wide-eyed, she stared up at him, still wordless.

"Is this unwelcome? If it is, I'll never speak of it again…"

"Not unwelcome," she said a little breathlessly, and curled her fingers through his. "Please don't think that. But as your wife? I had no idea."

"No idea of what?"

"I know that we're friends, but…"

He could see the faint blush on her cheeks.

Then, pulling his hands to her heart, she held them there. "I would very much like to be your wife, Alexander."

"I love you," he said. "I've loved you for a long while, but I've never had the courage to speak up. I don't want to ignore the feeling any longer. I want you too much. I want to make love with you, wake up with you in my arms every morning."

"I never imagined…" She caught her bottom lip in her teeth.

"That I wanted you?" He smiled, saw the gamut of emotions race over her fine features. "I needed to know you. I needed to know you cared about me. Those things were more important than simply taking you to bed."

"Alexander…I love you, too. Never doubt that. And I want you, so very much." She stopped, shook her head, as if with wonderment. "How incredibly fortunate we are."

"True." He smiled. "Life has given us a remarkable gift." Releasing her hands, he folded her into his arms, savored the feel of her, her delicate natural scent, her warm breath.

"Alexander?" Her voice was a caress.

"My love?"

"You're certain you want us to be married? We don't have to. I'll stay with you even if…"

He stopped her words with a deep lingering kiss. Then looked down at this woman he would always cherish. "Oh yes, we do. I won't have it any other way. We won't rush things, if you don't want. We can take our time. But I have to know that eventually you'll be mine, and that we'll be together for the rest of our lives."

"The rest of our lives, what a lovely thought. Why should we wait? But…" She stopped, and a little frown appeared between her brows. "Marrying me will cause a terrible scandal. With the people who know you. With your two sons, Edward and William."

"A terrible scandal? I hope so." Chuckling softly, he smoothed away the frown with gentle fingers. "There are few things that would give me more pleasure."

III

The Memory of a Village: 1948

Alas, you seek not happiness,
Nor do you escape a happy past.
                    ~Mikhail Lermontov, (1814-1841), *The Sail*

She kept the image of the village in her head. It was her secret place, the one she could go to no matter where she was, or what was happening around her. The lazy dirt lane was still there, just as it had been for hundreds, perhaps thousands of years, bumping its way out of Bobriki, rambling into fields of potatoes, barley, or rye, or clambering to forests, home to bears, wolves, to evil witches who led you astray, to wandering spirits that trapped you in twisted branches.

She remembered the blue-brown river, once so pure it could be used it for cooking and drinking, and all the brightly painted wooden houses, still intact, with their perfect cupcake trim. There, too, were the inhabitants: Olga, whose magnificent embroidery rivaled her own grandmother's fantastic roses, flirtatious Galina, handsome Grigory, old Akulina, drunken Pavel, and all the others, quarrelling, gossiping, spying, loving, and hating.

She could conjure up every single nook in her own blue and white house, one inhabited by Sergei's family over generations, for peasant girls, when married, went to live with a husband's family. That had been difficult enough, for a bride often became the slave of a domineering mother-in-law who held the real power, and Polina hadn't been spared. Treated rudely as punishment for having fallen in love with Sergei, only that vicious old lady's death had solved the problem.

It was her fault, in a way. She was educated, a music teacher graced with a superb voice; her father was a professional musician, a violinist, and he could travel by train to distant cities, lead a glamorous life. Her aunt Akulina had cautioned her: "Sergei's family is beneath us socially. You'll never be happy with them; there will always be jealousy." Suspicion, too, and that was dangerous, for times had changed, and denunciations could mean arrest.

But she'd loved Sergei, and he had loved her, that was what mattered, although the marriage was hardly perfect—were they ever? Sergei hadn't taken her side when his mother had been spiteful: "She's an old woman. You have to humor her." And that older woman had tried to wean away the affections of her own little son, Grisha, her darling. She hadn't succeeded: that victory had been claimed by typhus. Gone. Like Bobriki. No longer in existence.

Now, here she was, in this new world of unlovely streets, crowded sidewalks, and that brash banner overhead: "Reno: The Biggest Little City in the World." This was the life she had to negotiate: there was no way to bargain her way back.

****

"So what do you think?"

"What do I think?" Cal Hardy stared at the singer

117

standing next to the piano. She was the loveliest woman he had ever seen. And her voice? Rich, flexible, mellow. Utterly beautiful. His heart squeezed. "Where the hell did you find her?"

Luke Whistler looked smug. "She just walked in here ten days ago asking for work. She can hardly speak a word of English, but I liked the look of her."

"I'll bet you did." A broad face with prominent cheekbones, golden hair, she held her head high, and even from here, the other side of the piano bar, Cal could see the charm of pale blue eyes.

"I knew there was no use in training her and putting her on the floor," Luke continued. "She wouldn't understand what people were saying, and people wouldn't understand her either, her accent is that thick. I don't need cleaning or kitchen staff, and I get a thousand people a day asking for jobs like that. The difference is, they don't look like high-class ladies. But she does."

She certainly did. "What's her story?"

"Who knows? She says she's Russian. Another one of the refugees, obviously." Luke shifted from one foot to the other.

Cal noticed his discomfort. Even if they didn't see each other often, after long years of friendship, they could read one another like well-worn books. "In other words, no papers, no passport."

"She told me they were stolen." Luke's expression changed to one of stubborn defiance. "Yeah, I know what you're about to say."

Cal's mouth twitched. "Be a pal, and let me know what it is."

"You're about to say she probably lied. That I'm

crazy to believe her. But I do. There's something honest-looking about her." He shrugged. "Besides, she needed a job."

"And she just happens to be gorgeous."

"Okay, okay. I figured I could let her be a cigarette girl. With looks like those, she'll get some nice tips. Or meet Mr. Right and snag a wealthy husband."

Cal chuckled, but his heart wasn't in it. He wasn't certain he liked that classy-looking lady gliding around the floor in one of the casino's low-cut, ultra-short red and black dresses. Yes, he knew that cigarette girls were always chosen because they were lookers, and part of their job was flirting with the customers, but she didn't look like the sort who'd give in to a rich man's propositions in hopes of a bedtime tip...although he could be wrong. To hide his sharp interest in the woman, he teased his friend: "If the husband material is here in your casino, they won't be staying wealthy for long."

Luke's answering grin was wicked. "That's what I like to hear."

Cal looked over at the woman again. That blonde hair looked as natural as the glow on her pale skin. "The gag is, she's standing beside the piano in a black dress. She's not selling cigarettes."

"The cigarette job is only if I need her on the floor. Right after I said I'd give her a job, she tells me she knows how to sing, that she sang for Russian soldiers along the front, and for American soldiers stationed in Germany. That she knows songs in German, Russian, and English. So I sent her over to Bob, told him to see if they could work on a few numbers to please the punters."

"She can sing, all right."

"She's got a terrific voice, and I'm lucky to get her. This isn't one of the big casinos. I can't hire in stage shows or famous entertainers, but the lady already has a few fans coming in just to hear her. Male fans."

"Naturally." Cal felt a strange stab of totally unwarranted jealousy. What the hell was going on? He didn't even know the woman, yet here was his caveman instinct, stomping into the picture with a big nail-studded club. "And how does she react to having fans?"

"She doesn't. She's as warm as a patch of frozen tundra."

"Married? A boyfriend?" Cal held his breath.

"Doubt it. She's sharing a room somewhere out on Wilson with a couple of the girls."

"Her name?"

"Polina Yukechev." Luke threw his friend an inquisitive look. "You thinking of joining her fan club?"

"I'm already in. And I'll be coming back for more, too."

"And what makes you think she'll give you the time of day?"

"Nothing." For Cal had a fair notion of what the woman must have survived before making her way to America. He'd done volunteer work in displaced persons camps in Eastern Europe as the war ended, helping people patch together ruined lives, soothing crushed souls, and realizing how overwhelming those tasks were. He'd never forgotten the sight of burnt-out houses, destroyed villages, or the millions of homeless wandering shattered roads and searching desperately for murdered relatives. War: if you hadn't seen it first hand, you couldn't begin to imagine the horror and devastation. If you'd lived through it, would you ever be free from terror?

How had that vulnerable woman gotten as far as Reno, Nevada? How many casinos had she wandered into, hoping to be taken on? How had she avoided falling into the hands of some rotten pimp? Because they were out there, skimming the streets, haunting bus and train stations, preying on newcomers like her. Okay, she wasn't as young as their usual fare—in her late thirties or early forties—but with looks like those, some louse would think she'd be good for a few years' exploitation.

He pushed the negative thoughts out of his mind. In here, in Luke Whistler's casino, she was in a safe haven. Luke was a good guy, a pacifist like himself. He'd make sure she came to no harm. Polina Yukechev. He liked the name. Damn, but he liked looking at the woman, too.

Liked? Was that all? What was this? A case of love at first sight? He laughed at himself. Did such a thing even exist? Maybe. Maybe it had just happened to him. Finally, after all these years. *Damn.* Yes, he'd certainly be back.

****

She caught sight of him on the far side of the casino, and it wasn't the first time, either. He'd been coming in here every few days for the last two weeks. Why? She never saw him at the blackjack or craps tables, or by the roulette wheel, or playing the clunky slot machines. He often drank coffee, very rarely alcohol, and she knew he was a friend of Luke Whistler, her boss; the two men often sat together, talking.

She threaded her way through the crowd, passing the players, the change girls, the waitresses, and she could feel his eyes on her. Friendly eyes. He'd invited her for coffee, for a drink, for dinner each time he'd been here. Polite invitations. Which she'd refused, although she had the feeling he wasn't one of the lusty men, not like those she'd known, the American soldiers in Germany with their dirty thoughts and evil hands. But who could be sure? She certainly couldn't. Anyone could hide under a chummy, happy-go-lucky exterior. Why trust a man again? She was fine on her own.

Besides, how could anyone understand her life? In this country, everyone seemed comfortable, easy-going, but over-protected. They had no idea how things had been for people like her. They couldn't even imagine it. No one, certainly not her father, well read, an idealist, could have foreseen the burning of villages, the rapes, and the murders. The end of a way of life.

She'd survived. Following behind the advancing Red Army, blending into the interminable stream of refugees with their ragged bundles, she, too, had eaten what she could scrounge, had chewed grass, scooped drinking water from filthy puddles. The weakest lay down where they were, no longer caring what would happen. But she had a voice, and it had saved her. She'd sung old Russian folksongs to the soldiers as they marched into Germany, invented verses that reminded them of home, villages, and other times, of wives and children left behind. In exchange, they'd kept her safe.

And her dear Sergei? Where was he? She'd been so certain that, no matter what the danger, she would find him. That he had somehow survived. She hadn't known that German POW camps for Soviet soldiers were open fields fenced off by barbed wire and surrounded by watchtowers. With no barracks, no buildings of any kind, prisoners clumped together in holes dug into the ground. Exposed to wind, rain, snow, relentless sun, to beatings, torture, and starvation, over two and a half million had died within two years.

Believing in Sergei's survival had been an act of blind faith, as blind as the belief that her beautiful little Grisha could survive the typhus epidemic when no medical help was available. Only later, when she was in the relative safety of a displaced persons camp, did she learn that Sergei had perished in June of 1941, that her village, Bobriki, had been wiped off the map. That she had to start all over.

****

Cal adjusted the blue square in the pocket of his suit jacket and straightened his paisley tie before heading down the stairs and into the main room of the Red Nag.

"Howdy, stranger."

He looked over at the corner table. "Nancy."

"In the flesh." The redhead threw back her head in bright laughter.

Flesh, yes, that was the right word for it. So many pearly buttons on her very tight western shirt were undone, the view of cleavage was unhindered and enticing. Nancy was an attractive woman, any man would admit that, but it wasn't enough to make him indulge.

He'd seen many women like her pass through town, the new frolicsome crowd of divorce-seekers who had put Blake's Folly back on the map. With Nevada's population decreasing steadily after the turn of the century, the state legislature had tried stopping the exodus by legalizing gambling in '31. The gambit had worked. Big casinos had opened all across the state, and the entertainment industry was flourishing. When no-fault divorces and a residency requirement of only six weeks were added to the attraction, the economy boomed, and lawyers, hotel owners, restaurant and shop owners, dressmakers, laundresses, baby sitters, beauticians, hairdressers had all rubbed their hands in glee. Even dying Blake's Folly managed, once again, to spring to life.

Certainly, this backwoods community couldn't hope to compete with cities like Vegas or Reno with their flashing bingo and keno signs, their glitzy floorshows. But, just outside town, one local boy, Lucky Handy, was doing good business with his Get Lucky Dude Ranch where divorce-seekers waited out their residency. No modern ranch house with guest rooms, swimming pool, or other luxuries, it wasn't bottom of the scale either: a cluster of cabins with simple furniture—a bed, table, chair, armchair, and a desk—and a short distance away, toilets and showers in wooden huts.

What Lucky's lacked in luxury, it provided in discretion and good humor. There were also several good-looking local "cowboys" on hand, and they entertained guests, teaching them to milk cows, taking them out horseback riding, preparing barbecue and square dance evenings, or providing ladies with a lusty roll in the hay when no appealing male divorce-seekers were in residence.

Thanks to these temporary residents, two

hairdressers had reopened, the laundry run by Angie Bilk was doing a booming business, and Millie Sparks, the seamstress, was overwhelmed with work, adjusting the western costumes bought in Lawkes' General Store and Haberdashery. Elmer and Edna Grimes now ran the Mizpah Saloon and Restaurant—it had once belonged to Ned Hardy, Cal's pacifist great-uncle who had died in WWI—and they were doing well; and the old Red Nag, this saloon his grandfather Alistair had built back in the 1870s, doomed to close back in the days of prohibition, was now a busy place indeed.

Nancy came over to where he was standing. Reaching out, she let her fingers trail over the line of his jaw. "Come on, sit down with me, have a drink." Her voice was low, provocative, and filled with promise.

"Another time, Nancy. I'm off to Reno this afternoon."

"All alone?"

The grin he flashed her was definite. "Alone."

"That's sure a shame."

Cal slipped into his wool overcoat and stepped out of the high wooden door with its fine etched glass window. The dry whiff of desert autumn played in the air, a hint of winter days to come and a different sort of beauty, one of rusty reds and bleached yellows against the dun-colored earth. He knew how hard it was for people to imagine this rocky inhospitable flatland transformed into fairyland with each season, but that it certainly was, however brief and subtle those enchanted moments might be.

Lord, how he liked being back in this part of the world. He'd missed Blake's Folly over the years, this ramshackle community where he'd grown up. Living in far-off cities, he'd often dreamt of the shambling Red Nag, of the room where both he and his father, Smithson Hardy, had been born. True, the town had been sliding downhill for almost half a century. Outsiders, some from far away California, had stripped lumber and brick from the finest buildings, and in 1934, an exploding illegal still had caused a fire that destroyed many good wooden houses.

These days, Blake's Folly was so quiet, you could hear wind scratching dust along the road, the crack of old boards, and the collapse of a roof. But that didn't discourage him any. He intended to stay. He was forty-seven years old, and it had taken him a long time to discover that his roots might have been the best ones, after all: that sort of knowledge came with experience out in the big wide world.

If he could find a lovely lady to settle in with him, life would be absolutely perfect. A lovely blue-eyed woman? "Silly dreamer," he chided himself, as he slid the key into the ignition of his shiny De Soto Deluxe. What did he know about the beautiful Polina Yukechev? Nothing—not that he hadn't made an effort.

Was she intelligent, kind, or silly? What sort of life had she lived? Had she ever been married? Other than singing, he didn't know what her interests were, what she enjoyed. He also didn't know if he could ever win her over. Did she find him attractive? Probably not. He wasn't the sort of man women were instantly attracted to—he didn't have the dashing physique for that. But he had an easy charm, discretion, and humor, and he was a good listener. Traits like that went a long way with the ladies, he'd discovered. With Polina, too?

Things didn't look hopeful. He'd been back to Luke's casino six times already in the hope of getting to know her better but had had no success. She'd steadily refused his offers to sit, converse, drink a coffee, a cocktail, or dine with him, and he didn't have the faintest idea how to win her over. But that didn't mean he was giving up, not by a long shot.

To his immense satisfaction, the car's engine turned over after only the third try.

****

In the old days, life in Bobriki had been very different but equally difficult, Polina knew that. In pre-Communist times, power had been in the hands of the noble landowners and the Church. You always bowed when the noble's carriage passed; you never dared miss a church service. That had ended when she was a young girl, after the Bolsheviks took power.

Religion was outlawed, and revolutionaries closed churches, tore down crosses on rooftops, ripped out icons and centuries-old wooden sculpture, burnt everything on public bonfires or chopped it up for firewood. Church buildings and synagogues became storage barns for farm produce or social clubs; others caught fire or were burnt by arsonists. As for the priests, other members of the clergy, as well as the nobles and the *kulaks*—the rich farmers—they were either shot or deported to the Gulag as slave labor.

She, who had hoped to become an opera singer, found herself teaching music in a provincial school and married to the mild, peaceful Sergei, another teacher. Like everyone, she was sent to toil in the fields in summer and at autumn harvest. It wasn't a bad life; Stalin hadn't starved them to death as he had four million Ukrainians, but it was a world where dreams were rarely realized.

Her father had been one of the lucky ones. As a violinist, he had managed to have another sort of existence, one far from the collective farm. There had also been other women, and his long absences became more frequent over the years. Her mother must have known, but she bore the burden of an unfaithful husband patiently: there were two children to take care of, and she was a dutiful wife, not a brave or adventurous one. Had she shown interest in seeing the world, she could have followed him to the cities, lived a far grander life, but she'd chosen to remain in rural Bobriki.

Polina remembered the night she'd caught sight of one of her father's mistresses, an irresistible woman with knowing eyes and an elegant neck. With Sergei, she had gone to the city of Prem for his interview with the school authorities. That evening, as they made their way back through frozen streets toward the train station, they had passed a restaurant, brightly lit, smoke-filled, enchanting, the sort of place where musicians played the night away and rich foods could be tasted.

Pressing her face longingly against the moisture-streaked window, she'd glimpsed cellos, violins, and in one corner, a piano. There, inside, it must have been warm, comfortable, wonderful, but such a paradise was forbidden to people like herself, to Sergei, simple village teachers. Only an *apparatchik*, a high-up official in the Communist party, or a blindly devoted follower could enter. Or someone like her father, whose musician's skill gave him the right to be in bright warm places.

That was when she'd caught sight of her father, seated at one of the tables. Beside him was the mistress, a smart little hat perched perkily on her curls. How his fascinated, even greedy, eyes had watched her as she threw back her head, laughing. And she, Polina, standing out in the icy night, felt no shock at her father's concupiscence, only pure envy. Compared to that scene in there, her whole life seemed tiny, banal. The life of a provincial.

She wanted more. She wanted to be part of her father's world. She wanted to be inside, in that warm brightness. She, too, wanted to wear a smart, cockily slanted hat, to be the star of the evening, a woman men followed with their eyes. She wanted to step out in front of everyone, join the orchestra, to sing, fill the room with high pure notes.

But that was before everything had gone wrong. Before, suddenly dishonored and unable to find work in that politically unstable world, her father had chosen suicide instead of humiliation. And shortly after, everything else had gone.

****

She'd finally agreed to sit with him during her break. Cal could hardly believe it. Naturally, he'd made it clear from the start that their conversation would be about business. He loved the way she sang. He wanted to offer her a job out in Blake's Folly, the town where he lived. He was the owner of an old-fashioned saloon, the Red Nag, and he would be setting up a concert weekend for the tourists and temporary residents who were his clients. Much of the music would be popular sounds, dance music, and even that well-known crooner, Max Wilty, who was in town waiting for his divorce (accompanied by his newest lady, an ambitious Hollywood starlet) had agreed to sing. But those performances were very different from what she did, and he was certain she'd be the hit of the evening. He'd already spoken to her boss, Luke, and he had agreed to let her go for the weekend…if she were willing.

She watched him expressionlessly. Was she pleased by his offer? Flattered by his praise? She remained silent for a long time, and only reacted when the ripple of the piano's first notes reminded her that the set was about to begin, that it was time to go sing.

"Where is this town?"

"It's not close, but there will be no problem getting there, I promise. I'll pick you up here in Reno, take you there, bring you back again. While you're there, you'll be lodged in the local inn, and all meals are included."

She stood. "I will think about it."

"Please do. I'll come back in a few days. Give me your answer then." He also stood, smiled at her. "I really would like you to come and sing at the Nag. You'll be a sensation, I'm sure of it."

She didn't smile back. She didn't thank him. No, he knew she wouldn't think about his offer. She'd already made up her mind to refuse him. Turning away, she returned to the dais. Without a nod, without the slightest acknowledgment.

Cal sighed. *It's a hopeless enterprise. Just give up, move on.* But he didn't want to, not yet. And when the first rich notes of her song filled the room, he was even more determined to try and win the very appealing Polina Yukechev's heart.

****

She opened the door of the boarding house with her key. Tiptoed up the stairway, making sure she disturbed no one. The living room with its square table and shabby worn armchairs was empty at this time of night, and she shook off her too light thrift-shop jacket, sat down.

The others—the young American women who lived here—were either sleeping or working late. She shared the bedroom with three of them, and it was a crowded space with a scramble of clothes, and heavy with the scent of makeup, of cloying perfume. She hated the promiscuity, would have given anything for peace and quiet, for a room of her own. Yes, she'd have that, eventually. It wasn't too much to ask for, was it? She'd spent so many years in close quarters with others.

She thought of the other women she had known, those who had come to America with her, Edita, Anichka, Klara, and Irena. Like her, they had been tossed up onto the bleak postwar landscape of barracks in refugee camps; like her, they'd lost all—families, husbands, sweethearts, children, homes. Working in kitchens, canteens, and soldier's clubs, they all hailed from different countries, but since they were Slavs, they could understand each other. Their languages, although dissimilar in pronunciation, vocabulary, alphabet, and melody, shared grammar. And because they had survived and life would continue, they adapted, made plans, took American soldier sweethearts.

The men were more than willing to indulge, make vows they would never keep, brave the very real danger of venereal disease. Far from home and triumphant now that the fighting was over, some even frequented German girls, although that was strictly forbidden. Yet,

Polina understood their abandon. They had seen war and horror; they, too, were exhausted, traumatized. Having lost friends, they were consumed by guilt, and to bolster egos, to keep demons at bay, they took to whoring.

She was singing in the American cabaret at the time, and it had been Irena, one of the barmaids, who encouraged her liaison with Bob. Although initially outgoing and friendly, he was someone Polina never would have chosen. She couldn't understand him, for she didn't speak a word of English, but hearing his raucous laughter, his loud banter, she knew he was vulgar. Undiscouraged, he pursued her, overwhelmed her with promises.

"Just think of the future," Irena said. "Think of life in America. This is how we'll get there, through these men. Think of how easy life will be then. Just think."

But for the moment, it wasn't easy at all.

"You'll marry me, won't you, Polly? When we get back to the States, to Vegas, you'll be my wife. We'll live in a pretty little house with a nice neat lawn, and we'll be happy together, won't we? Come on, Polly. Come here, babe." Bob, sweaty and mean when drunk, groping her, squeezing her breasts, pushing her against a wall, forcing himself on her.

She learned to tolerate the ugly sex. It was the price to be paid for leaving the camp. It was her ticket out. It had nothing to do with love or respect. With her beloved dead Sergei, she had made love. With Bob, it was submission in order to survive. She would never marry him, no matter what happened. Once in America, she would find a way to escape.

When did she realize nothing was the way it

seemed? That Bob's story was false. Little by little she was learning English—it was possible to do that with all the bright chatter around her—although she could hardly speak a word of it. Convinced she understood nothing, the men were open in their talk of Russian girls, of making money with them, of Vegas, and whores. There would be no pretty little house, as sweet as those in glossy American magazines. There would be no marriage, but she played along, waiting for the right moment. Hadn't she spent the last eight years learning all about survival?

Now, safe and sound, sitting in this calm dark room in Reno, Nevada, she thought about tonight, about Cal Hardy and his offer to go sing in a music festival in some town she'd never heard of. No, she didn't think Cal was a bad man, and she didn't think he was trying to trap her, but why take chances? Why risk stepping onto unsteady ground? Yes, it was crowded in this boarding house, and it was disagreeable hearing men's drunken propositions when she walked around the casino in that ridiculous cigarette girl costume, but there was no real threat.

And if things became intolerable, she could always retreat into the village, the one in her head, eternal and untouchable.

****

Cal entered the casino, pausing, letting his eyes adjust to the flashing lights, his ears, to the bleeping roar, his nose, to the blanket of cigarette smoke. This was a world away from Blake's Folly; it was like stepping through a time barrier, and he needed to adapt. His eyes searched for Polina. Was she doing the rounds as a cigarette girl? It was too early for her to be beside the piano, singing. No, he couldn't see her. He went over to the bar, settled, and ordered a drink. Waited. Would she accept his offer or not?

Thirty minutes later, she still hadn't appeared, and that was strange, very strange. He got up, went over to the cashier's window on the far wall.

"Hi, Mike. Is Luke around?"

"In his office."

"Get someone to buzz me in."

Mike nodded, and Cal strode in the direction of the discreet door marked Employees Only.

Luke rose to his feet when he saw his friend enter. "What brings you to town?" Then, eyes twinkling, he raised a knowing hand. "You don't even have to confess. I've never seen your gorgeous face as often as I do these days. I know you don't like Reno, but I refuse to believe you're here because you've fallen in love with me."

"How about if I just say I like stepping into civilization from time to time?"

"Liar. Who said Reno was civilized? No, I think it's because you have a hankering to hear some Russian songs. But you haven't managed to get her away from me and into your lair, yet, have you?"

"No, I definitely haven't. Which is why I'm in your office at the moment. Where is Polina? You haven't fired her, have you?"

Luke looked surprised. "She's not on the floor?"

"She isn't."

"She didn't say anything to me. Let's go take a look."

Together, they returned to the casino's main room with its buzz, whirrs, beeps, and bells. The punters were arriving en masse, and the place was filling up.

Luke went up to Sam, the bartender. "Polina hasn't shown up yet?"

Sam wiped a glass, shrugged with indifference. "You know how these girls are. Easy come, easy go. Here one day, gone the next. Lady probably found herself a big spender to run off with."

Cal glared at Sam, annoyed, but was the man wrong? Not where some other women were concerned, but not Polina, he was certain of that. She was too skittish, too self-protective, and too wary. There had to be a valid reason for her absence, and that was worrying him.

"I'll go look around," said Luke tersely. Either the situation also bothered him, or he sensed Cal's unease.

"So will I."

Which was when he caught sight of her. She had just come in from the street, racing into the casino like a whirlwind, frazzled, nervous. Gone, that casual sensual way she usually moved, and her expression told him something was very wrong. She stared around the room, her eyes frightened. Then spotted him and began heading in his direction.

He met her halfway, noted her extreme pallor. "What's wrong, Polina?"

"Outside, there is one man..." She stopped, clutched the collar of her coat.

"You know this man?"

"This man, he look for me. He want to make me come back. But he is bad. They are five, all bad men. They want me to work for them like prostitute. I run away in Las Vegas. They very bad when woman refuse."

"Okay, Polina. Don't worry." He almost felt like smiling, although the situation was hardly funny and might be dangerous. Still, he was in the right place at the right time, and she had sought him out—that implied she trusted him in some way, didn't it? That made him feel good, mighty good. "Nothing bad will happen to you. You're safe here."

She stared up at him mutely.

Luke had reached them. "What's going on?"

"Some guy is after her, some lousy pimp, from what I can understand."

"Someone in here?"

Polina looked around the large room. "No. I see him out in street. I run to other place, he run, find me. I run more, I come here."

"Good," said Luke. "Then, let's wait for him. He won't stay outside for forever. If he steps in here, some of the boys will take charge. Keep him nice and calm."

"Should we call the police?"

"What could they do?" Luke shrugged. "The guy hasn't done anything yet. He hasn't hurt her or kidnapped her, even if that's what he intends to do."

"And we won't give him the chance."

"He not alone," Polina interjected. "I see a big car with two other men. I know these men, too." Her eyes went to Luke, then back to him. "You believe me?"

"Of course we believe you," Cal said.

"Let's go into the back," said Luke. "Hear what this is all about."

Cal couldn't miss the relief in Polina's eyes. Catching her elbow in his hand, he led her through the employee's doorway. She didn't resist. She was too frightened for that.

Once inside his office, Luke jerked his head in the direction of a few armchairs in one corner. "Sit down, both of you." Going to a low cabinet, he pulled out a bottle of rye, served them all a glass. Polina didn't refuse.

"Who are these men? They're the ones who kept your papers?"

She nodded.

"Why?"

"Money. They spend money, bring us to America. They say they want their money's worth."

"How do you know them?"

"They are soldiers in Germany. They promise good life in America, but they lie. I understand too much, and they say we are investment. Bob, say that. We make money for them." Her hands were knotted together into a tight fist in her lap. "One girl, Klara, she Czech woman, she try to get help on boat. They beat her bad. Broken hand, arm, broken face…" Her lips trembled.

"It's okay now, Polina." Reaching out, Cal briefly covered her hands with his own, not an intimate gesture, but a reassuring one although, for a split second, he thought she would misinterpret it and pull away. She didn't. "Nothing will happen to you. You believe me, don't you? We can help you."

Her eyes were unreadable. Trust. If she didn't trust him, then there would be nothing he could do for her.

"How? How you can help me?"

"I can take you away from here. To Blake's Folly, the place I told you about. It's where I live, an old silver mining town quite a distance away. No one will look for you there, and only Luke will know where you are. First, we can go pick up your belongings. Then, we'll drive out there tonight." He held his breath.

She was silent, her face still expressionless. Then, to his considerable relief, she nodded. "Yes, that is good."

****

How long had they driven through the night? She knew they were far from Reno. Outside, the night was cold, almost as cold as late autumn in Bobriki, and she had only this shabby thin jacket to wear. But in this comfortable car, the air was reassuringly warm. Had she been foolish to trust this man, to have followed him meekly? *You can always run. You did it before, you can do it again.* The familiar little refrain calmed her, yet the fear wasn't overwhelming. Oddly enough, she felt strangely peaceful on this lonely road. No towns, no lights, just darkness out there, and from time to time an animal caught in the car's headlights. Carl slowed for all, and she understood he was a steady, kindly man, one who would harm no creature.

The car slowed, turned off the main highway, took another road, bumpier. Where were they? There was nothing out there, just scrub, just emptiness. Not a tree, not a house, not a building. Fear rose again. Had Cal sensed it?

"Just a few miles more, Polina." His voice was gentle, calming. "I know it's hard to believe, but this used to be a main highway leading to one of the busiest boomtowns in the state. Since the silver ran out long ago, no one maintains a road to a place that no longer counts."

She told herself to relax. And soon enough, buildings did come into sight although it was hard to make them out. Wooden buildings? Shacks? A main street, of sorts, but there was no one around, and there were no lights. What a strange place. He turned onto another road, even bumpier, drove over a little rise. Then stopped.

In front of them, a large wooden house towered. Despite the dark, she could see its yellow paint, make out a broad porch. There was a light in one downstairs window.

Cal came around the car, opened her door, and held out his hand.

"What is this place?"

"Come. I'll introduce you to the lady mayor of Blake's Folly."

The woman who answered their knock was old but spritely, although her powdery white hair was worn in a style Polina had only seen in ancient photos. Shrewd eyes took her in from head to toe, summed her up. "Well, Carl, what have you brought us?"

"Polina, meet the formidable Susanna Treemont."

"Formidable," the woman scoffed, but her mouth curved into a merry smile.

"Polina is a Russian singer, and with any luck, she might become Blake's Folly's newest star resident."

"Well, it's good to meet someone who's coming into town and staying, for a change."

Cal grinned and looked down at Polina. "Susanna might be rude, but she keeps us all in order."

"Hah! I'd have better luck putting order into a family of tricky coyotes."

Followed by two huge, shaggy dogs, they passed through an entry hall and into a large room. Surprised, Polina stared at the paintings covering every wall, at the heavy old furniture, the silky oriental carpets scattered over the wide-planked floor. How strangely familiar it all was, old-fashioned, different from anything she imagined she'd see in America. She felt as though she had stepped back in time, was again in the comfortable house of the rich peasant Bunin. She'd gone there when a tiny girl, accompanying her father who would play for a private party. But Bunin had been shot long ago, and his stately house with its grand library and elegant furniture, pillaged and ruined.

An elderly man seated in a deep settee rose somewhat stiffly to his feet. Reaching out, he enfolded her hands in his own bony ones. "Welcome, my dear. I see Carl has managed to bring a delightful fledgling to the backwoods."

Polina didn't know what he meant, but she saw the humor in his eyes.

"So I have." Cal chuckled. "Polina Yukechev, this is Alexander Treemont, the most talented male charmer in Blake's Folly."

Alexander scoffed. "That's no outstanding achievement. I'm one of the few men left in this town."

"Are you hungry?" Susanna asked. "Have either of you had anything to eat? Go sit down, and I'll bring in some sandwiches, tea, and biscuits. Then you, Cal, will tell us what this is all about."

They made themselves comfortable, and easy conversation flowed between Cal and the Treemonts. Polina felt so tired, and the words were hard to follow, but did she have to make the effort? No, not really. She already trusted these people, knew, instinctively, they had her well-being at heart. They could decide her fate; it was out of her hands at the moment. Strangely enough, that felt good. The tea she sipped was a mixture of herbs, very unlike her grandmother's dark brew, but the biscuits were light and buttery, and even the soft puffing of the dogs snoozing around their feet reminded her of her own, long dead Bimka.

"I was thinking she could stay in a guest room in the Mizpah Saloon," Cal was saying.

Stay in a room? In a saloon? She sat straight, suddenly wide-awake. How could she pay for lodgings? "It's not possible. No! I don't…"

"You don't have the money?" The older woman smiled. "Don't worry. The saloon belongs to me these days, and there's a separate room upstairs in the back that I don't rent out. It will be perfect for you. I'll give Elmer and Edna a call right away and prepare them for your arrival."

They went back out into the hallway, where icy night air was slipping under the door. Quickly, Polina slid into the jacket Cal held for her.

Susanna took in the shabby garment with her sharp, critical eye. "That's not good enough for the weather out here."

"Is good," said Polina, embarrassed.

"No, it isn't. You wait right there." Susanna disappeared, reappeared moments later with a large, flowing, full-length wool coat in a deep honey color. "Put this on."

"No, please."

"Put it on right now." She was not someone to be argued with.

"See if it fits," Cal encouraged.

How couldn't it fit? Elegant, its soft cashmere warmth enfolded her.

"It's yours."

"Thank you, but I…"

"Wear it in good health."

Cal chuckled softly as they went down the front steps. "You might as well argue with the wind. Susanna never accepts a 'no.' "

"Who are those people?"

"Susanna and her husband Alexander are almost as old as this town. She's a businesswoman, and he was a famous painter in his day. He's in his eighties now, and sometimes has trouble holding a paintbrush steady, but he still paints and shows his work in a San Francisco gallery. Young artists come all the way out here to meet him, and Susanna has been his agent for years."

Cal drove back into the dark town, stopped in front of a large old-style western building with a balcony running full length around its upper story.

"Home sweet home."

Grabbing her small cardboard suitcase, he headed up the steps toward the high double doors. She hung back, uncertain, unwilling to accept charity. "I can't stay here. You are nice, but I can't…"

He looked down at her with his calm eyes. "Yes, you can. Sometimes, we need the help of others. We also have to accept that other people want—and like—to give."

"But…"

"No, not another word." His teeth flashed white in the night. "Besides, I have my own interest in this."

Polina waited.

"As you well know, I want you to sing in my saloon, the Red Nag. If you'd like, you can start right away."

"You are serious?"

"Perfectly. I have a pianist and a guitarist who'd both enjoy working with you. If you'll accept, that is."

Did he think she'd refuse? Did he even look uncertain? How was that possible? "I would like that," she said. "Very, very much."

"Perfect. Okay, let's get you settled in. Get a good night's sleep, and I'll show you around town tomorrow morning. Is ten o'clock a reasonable time for you?"

"Is good." Ten o'clock, eight o'clock, four o'clock, any time was perfect as far as she was concerned.

"And make sure you eat a good breakfast in the Mizpah's restaurant." He laughed. "It's all included."

What did that mean? There had been too much to take in this evening, leaving Reno, coming here. Nothing was familiar—not the scent in the air, not the shape of buildings—yet, for the first time in many years, she had the strange and comforting feeling she was on firm ground.

****

He came for her at ten o'clock, as promised. She had been sitting at a table and watching for him at the window of the Mizpah's large main room. She was certain Cal wouldn't be late, yet when she caught sight of him, relief washed over her. Unless it was something else. Optimism?

She noted his springy step, the way he took the steps two by two. He wasn't a handsome man, nothing like her beloved Sergei who had been tall, lean, with high Slavic cheekbones, and a firm jaw. Cal's hair was thin and pale, his hairline had receded, and he was squarely built, although his broad shoulders and flat stomach told her he took care of himself. Best of all, his was a mouth that smiled, and that smile was broad when he caught sight of her. Her heart warmed.

He came to her table, sat. "Did you sleep well?"

"Yes, thank you," she said, although it wasn't true. Everything had been too new, too strange: the unusual silence of the icy night, the shooting stars streaking across an inky heaven, the unfamiliar shadows of dark furniture, and a strange scent of the past in the dry, cool air. The room seemed full of ghosts, but surely that was just her imagination running wild.

"The Red Nag where I live and you'll work is on the other side of town. That means it's only five minutes walking distance away. Even the word 'town' has been an exaggeration for the last fifty years or so."

"I don't care when it is close or far. I like to walk. I like to see things slowly."

"Good. Then, if you're ready, we can get started."

The broad main road was very calm, almost as still as it had been the night before. A few shops were open—a laundry, a clothing store, a general store, a beauty parlor—but there were many abandoned wooden buildings, too. A few, more imposing, were in brick, but everything looked shabby, run down, half forgotten. Like a town after a battle, and she'd seen many of those. But there had been no war here: there were no bullet holes in the walls, and there was no shattered stone.

"The place has changed a lot over the years."

"How…" She hesitated, vocabulary and grammar fighting in her head. She knew she made terrible mistakes each time she spoke, and she was ashamed. She didn't want him to laugh at her. "How it…how do…it change?"

"I was born here forty-seven years ago, but back

then, in 1900, Blake's Folly had a school, churches, a theater, and a big hotel. This, Main Street, was the business district. You can still see some of the old signs even though they're quite faded. Look, over there. That's Cigars, Bert Freedman proprietor, then J.W. Chrisman, Drugs and Patent Medicines, and Luigi's Barber Shop. We even had a thriving local newspaper, *The Morning Sun*. The office is still there, but it's an empty, battered ruin, these days. One crazy coot used it as a furniture workshop back in the twenties, but seven years later, he went broke. Even when I was a kid, the town was dying. If you wanted to make a living, do something in life, the only choice was to get the hell out. So, that's what I did."

"But not everyone."

"Some who stayed on continued to eke out a living in the few mining ventures that were left, but it was a far cry from what the Progressive reformers had planned for Nevada at the beginning of the century. They'd wanted to create a state free of capitalism's greed, where universities and culture prevailed, like in Vienna, Austria, back in the late 1800s. After the economic bust in the early 1900s and the decline in population, dreams of a society based on reform, equality, and justice vanished. Nevada became known as 'the beautiful desert of buried hopes.' "

It was strange, she thought. Despite the all-pervading air of a place almost abandoned, the few scrubby leafless trees, yellowed weeds, and spiky shrubs, there was a familiar small-town atmosphere that touched her. "Why do people go from here?"

"Because of the town's isolation. Blake's Folly is many miles from Reno, and the violent, always unpredictable weather makes it unappealing for most. Shops are opening up again because of the divorce market. However, if other states start adopting their own liberal divorce laws, I'm afraid Blake's Folly will slump back into its former torpor."

She looked up at him. "What is divorce market?"

"Well, in other states, if you want a divorce, even if you have a violent drunk for a husband, you have to prove adultery. In Nevada, a resident can get a no-fault divorce, and the residency requirement is only six weeks, the shortest in the whole country."

She hadn't imagined something like that here in America. Divorce had been easy in the Soviet Union under the Bolsheviks. Only under Stalin had it become harder to obtain: women were expected to stay married, have many children. But a divorce market? Imagine! Then she sighed. There was much she had to learn. Would she ever understand it all? Fit in?

They arrived at the Red Nag, and it wasn't much different from the other wooden buildings in town, two stories high with overhanging eaves and a wooden sidewalk. Inside, a long bar ran down the right side of the room. Behind were a large mirror, a few paintings, and dark wooden shelves covered with glasses and bottles. Golden sun shimmered merrily across the polished plank floor.

"It looks like Russian bar." She turned to him. "This…is…this belong to you?"

"Yes, it does. Built by my grandfather when the town was starting out."

"It is nice." She felt strangely shy.

"I'm glad you like it."

"This is where I sing?"

He laughed. "Don't worry. It's empty now because it's too early for customers. The place starts filling up at noon, but you'll only sing in the evening. That's when the other musicians, Will and Louis, show up."

"I meet them tonight?"

"Why wait? We'll go to Will's house after lunch. You might need a few days rehearsal before you can start working together, but there's no rush. You have all the time in the world, Polina. Remember, there's no pressure." He led her to a corner table. "Would you like a coffee?"

"Thank you. Very black." Then she smiled. "Coffee is too weak in America."

He smiled back at her. "Thanks for the hint. I'll do my best."

She watched while he went behind the bar, made a fresh brew, and brought two cups to the table.

"Okay, Polina. We have to talk. I want to know what you were afraid of back in Reno. I also want to know how you got to Reno in the first place."

Her stomach tightened. She didn't want to tell him that ugly story. She wanted to push the details far away, out of her mind. If she brought it all up again, she would somehow sully the pristine air around them, destroy innocence.

"Look, it's the only way I can be sure you're protected."

He was right. But it had been so long since she had told anyone what she was feeling, what she feared. She'd kept everything locked up inside for years now. That had been the only way to get by.

"Also," he continued, "by letting me know what happened, we can do what's necessary to regularize your situation here, get you official papers."

She was silent for a long time, turning her coffee cup one way in its saucer, turning it back. "It isn't good story. There are no good people in it."

"There are some good people in every story, even in bad stories, but I understand what you're saying. I was in Europe doing volunteer work in displaced persons camps after the war."

Her eyes met his. "You are a doctor?"

His smile was rueful. "No, far from it. I thought about becoming a doctor when I was young, but dropped out of university when I realized it wasn't for me. I ended up in Hollywood, working on film scripts, and that was exciting...but only for a while. Pretty soon, I was wanting out. When the war started, I became a medic."

"Because you knew medicine?"

"Not really. A few of us had some medical expertise because we'd studied for a while, but it wasn't enough to prepare us for the battlefield. Basically, we had to be trained from scratch, learn how to stabilize the wounded, stop bleeding, apply dressings, sprinkle antiseptic sulpha powder, and administer morphine to kill pain."

"But you were not soldier?"

"Never. I was a conscientious objector. A lot of medics were."

She shook her head. Oh, why were some things so difficult to understand? "What does that mean?"

"Conscientious objectors are people opposed to war. During the first war, objectors were badly treated. Some went to prison, others to work camps where life was extremely hard. Nobody cared about treating them fairly, because if you were opposed to war, you were considered a traitor. Only pacifist religious groups like the Quakers, the Brethren, and the Mennonites urged humane treatment. Like other people in my family, I've always been averse to combat and warfare in any form, but I did want to support the Allied forces in this last war. The best way I could do that was to go to the front as a medic."

"You go to front?"

"Yes. I was on the front line with other men from the Allied countries, but it was the same for German or Axis medics. It was very difficult, because we were terribly understaffed—about thirty medics for a battalion of four or five hundred men, and it was a hell of a job. We had to prepare the wounded for evacuation to field hospitals, to decide who was beyond help, and who we could save."

She caught the pain in his eyes, the sadness. *We all have them, those bad memories. No matter what life we were born into.* "Why you are against war? Because you are religious man?"

"No. I'm a secular humanist. That means I believe humans are capable of honorable behavior without a god and without religion." He leaned forward. "That's enough about me. It's time for you to tell your story."

"My English too bad…"

"You're doing very well. Besides, this isn't a grammar lesson. If I don't understand something, I'll say so."

She had no choice. He had paved the way, and now she had to confide, too. Where to begin? With the camp where she had sung. With Bob and his proposal. She told him about the ship where she and the other girls had been isolated, spending long hours locked into the cabin they shared. How she had been smart enough to know that, once in America, a country where these men felt comfortable, where they knew all the rules and she didn't, she would need to rely on her wits, keep her eyes open, seize the moment, then run for her life.

"I had money," she told him. "A little money, dollars soldiers give me when I sing, but Bob, he know men give me tips."

Cal's eyes glinted. "But you managed to keep a little part of it."

She looked smug. "In my hat."

"Hat?"

"I have hat with secret place inside."

"Ah, yes, I understand."

"And we come to Las Vegas, all of us, in train. The men keep us like sheep, all together, all the time. And all the time, I look, look, look, look for my one chance. And it come. We are waiting in noisy place, a bar."

A place run by a man Bob and his friends knew. Waiting for someone to show up? Who? She didn't know. The other women didn't, either. They were supposed to obey, and the simplest question, or even a word said in the wrong way could elicit a slap, a beating. Because things had changed, just as she'd known they would. The men were feeling powerful. They were home, on solid ground. They could do what they wanted. The women knew nothing, how things worked, or if they had rights. They had only each other, and a certain solidarity.

She'd gone to the ladies' room, but had mistakenly taken a wrong turning, gone right instead of left. Ended up in a kitchen where the steam was dense, and people raced back and forth. No one had looked at her, just pushed past with loaded plates and trays. Straight ahead there was a wide-open service entry, and she'd walked toward it, without thinking, without a plan, hardly breathing, not daring to hope. Never considering the consequences if one of the men came after her.

Outside, over there, right across the street, were rounded vehicles. Buses. A bus station. One bus had its motor idling. About to leave, its door was still open. She raced over to it, leapt up the steps. It was filled with well-dressed people, men and women, making themselves comfortable, on their way to somewhere pleasant, to an agreeable life, to freedom.

"Your ticket, lady," said the driver.

She turned, stared at him. "No ticket."

"No ticket, no travel." He sneered.

"I can pay. Please."

The driver had looked at her oddly. "Then go into the station, buy a ticket. You got two minutes."

Get back off this bus? Go buy a ticket? No, that was impossible. The men would soon realize she was gone. They would send someone to look for her. They, too, would see the open door, the waiting buses, and they'd come after her.

"No, no, please. Let me stay. I can pay you."

"Whatssa matter lady? You got problems?"

"Please. Help me. I must leave here. Very fast."

The driver only looked at her for a long moment. "This bus goes to Reno."

She reached into her hat, slid her fingers into the secret compartment, pulled out a few bills although she had no idea how much a ticket would cost. The driver stared at the dollars, looked at her again. Jerked his head toward the empty seat just across the aisle. "Go sit down."

He was letting her stay? Incredible. She was really getting away?

The bus door slammed closed.

"Thank you," she said.

"Don't make me regret this," he muttered. Began backing the vehicle out of the station.

She slid low in her seat. Bob, the others, oh yes, they must have realized she was gone, by now. They must be looking for her. The bus turned a corner, began rolling down the main street. Pulling on her hat, she hid her face with her hair, although they'd recognize her easily enough, she knew that. But the bus kept going. To Reno? Where was that? It didn't matter. Any place else was far enough away.

****

She was an instant success; Cal had known she would be. She'd only been here for ten days, but that glowing beauty of hers, that flexible rich voice had easily won hearts. She'd shown up that very first evening, stepping confidently into the Nag as if she'd been coming in here for years, head high, like the star performer that she was, like a professional singer with years of experience behind her. She and Will hadn't needed more than a few hours of rehearsal, and when Louis had shown up with his guitar, he'd been as charmed as Will. Even the noisy party crowd had fallen silent, and that was nothing short of a miracle.

"She's wonderful," Will had told him later.

That was the problem. Polina and Will had hit it off right from the beginning, and as the days passed, they seemed to be getting along well…very well. Too well?

She seemed easy when in Will's company, laughing, joking. Was it just the easy companionship between musicians who work together? Perhaps. But it wasn't encouraging. Not only that, she was gaining solid fans among the male divorce-seekers—that had been the risk he'd taken when bringing her out here. At least with them, she was her usual cool self.

Still, it looked like the lovely Polina would never be his either, and since that was the way things looked, so be it. He'd given her what she'd needed, a safe haven, a job, and he had to be satisfied with that. She'd been through much, but she was rebuilding her life, and that made him feel good, very good.

However, he did wonder how she passed her days. He'd told her she could take her meals at the Nag, and in the evenings, she ate here with Will and Louis. But aside from those first two days, she hadn't taken him up on his offer of lunch, which was a shame. It would have given them a chance to be together. He'd even gone to the Mizpah to look for her, but Edna Grimes had told him she went out early every morning. Where did she go? Blake's Folly was only a few streets, these days. Where could anyone disappear to? It was a mystery, all right, and he didn't feel he had any right to ask her about it. *Because it's none of your business.*

The Nag was filling up, and the two bartenders had their hands full, filling drink orders for the usual noisy crowd. Sitting at a quieter table near the back were Susanna and Alexander Treemont, as elegantly dressed as always, throwbacks to an earlier, more refined era. Age notwithstanding, they were loyal customers, and he loved chatting with them: they were the most delightfully wise and generous people he knew.

He went to their table.

"Come, sit with us, Cal," said Alexander. "We're in need of a little gossip. Life gets dull in that big rattling old barn of ours."

Cal didn't believe that for a minute. These two were the least likely people to let boredom get the upper hand. He knew for a fact that, aside from Alexander's passion for painting, both he and Susanna were voracious readers and fanatical gardeners (although their prickly unrewarding garden was far from lush).

"Okay. What sort of gossip are you looking for?"

"Don't you pay attention to him." Susanna threw her husband a scolding look. "There's no reason to satisfy his nosiness."

"There certainly is," Alexander answered. "Tell us how things are going with that lovely lady you brought to our house that night."

"Ah." Of course, they'd be curious. In the same situation, he would be, too. "How what things are going?"

"You can't fool me. The lady's too beautiful for any male to remain completely indifferent."

Rueful, Cal shook his head. "I'm not indifferent, I'll admit that. But don't go dreaming up a romance. If Polina ever does get interested in a man, I'm pretty certain I'm not the one she'd choose."

"Nonsense," chided Susanna. "You're a charmer, a subtle but very effective one. Give the poor woman a chance. She's just settling in, getting to know the town, the culture."

"I know. She needs time to find her feet and a little peace. She's had a tough life, from what she's told me." And he was certain there was a lot she hadn't told him either.

"She's doing fine."

Cal stared at her. "How can you know that?"

"Because she came over to our table to talk to us the other night. Said she wanted to start paying for her room at the Mizpah. I refused. Told her she was our guest, but she just got that stubborn as a mule look on her face. I don't think we've heard the last of it either, because she said you pay her good money as a singer, and she also has another job as a seamstress. That she was perfectly capable of paying her own way."

"A seamstress?"

"Over at Angie Bilk's laundry." Susanna laughed outright at his confusion. "She's a tough lady. Don't you worry about her."

"Okay." He stood, feeling like a jerk. "She managed to get pretty far without my help. I'll back off."

What had he expected? That Polina would remain dependent on him only? That she would eventually fall into his arms, declare undying love because he'd helped her out? Was he that selfish? That manipulative? If so, he didn't like himself very much. But he didn't have time to take the thoughts further. The door of the Nag opened, and there she was.

She looked around the room, saw him, smiled. A smile that warmed his heart as surely as a bolt of pure white lightning. That's all he wanted, to keep her smiling. He needed that smile like a man needs fresh air. No matter what happened. *Even if she does fall in love with someone else.*

She began threading her way through the crowd, heading toward him.

"Cal. I have surprise for tonight."

He noticed how her eyes danced. "Surprise? What kind of surprise?"

"You wait. Maybe ten minutes. Maybe five."

But he didn't even have to wait that long. In came Will with his usual piano virtuoso strut, as if about to go on stage at Carnegie Hall. And right on his heels...

Cal gaped. Ralph Grimes? Hadn't Ralph, a notorious grump, vowed to never set foot in the Nag because it was the rival of his brother's Mizpah? But here he was, all right, and lugging a big case. Cal even knew what was inside: an accordion. Ralph was one of the best musicians around.

Polina was grinning openly and looking very proud of herself. "You see?"

He grinned back at her. "I see, all right. What's going on, Polina?"

"Ralph, he hear me and Will and Louis rehearsing, and he say he want to play here, too. A whole band, almost. This is good, no?" Then, she tapped her head with one finger, a gesture indicating she thought Ralph a bit of a crank—which he definitely was. "Ralph, he say he don't care about money. He just want to play."

"That's even better news." Although Cal was certain money wasn't something he'd have to worry about: these four musicians were bound to make a success of things, turn the Nag into an attraction for more than just the local divorce crowd.

****

Polina perched on a bench—well, she couldn't really call it a bench, just a halved log propped up, at each end, on two large rocks. She liked coming to sit here, right at the end of Third Street, although there was nothing much to see, and this was certainly no bustling community. Yet, it reminded her of Bobriki, of the benches where elderly folks had sat each evening with their canes stretched out in front of them, gossiping, scrutinizing every passerby, looking for signs of sin, unseemly behavior, anything that could turn into juicy gossip. She'd always hated walking by them, bidding them good evening, knowing that, as soon as she was out of earshot, their tongues would wag.

Nowadays, she thought of them with affection. She even missed them, but knew there was no chance they were still alive. Few had been as lucky as she. Fate had certainly worked overtime, granted her a few mighty precious assets: a singing voice, good bone structure, determination, and excellent health.

She looked down the gritty road. Although the nights were desert cold just before sunset, the air was fresh and dry, and even the glancing wind was a delight. Somewhere behind her, the planks on an abandoned house creaked nervously, and pale swirls of dust rose, pranced across the road's ruined surface. How good it felt being here. Even if Cal claimed Blake's Folly had been a wild, roaring place in earlier days, it was the peace and the silence of now that appealed to her. Noise and turbulence were things she could live without forever.

Wasn't life funny? She'd come from a village on the other side of the world, and here she was, back in a village. A very different one, without rich greenery, a rushing river, or little paths winding between fields. Without the traditions of long centuries, without the songs, the crafts, or the language she loved. Yet, Blake's Folly was still a village, and she felt good here.

Almost as if she'd found home.

She glanced at her wristwatch. Soon she would go to the Red Nag, to sing, do what she loved. In the Nag, no one bothered or opportuned her. She wasn't unaware of the looks the men sent her, those free and easy males waiting for their divorces to go through, men on the lookout for short spicy affairs for the duration of their residency. She knew Cal also saw their looks—his watchful eyes missed nothing, she was sure of it—and he would always make certain she was safe.

She particularly loved the last part of each evening, after the music ended and customers went home, when she and Cal were finally alone. Sitting together at the back table, they drank cups of strong tea, just the way she'd always done in Russia.

And little by little, she told him about Bobriki, about the vats of pickles they had prepared each autumn, about old Zinaida, the worst gossip in town who sat under people's windows, her ear pressed to the wall, overhearing conversations. She told him the old stories, about how, when she'd been a little girl and lived in a house outside the village, it had rained for such a long time that roads were impassable and it had been impossible to attend church. A week later, the priest had come to the house and said to her mother she would have to pay a fine, do penance, chop the priest's own wood, and do extra work in his fields. How unfair!

But the church had been so powerful in those days, and every family had to give a part of everything they produced to the priest: If you had ten kilos of wheat, you gave him one; when you killed a pig, you gave the priest the best cuts of meat, and he always showed up at exactly the right moment. No one complained, because he was the most educated man in the village. He read and wrote letters, filled out official forms, because most peasants couldn't read. No one wanted to educate them: they were needed in the fields. Only later, did things finally change.

She talked about Grisha, finally, for the memory of her son was a hard painful knot begging to be freed, and Cal listened, never interrupting, never judging, and never hesitating to smooth over awkward moments or share his own stories. Then, tea and conversation finished, they would go out into the night, head for the Mizpah—Cal would never let her return alone in the dark. And every evening, she tucked her hand into his elbow as they walked, savoring his closeness, the lovely feeling of being beside him.

She smiled. Perhaps Cal coming into her life was the biggest stroke of luck she'd ever had. Because of him, she had again found a village: Blake's Folly. Her heart filled with warmth. And in a little while, just as soon as the sun slipped away, she would be seeing him again.

****

This morning, he would go see for himself, although he knew it was none of his business. Still, wild horses couldn't have kept him away, and who needed wild horses when Angie Bilk's laundry wasn't even four minutes walking distance from the Nag? He still had to have a good reason for showing up there, and laundry wasn't one of them.

As a bachelor, he'd always insisted on being as independent as possible, and that required investing in work-saving devices like the latest model Bendix front-loading automatic washer sitting in his laundry room. It was an excellent machine, far in advance of anything else on the market, and equipped with a rotating drum. Why, that crafty Bendix could even auto-fill, wash, rinse, and spin dry—a hell of an advantage over those inferior appliances with motorized ringers, notorious for trapping hands and fingers. Of course, he'd had to bolt his washer firmly to the floor or it would have shifted itself all through the Nag, heaving and roaring like some incontrollable Frankenstein monster.

Perhaps if he claimed it was out of order? It would be a fib, but he couldn't come up with anything better, not even sewing. He knew the seamstress, Millie Sparks, also worked in the laundry with Angie, but since he was quite capable of handling a needle and thread to sew on his own buttons and mend his clothes, vanity wouldn't let him use that as an excuse.

So, feeling as guilty as hell—he hated telling lies, even little white ones—he neatly folded his sheets, slipped them into a pillowcase, left the Nag, slunk down Main Street toward the red-brick building housing Angie's laundry. No sooner was he in front of it, he saw he hadn't needed subterfuge to find out if Polina really was working there. Both she and Millie were seated in full view, right there in the shop's big window, their hands filled with fabric.

It was too late to turn back. Both women had seen him out on the street. On Polina's face, he could read complete surprise…something else, too. Would she be annoyed? Feel that he was spying on her? She might, and she'd be absolutely right. He felt ashamed of himself. Deeply regretting he was here, but unable to do anything else, he pushed open the wood and glass door, entered.

The odor of soap and hot irons filled the steamy air. Three round electric washing machines chugged percussively along the far wall, but noisy as they were, they couldn't drown out Angie Bilk's first insolent words: "Well, look what the cat dragged in."

No one had ever accused that raw-boned woman of subtlety or refinement.

Polina's big grin was more welcoming. More than that, even. It was…what? Radiant? As if pleased to see him. "Good morning, Cal."

"Hi, Cal," Millie called. "What brings you here?"

Angie stared pointedly at the filled pillowslip he was carrying. "That fancy machine of yers give up th' ghost?"

"Certainly not," he said, refusing to admit a false defeat. "The machine is in perfect working order. It just needs a few more bolts to secure it to the floor. Before I get around to doing the job, I thought I'd bring a few things here." That sounded plausible, didn't it? Or was his tone too jolly?

"So you've finally decided to avail yerself of my services, huh?"

Ah, Cal thought. So, that was the problem. Angie was huffy because he wasn't a regular client. "You see, I just got used to doing things on my own over the years," he said, hoping to mollify that harpy. "That's what happens when you're a long-time bachelor."

She only harrumphed.

He put his bundle on the wooden counter, turned to the other two women, and wondered if he'd have to pretend surprise at finding Polina here. He didn't. She was the one who held up the needle she was holding.

"Look, Cal. I have new job. Sewing."

"And she's real good at it, too," added Angie.

"Normal. I always sew in Russia. Every woman do fancy work in my village."

"Doan know what we'd do without her. All them city ladies coming in here, wanting their new cowboy togs to fit just so. Poor Millie couldn't handle all the work."

"I can imagine," said Cal, thinking of the seductive shirts red-haired Nancy had sported in his saloon.

"So we go an' put a sign in the window askin' for a seamstress, and not ten minutes pass when Polina walks in," Millie added.

"Yes, I walking on road, see it, come in."

"And I says, if you can sew, come on, join us," added Angie.

"And we talk all day, so I soon speak good English," said Polina proudly.

Cal tried not to wince. In Angie and Millie's company, she'd certainly learn a sort of English, but it wasn't of the variety anyone would call "good."

Millie stood. "You want to eat with us, Cal? We're just gonna have some lunch, and I'll bet we got the fixings for another sandwich."

"Thanks, Millie, I can't. I have to get back to the saloon."

He hoped his exit didn't look too hasty, but he had no desire to tarry. He didn't like the image of himself as just another Blake's Folly nosey parker.

****

He was over on the other side of the saloon, talking with Lil, a brassy fake blonde, and Polina didn't like that one bit. She knew her type, all right. Just like the other divorce ladies, now that she was away from hometown disapproval, Lil was determined to live it up, do the kinds of things she'd only dreamt about in her married days. Surely Cal could see how vulgar the woman was, couldn't he? But what if he liked that kind of thing?

Polina tried to fight down the raw jealousy…and failed. She knew she was being unreasonable, and the violence of her feelings stunned her. What claim did she have to Cal? None at all. He'd helped her out because that was the sort of man he was. He'd help anyone in trouble, that's what he'd explained when he'd told her about being an *eticheskiy gumanist*—what were the English words for it? Oh, yes, she remembered now, an ethical humanist. Would she have to accept she was nothing special to him, that she'd only been on the receiving end of a good deed? The thought wounded her deeply. She'd been sure…sure of what? That she'd mattered to him?

Then Cal looked over in her direction, met her eye, and something in his gaze reassured her. The hint of humor? Warmth? Something far more potent? Unless she was getting everything wrong, letting her heart dictate, turn wishes into reality.

"Polina? Shouldn't we get started?"

She turned to Will, Louis, and Ralph, nodded. There was one more set to do tonight. After that, she'd cross the room, stake her claim. Or see if she could. At the very least, she'd pry him away from that silly seductress with her dyed hair and loud giggle. She'd get his attention, all right. Just another twenty minutes to go.

****

Ralph packed up his accordion, left. Will and Louis

headed out into the night together.

"See you tomorrow, Cal."

The last clients pulled on their coats and gloves, and the bartenders fetched dirty glasses, wiped down tables. This was the part of the evening he loved best, when silence returned to the Nag. When he sat down with Polina, drank tea with her before setting out into the night, escorting her back to the Mizpah. It had become a ritual, one he wouldn't have given up for anything in the world.

She was waiting for him at the back table, the honey-colored coat slung around her shoulders, her beautiful eyes limpid, soft, watching his every move, her rosy mouth smiling, her hair a golden sheen. On the table in front of her was a flat paper parcel. He went to her, put down the tray with the teapot and two cups, sat.

"It was a good night," he said as he poured out the tea. "We're getting more people in here than ever before. And that's because of you, you know. Because they're coming to hear you."

"That is true. But also true for Will, and Louis, and Ralph. For all four of us."

"All four of you," he acknowledged, although, as far as he was concerned, she was the real star, the one who pulled everything together. "You're right. The combination works perfectly."

She lifted her teacup, then put it down again. Did she look uncertain? Picking up the packet on the table, she handed it to him. "This for you."

"For me?"

"Another surprise."

He chuckled. "Good. I always like surprises. Can I open it now?"

She nodded, but still looked uncomfortable, as if afraid he wouldn't be pleased by her gesture.

The flat bundle was of simple brown paper loosely tied with string. Amused, certainly intrigued, he undid the bow, lifted back one flap and reached inside. His fingers touched something soft. Pulling it out, it unfolded into a long-sleeved shirt in soft white linen. Around the cuffs, the neck, and part way down the front, was the finest embroidered pattern in creamy beige: leaves, tiny flowers interspersed with squares and triangles. It was handwork of the highest order. He looked at her, lost for words.

She was watching him, trying to gauge his reaction. "It is traditional Russian shirt."

"Yes," he said, quietly. "I know what it is. Did you make this?"

She nodded, her eyes still wide, anxious in the room's soft light. "I make shirt by hand, and I do embroidery with pale beige color, not normal red or blue, so you can wear it with not much difficulty here in America. But please, don't worry. You don't have to wear. It is just as gift."

"Why wouldn't I wear it?" He'd wear it, all right, no matter what color—red, blue, green, or shocking pink—with pride. And with love. "Polina...it's magnificent. It's..." Adequate words still escaped him. "Thank you. I know that sounds terribly weak, but this gift means very much to me."

She smiled faintly. "No. To me. It is to thank *you*. For everything. For giving me the chance to have a life that is beautiful again."

****

They were both silent as they made their way to the

Mizpah. The night was dark, moonless, and no stars twinkled through a heavy layer of cloud. His heart was so full, he didn't dare utter a word in case the spell was broken and everyday banality slid back into the picture. He left her on the steps of the Mizpah, just as he did every other night, although he ached to take her in his arms, kiss her. And didn't dare.

"Sleep well."

"Yes, you, too."

He waited until she was safely inside before turning back, heading home.

Then stopped in his tracks. He knew what he wanted. He knew what his dreams were. He had given her a life that was beautiful? Perhaps. But hadn't she done the same for him? Everything had changed since he'd first seen her.

He turned, jogged back toward the Mizpah, charged up the front steps, ripped open the door, and entered. Elmer Grimes was behind the bar, wiping down the counter with a rag that had seen its cleanest days half a century before.

"Polina?"

"She's gone up to her room."

He took the stairs two by two, turned left on the landing, followed the long corridor to its end. Knocked.

She opened the door. "Cal?" Frowned. "Is something wrong?"

"Nothing is wrong. I have to talk to you. I… Look, Polina, if you don't want us to sit in your room, we can go…"

"You are a silly man." Taking his hand, she led him inside. "Please."

A table lamp touched the old furniture with soft

light, caught the shine of her hair, shadowed her eyes. How he loved her, wanted her, but if he revealed his feelings, he might ruin everything, their friendship, and the trust that had grown between them. Still, he had to take the chance. Just in case.

"Sit down." She gestured to two ancient leather armchairs.

He didn't even glance at them. "No, Polina, I can't sit. I...I don't know how to begin."

"Begin?" Then, she smiled at him, that wonderful smile, the one that meant so much to him. "Just tell me. It is so very easy."

"Is it?"

"Yes. Easy. I love you, Cal. You are here because you love me, too, is that not true?"

"Yes. It's very true. Unbelievably true." He stared at her with wonderment. "How did you know what I wanted to say?"

"Because the way you look at me."

"Do you love me enough to marry me? Be my wife?"

She laughed, a bright tinkling sound. Was she laughing at him? No, she'd never do that, not at a moment like this. Reaching out, she caught his hand again, brought it to her lips, kissed his fingers. "I want very much that you be my husband. Is okay?"

"Oh yes. That's very, very okay." And unable to resist another minute, he bent, feathered her lips, let himself sense her need before deepening the kiss.

Opening to him, curling her arms around his neck, she leaned into his strength. "You will be my forever husband, yes?"

"Yes." He chuckled with pure delight. "And you

will be my forever wife. "
   "Promise?"
   "Promise."

IV

At the End of the World: 1972

For each age is a dream that is dying,
Or one that is coming to birth.
~Arthur O'Shaughnessy, (1844-1881), *Ode*

"You gotta be joking." Mike Barnes stepped out of the car and looked up and down the town's main street—if that's what it was: dust, a cluster of abandoned buildings, a wilderness of empty lots. Behind, a hill dotted with shanties and abandoned trailers resembled the flea-covered flank of a hairless dog. People still lived in places like this? Blake's Folly might have been something once, but those days were gone forever.

Barry Grimes looked at his friend, read his expression, and laughed. "Yeah, I know what you're thinking. But believe me, it wasn't a bad place to grow up in."

"Maybe. But it's a ghost town now, and something tells me it's been a ghost town since the turn of the century." And he was going to be stuck here for five whole days?

"Well, a semi-ghost town. There are still sixty-five residents." Barry looked rueful. "I admit it's gotten worse in recent years. People used to come here from

169

all over the country when they needed to establish a six-week Nevada residence to get a divorce. Now that no-fault divorces are available in other states, or you can go to Mexico for a cheapie, that migratory trade has faded away. There was even a dude ranch outside town, the Get Lucky, but it closed down when modernizing became too expensive. A few hippies live out there now. You see? Even a semi-ghost town has a lively side."

A very tranquil lively side, Mike wanted to say, but he saw the look his friend was giving him and held his tongue. He was sounding like a snob, a city slicker, sneering at any place that wasn't San Francisco.

"Come on. Let's get our gear inside."

Mike stared at the building where they'd be staying, shabby, two stories high, and with a long balcony running along the second floor. There was a broad front porch and a wooden sidewalk, but both looked as though they'd give way under their feet. Still, the place did have a sort of rustic charm…if you liked that kind of thing. "This is the Mizpah Saloon? The bar your parents ran?" And the place where—according to family legend—his grandmother had once played the piano.

"This is it. It now belongs to my older sister and brother-in-law."

Once inside, things were different. This was the real McCoy, all right, authentic, even majestic. A long wooden bar ran down one side of a large main room, the old-fashioned tin ceiling had authentic cornices, and mirrors vied for space with paintings on all the walls. There was even an old piano near the back, almost invisible behind the rows of modern un-beautiful slot machines.

"This place is incredible." Although he knew the words were inadequate.

"I know," said Barry, his face beaming. "Back in the old days, saloons were usually the best-built buildings in town. They had the town's only public toilets, too."

"How's that for progress," Mike mocked.

"Don't be fooled. Saloons did represent civilization, not just depravity. Many opened at five or six in the morning, and men came to drink coffee, eat breakfast, read newspapers, smoke, meet with others, and conclude business deals. They could even buy bonbons to pacify the wife who was always stuck at home, being respectable."

"Hey, big brother." A rosy-cheeked young woman with deep dimples stood behind the bar, grinning at them. Throwing down the towel she was holding, she loped around the mahogany. Barry caught her in a hug, gave her a huge smacking kiss on the cheek. Then, he looked over at Mike. "Meet my bratty baby sister, Laurie."

"Bratty." Elbowing her way out of her brother's arms, she appealed to Mike. "He made my life so miserable, I had no choice." Then, held out her hand. "Pleased to meet you, even though you probably are a friend of his."

Mike laughed, took the proffered hand, shook it, admired the young woman's candid-looking blue eyes, the straight brown hair falling to her shoulders in a shining curtain. A tight T-shirt emphasized her slender, gently curving figure, and well-worn jean shorts gave a very nice view of shapely tanned legs.

"Hey sis, what are you doing behind the bar? I thought you're supposed to be combing the countryside, hoping to find a little vegetation."

With a mocking smile, she turned to Mike again: "That's what happens to formerly good people who go work in advertising. They're corrupted. My brother used to be normal."

Barry laughed. "You're appealing to the wrong man. Mike and I are the advertising world's dream team."

"Sad world." She winced, but Mike saw the dimples deepening.

"Come on, buddy." Barry picked up his holdall and headed toward a broad stairway near the back of the room. "Let's not waste our time talking with a tree hugger."

Following behind, Mike couldn't help smirking. "Tree hugger? Out here there are trees?"

"You see?" she called after them. "I might have met a defender."

Mike half turned, grinned back at her. "No, just a realist."

Barry led the way upstairs, along the hallway, and into a square white room. "Make yourself at home."

Mike looked around. Home? There was an old iron bed, a few sticks of tacky furniture, all leftovers from some makeover, circa 1950. The walls needed a good coat of paint, the curtains sagged, and the broad window led out onto that rickety-looking upper story veranda—although going out there definitely meant you had a death wish.

"You still get clients staying in this place?"

"Nah. Not modern enough for people these days,

and my sister and brother-in-law can't be bothered running a hotel. Besides, Blake's Folly is too far off the beaten track. Who'd imagine there'd be accommodation at the end of a ruined road?"

"How do they make a living?"

"With the restaurant and the bar. They have country music groups every weekend, and those pull in quite a crowd. And since this is the only place for miles around, the locals, ranchers, feed salesmen, veterinarians, wannabe miners, tall talkers, and con men fill the place every evening. You'd be surprised at how good business is."

Country music? Wouldn't you know it. *Grandma must be rolling around in her grave.* Mike tried not to groan.

"Besides," Barry continued, "a bar with slots will always find customers. It has to. You'd never call my brother-in-law Bob an ambitious man. Born and raised in this town, I don't think he ever leaves it."

"And your sister?"

"My older sister Ruthie? She's as lazy as he is."

Which is why the place looks the way it does, Mike thought, but didn't say. Anyway, it was none of his business. He wasn't here in Blake's Folly for forever, and who was he to tell people how to run their show? *Live and let live.* He had problems of his own. Big problems.

He grimaced. Tracey-Ann: she was a problem, all right. She was the one trying to mastermind him at the moment, oblige him to change his own life. He pushed thoughts of her out of his mind. He hadn't left her behind in San Francisco just to conjure up her image. Be forced to think about what he'd come to call "the problem." Problem? Disaster, more like. Damn!

****

A tour of the town didn't make the place more endearing to him. Sitting on a little quadrangle of half logs propped on stones and pretending to be benches, an alert-looking older couple watched life—such as it was—go by. They nodded politely as he and Barry passed, then stared unabashedly.

Barry stopped beside one empty lot with a tumble of ruined bricks that might have been something…a very long time ago. "Right here, once upon a time, there stood the most famous brothel in the state: the Hot Red Star in the Desert, some people called it." He looked regretful.

"A brothel?" Mike leered. "A place you knew well?"

"If only." Barry laughed shortly. "I was born too late for that, but it was said to be quite a place in its heyday. When I was a kid, people still talked about its sumptuous theme rooms and the sexy ladies who used to work there. Unfortunately, the place burnt down in one of the big fires that destroyed a lot of the town's good buildings, a few former saloons, and a whole row of interesting wooden houses."

"A shame."

"It is. Fires have always been common out in these prairie towns, but back in the old days, people pitched in, built everything up again. Even in places that were virtually wiped off the map, it only took a year or two before everyone was back in business. But in ghost towns or semi-ghost towns like Blake's Folly, who'd rebuild?"

"Who'd even come to live here?"

Barry looked at his friend. "You don't see the charm in the place, do you." It was a statement, not a question.

"Let's just say, I can see why people left. How can you make a living out here if you don't run a bar with slot machines and country music concerts?"

"There's a mechanic and a gas station, a small grocery and general store, although I doubt the people running it make decent money. Years ago, a famous artist lived out here, and a few writers and scientists come through, too. But since the Mizpah is now a has-been, not a hotel, they don't stick around."

"Hard to imagine that this town supposedly had its own newspaper." Which was why he was out here right now, following up on that story—unless it was just another tall tale, or the brag of an old man who wanted to think his youth had been an exciting one.

"You're referring to the paper your grandfather claimed he wrote for?"

"That's the one. My grandfather's name was Westley Cranston, and the paper was called *The Morning Sun.*"

"Would be, out here." Barry snorted. "Okay, your grandfather was telling the truth. Come on, the old newspaper office is just one block away."

"It's still standing?"

"Sure, it is. I heard it was taken over by some small company back in the 1920s—there's still an old sign saying something about furniture tacked on the front." Barry shook his head. "Somebody must have been nuts, thinking a business could thrive out here."

"What about your younger sister? Laurie. The one we met in the bar. What's she doing here?"

"She's only temporary. She's finishing a doctorate in botany over in Sacramento. During the holidays, she comes to Nevada and gathers seeds for replanting in burnt-out areas. But she can tell you more about it than I can."

"Good-looking lady."

"You bet she is. But don't let the pretty exterior fool you. The woman's one hundred percent old-fashioned and radical bluestocking." Barry shot his friend an admonishing look, although his grin remained jovial. "Anyway, lecher, keep your hands off. You've got enough problems in life."

Which was a mild way of putting it. "Don't worry. All I have in mind is friendship. Let's just say this is a five-day holiday away from Tracey-Ann. I'm not in the market for romance. Far from it."

Tracey-Ann. Just saying her name depressed him. He'd met her when they'd both been students, in the days when they'd both dreamt about becoming writers—that had been the glue that had cemented them together. Had love come into the picture? Perhaps…in the beginning, but that stage hadn't lasted long. It had become familiarity, companionship, petty disagreements, and nasty arguments, all the things that make up a relationship when the zing goes. His parents' marriage functioned on just such an irritatingly dull basis, and he wasn't ready for that.

He was still young; he wanted stimulation, travel, and adventure out in the big wide world. He wanted to smell olive trees in Greece, experience life in Paris, fly to Morocco, go join the Kurds on some mountain in Turkey. Yet there he was, stuck in San Francisco, sharing an apartment with Tracey-Ann who'd been his girlfriend since 1967, working for an advertising agency and writing copy. How had that happened?

It had been an easy trap to fall into. He and Tracey-Ann had planned to work for a few years, save enough money to take off. But Norwegian fiords and Machu Picchu had been replaced by Tracey-Ann's determination to get married and start a family. It was this last—family—that she was now using to get the first. A few "forgotten" birth control pills: a surprise pregnancy. Under the heavy weight of parental disapproval, marriage was no longer a subject to be argued about.

The idea of being married to her filled him with horror. Okay, horror was too strong a word for it, but he'd been trying to end the relationship with Tracey-Ann for over a year. Only her threats of suicide and her crying jags had kept him in place. Waiting for the right moment to escape, it had passed him by, and now he really was stuck.

He didn't want children. He didn't want a lifetime with a woman whose values were unlike his, a woman he no longer desired—yes, that was another one of Tracey-Ann's complaints: he didn't make love with her as often as she wanted. No, he didn't. But jerk that he was, he'd made an effort. And look how that had ended.

"Here we are."

Here was what? Just another run-down building with boarded-up windows and a rotted front door hanging half open. Inside, a perfectly empty office was caught in afternoon's half gloom. Behind, in another, sunnier, room, a few long wooden tables were in surprisingly good shape—they'd made things to last in the old days. Other than those, a thick layer of dust, and considerable rodent excrement, there was nothing. No sign that this had once been a noisy newspaper office with brisk journalists, typesetters, and apprentices. There were no type cases, and no presses; no oily tar stink of printer's ink remained in the air. The place had been cleaned out, probably by pillagers who'd carried off all they could, then sold it in junk shops as "authentic" Wild West antiques.

Yet, this old office, picked clean, and with no memories left, touched him in some way. This was the place where his grandfather had worked; this town was where Westley had met his future bride, his grandmother, Hattie. How? What were the circumstances? Where had they both come from? Somewhere in the east, he knew. But how had they ended up here? Had they been in love, or had it been a marriage of convenience?

It was too late to get the answers. Too much time had passed. Both Westley and Hattie had died some years ago, and his parents, never curious, hadn't asked them the right questions. Still, he could consider himself lucky: some people knew nothing at all about their grandparents. At least he had this. This what? Shanty? Wreck? Pile of old boards? Inwardly, he sneered at himself, at the sentiment that had sent him out here. What sort of secret was he hoping to uncover?

****

"A little peace and quiet. Finally." Mike's lip curled. The live music was awful. Thank goodness, the set seemed to have ended. The guitarist put down his instrument, the scratchy-voiced singer pranced off the low podium, wriggling her bottom for maximum effect, and both the bass player and saxophonist buried their noses in beers.

Standing beside him at the bar, Laurie winked. "Didn't my brother Barry warn you?"

"He only mentioned there were country music groups coming here on Fridays and Saturdays."

"Oh sure. Country music? That's not the worst of it. We get Dylan copies, Guthrie copies, Elvis Presley acts, pseudo-Beatle routines, you name it."

"Sounds grim. I guess Barry didn't want to discourage me."

"Barry," she scoffed. "What does he know? He's never around."

"But you are?"

"Well, since this place is only a hundred and seventy miles away from Sacramento, I get to come back quite often."

"As punishment?"

She looked at him oddly. "You think Blake's Folly is that bad?"

He realized he'd offended her, just like he had upset Barry, and that was the last thing he'd wanted to do. He liked her, liked sitting up here at the bar with her. There was something earthy and honest about her, and he enjoyed being with a woman who didn't shy at keeping pace with him, beer for beer. He also liked those blue eyes, that perfect skin. "It might take some getting used to before I can actually come out and say I'm ready to take out a mortgage."

She grabbed a handful of peanuts from the bowl to her left, began shelling them, popping them into her mouth. "Okay. The next question is, do you always see the negative side of everything before coming around to the positive? Or is the positive dangerous territory you'd prefer to avoid altogether?"

He squirmed. That was the problem in conversing with intelligent people: They saw through you too easily. "No, I'm not that bad. I'm all for enthusiasm and the sunny side of life. I just like to creep up on it slowly."

"Right." She laughed shortly, and those seductive dimples appeared again.

"You flirting with my sister?" Barry had come back into the bar. With him was an absolutely stunning woman, as close as you could get to the ideal: bombshell figure, a broad face with well-defined bones, pale blue eyes, and a lush rosy mouth. How the hell did a town like this produce something like her? Mike knew very well who she was, too. Hadn't Barry been talking about her for months? "Elsa Hardy? Meet my pal Mike Barnes."

Elsa barely acknowledged him. Instead, her eyes roved around the room. Looking for someone, Mike thought, and instantly felt sorry for his friend. He knew of Barry's obsession with Elsa, but that one glance had told him all he wanted to know: Barry didn't stand a chance.

Sure, his friend was a nice guy, not bad-looking, sporty, good-natured. He was a dedicated advertising man who would build up a good career because he had talent. He was also naïve, which made him excellent husband material. And that was the problem: Girls like Elsa Hardy didn't even give guys with qualities like those the time of day. They were bored by them. Mike knew he was right, too, because he could suss people out—wasn't that the job of any serious writer?

Okay, he was almost thirty years old, and he hadn't

written much of anything yet, just a few short stories that he'd sent off to magazines and that had been rejected. For the moment, all his energy went into writing shitty commercial crap: "Harley's Ground Meats—the Real Chef is YOU." Not a brilliant start for a would-be Vonnegut or an angry Barth.

"What are you drinking, Elsa?"

"Vodka."

"Right." Barry leaned over the bar, signaled to his brother-in-law Bob.

Mike continued to observe Elsa, noticed she was watching a man on the other side of the room. Yes, Mike knew his type, too. A fast-talker with an answer to everything. A womanizer. A bad boy. When the man's eyes slid over toward Elsa, she looked away.

Mike almost laughed out loud. Small town nowhere that this was, all the elements for a good story were well in place. Or a bad story. He looked over at Barry. Poor man. Oblivious to the mini-drama being played out, he handed Elsa her drink. Mike noted his flushed face, his too-evident bliss at being beside the woman he was crazy about: "Hey Mike, Elsa's not only gorgeous, she's got a singing voice you won't believe. She's star material."

Poor besotted Barry.

Mike saw Laurie was watching him, a knowing smile on her lips. Did she think her brother's obsession was ridiculous, too? Her eyes slid briefly in Elsa's direction, then back to him. Yes, she did. He felt like chuckling. Then realized he was looking forward to a little more conversation with Laurie. But that was impossible...now. A painful squeal ripped through the air. The guitarist was back on stage, adjusting his lousy sound system. Beside him, the singer pulled self-consciously at the hem of her too-short, too-tight mini skirt. The so-called music was about to start again.

****

"Well, what do you think?"

"About what?" Mike picked up his coffee mug, sipped. They were sitting at a table in the front of the bar, watching sunlight shimmy across the wooden floor, touch up the brass foot rail, make mirrors sparkle and wood glow. This place had a good feel to it, one that knocked you back a hundred years or so. Not too difficult to imagine the gunslingers, cattlemen, and cowboys that had filled the place in the town's heyday. And a few saloon ladies, too. Those bedrooms might well have seen some torrid things. *If only the walls could talk.*

Barry was looking at his friend and shaking his head ruefully. "Don't tell me you didn't notice Elsa. No male in the entire universe could ignore her."

"Elsa?" He pretended ignorance for a moment more, and then gave up. There was no way to avoid this particular subject. "Okay, okay. The woman you wet dream about every night."

"Wouldn't you?"

"Dream on, buddy."

A frown appeared between Barry's brows. "What's that supposed to mean?"

Mike put down his cup. "Forget it. She's a professional flirt. She's interested in herself, not in you."

"Oh yeah?" Now Barry was looking belligerent. Angry, even. "Except I know what happened last Easter, when I was out here, when me and Elsa were alone together. Believe me, she was plenty interested then."

"Okay, okay. Have it your way. I'm just warning you."

"Warning me?"

"About professional flirts."

Barry leaned back in his seat, looked down, was silent for a long minute. Fighting down aggression? Or just disappointment.

"Come on. Finish your breakfast. If we're going out walking in the hills, you'll be sorry you haven't eaten much of anything."

"I guess she's an obsession," Barry said quietly.

"No kidding."

"She said she was planning to come to San Francisco, meet someone in the music world. I told her she could stay with me."

"And what did she say?"

"She said yes, she'd like that. So you see?"

Sure, she'll stay with you. Unless something better comes along. But he kept his mouth shut. A change of subject was the best tactic at the moment—if he wanted their friendship to continue. "Where's your sister?"

"Ah ha! Talk about obsessions." Barry laughed.

"Laurie is hardly an obsession, but I like her. She's intelligent. It's fun talking with her."

"Don't tell her that. She already has a good opinion of herself." Although the proud look on Barry's face said something quite different. "She was always the smart one in the family."

"The pretty one, too."

"Shucks. Don't I appeal to you?"

Mike grinned back at his friend, pleased that the

tense moment was over. "I never mix business with pleasure. How will we write good copy about pork sausages if all I do is stare into your sweet little eyes? No, I like the sparkling blues of your sister a lot better."

"Where does Tracey-Ann stand in all this?"

"Tracey-Ann is two hundred and thirty miles away. And you know perfectly well I want out."

"Yeah. I know. But you'll have to convince Tracey-Ann of that. I'm getting mighty tired of being the shoulder she weeps on every time you say it's over."

It was even worse than he knew, Mike thought. He hadn't told his friend about the pregnancy yet. He hardly even admitted it to himself. Doing so would make the whole thing more real, more nightmarish. Especially since Tracey-Ann had no intention of terminating. What was the point of living in California, the first state to legalize abortion three years ago, if women like Tracey-Ann were still using pregnancy to force men to marry them?

"And what about Marsha? You haven't forgotten her already?"

Mike felt the annoyance ripple over him, followed by an uncomfortable wave of embarrassment. Why did Barry have to bring that crap up? What had Marsha been but a few fun afternoons? She was a long, lean party girl, a graphic artist with a wild social life. He and Marsha didn't expect fidelity from each other. What they had was pure fun, smoking dope, having sex, just part of the free life back in Frisco. He was out here now, here in this hot dry air, and a world away from ads and casual affairs.

"Look, I didn't say I was in love with your sister. I

said I like talking with her."

"So you did." Barry threw him a knowing look. "But you'll just have to wait until this afternoon to see her because she's out in the field. She gets up really early, before it gets too hot, goes to collect seeds out in the middle of nowhere."

"Fine. I'd also like to go speak with those old timers, the couple we saw sitting on those makeshift benches yesterday. Maybe they know a little about local history."

Barry guffawed. "Don't kid yourself. They'll probably clam right up because you're not a local boy."

****

They trudged over a seemingly endless beige plain covered by dry, pale scrub. It was a hostile landscape where each step meant avoiding, as best as possible, branches that snagged clothing and ripped skin. Those distant curved shapes undulating at their approach had to be rattlers—no, Mike really couldn't see the charm of it.

There were still the remains of old mines, a few buildings in stone and wood that no longer served any purpose, but everywhere you looked, were bullet holes—on road signs, on forgotten bits of metal, on boards, and on discarded heaps of old furniture. What kind of armed cranks came out here? Loonies probably populated the whole state. He tried not to think about them, did his best to imagine this area as it once had been, to see something positive, but failed.

"When I'm in a landscape like this one, I think about the poor jerks who worked in those old mines. It was a hell of a job: long hours, heavy machinery, poisonous fumes, and dust. Most were lucky if they lived to the ripe old age of forty-two."

"True." Barry wiped a sweaty brow with the back of his hand. "But they all flocked out here, right alongside the gamblers, the criminals, and the prostitutes. They were willing to work hard, too, even if that just made the big boys on top richer. Think about cowboys. Those guys dreamed of freedom, and the cowboy myth still plays on that. In reality, they were only lackeys on horseback."

Mike looked at his friend with amusement. "Negativity is supposed to be my game, not yours."

"But it's the truth. All of them, the miners, railway workers, and cowboys slaved for long hours, then spent every penny they earned in the saloons and brothels all along the railway lines. There was even a branch line in Blake's Folly, and that kept the Mizpah going for years."

"Brothels, huh? I was wondering about those, although that sort of thing was never mentioned in my family—especially since Grandma supposedly played piano in saloons. But do you think the Mizpah used to be a brothel?"

"Who knows? Might have been."

"Wow." Mike snickered. "Straitlaced Grandma Hattie a seductress? No way. I can't even imagine her thinking of sex, much less indulging in it."

"So your mother is the result of an immaculate conception?"

"Sounds about right."

"Well, my family has no idea about what went on back then. Just, with all those bedrooms and the old piano, it's easy to imagine dancing girls working the place and taking men upstairs."

Mike sobered. "Then dying from botched abortions, or in giving birth, because the only medical men on hand were doctors without diplomas, or quacks selling snake oil."

"Hey." Barry clapped his friend on the shoulder. "Sellers of snake oil: you know the origin of that?"

"No, old buddy, but you do, obviously, or you wouldn't ask."

"The Chinese laborers who worked on the transcontinental railway line used a lotion made from oil extracted from water snakes to treat inflammation. Because there are no water snakes on this continent, shysters made oil from rattlers. It doesn't work, but people will believe anything."

"Which is why we're good at what we do."

"Yeah. You're right. That's us," Barry crowed. "Modern snake-oil salesmen."

****

Laurie sat in the main room of the Mizpah, happy to be out of the late afternoon's heat.

"Mind if I join you?"

She looked up, saw Mike coming down the stairs. "Not at all. Take a seat. If you want a coffee, there's a fresh pot behind the bar."

"Cool."

She watched while he served himself, came to where she was sitting. He was a very good-looking guy with his curling hair worn long, his dark eyes surrounded by enviable long lashes, and his well-toned body. But there was a dissatisfied surliness about him, something that hinted at frustration. She didn't know if he was seriously interested in her or not, but the suspicion of something negative, possibly destructive, told her to keep him at arm's length.

"So, how did you meet my brother?"

"It's a funny story, really. After we left university, we both found ourselves working at Lawson and Solmes Advertising, writing copy. We'd studied different things. As you know, Barry's main interest was philosophy, mine was history, but unless you want to accumulate more degrees and go into teaching, those subjects don't get you anywhere. So there we were, both of us writing about perfume and plumbing…" He paused, grimaced, before continuing, "And we got along. Soon enough, we discovered that, putting our heads together, working as a team of two, we produced higher quality work and were able to present a client's brand more efficiently."

"But you don't feel satisfied?" There was no way she could ignore that grimace of his.

"Let's just say, it's not exactly how I planned my life. Barry and I are still writing about perfume and plumbing, but there are a hell of a lot of other things I want to do in life."

"Such as?"

"Write." He laughed shortly.

"Which is what you're doing now, right?"

"Sure. People will tell you that copywriting is all about creativity. That you need talent for that sort of work, and maybe it's true. But I've always wanted to write stories, not copy. Pushing products to gullible consumers isn't very satisfying, morally speaking."

"Does Barry feel the same way?" She never saw her brother long enough, these days, for this sort of conversation to take place. Their lives had become so dissimilar since leaving town.

"Barry's more easy-going than I am. He has patience. Maybe that's one of the benefits of growing up in a place like Blake's Folly."

"Maybe." Although she knew it was really a question of character. Even as an adult, Barry had retained a refreshing enthusiasm, and he'd probably be like that his whole life—which was why he'd fallen hook, line, and sinker for a manipulating bitch like Elsa Hardy. Laurie had hoped that the time spent away from home would have cured him of that misguided passion, but last night, seeing him in Elsa's company, told her, very clearly, it hadn't. "This doesn't explain how you came to be here in Blake's Folly. Or did my brother make the place sound irresistible?"

Mike leaned forward, his elbows on the table. "No. It's even better than that. We discovered, by a very strange coincidence, that we both have a family connection to this place, as crazy as that sounds."

"Crazy?" She had to laugh. "I don't know if that's the right word. Amusing, maybe. Astonishing. Come on. How does Blake's Folly fit into your life story?"

"It's sort of a family legend. My maternal grandfather, Westley Cranston, was one of the journalists who worked here in the late 1800s. This is where he met his future wife, Hattie, my grandmother. She used to play the piano right here in the Mizpah—or so I was told. They didn't stay here long. They left, went to the Yukon, lived there for a few years, then came south, to San Francisco. They had one child very late in life—Arabella, my mother. One day, my grandfather had a visit from an old friend of his, a guy named Ned something-or-other, who told him he'd had another child, a daughter, with a woman he'd been involved with here in Blake's Folly."

"Really? Did your grandfather try to contact the woman?"

"No. Maybe he didn't know how—this Ned person went to Europe and died during the First World War. Actually, what I figure is my grandfather didn't want my grandmother to know he'd been messing around, so he kept the secret until he was very old. After my grandmother Hattie died, Westley told my parents. He claimed he'd really loved that other woman, and had never forgotten her."

"If he loved her, why didn't he make an effort, come back and look for her after your grandmother's death?"

Mike shrugged. "Because he couldn't. By then, he'd had a stroke, and he wasn't going anywhere. He asked his son-in-law—my father—and my mother to try and find out if she was still alive, who the child was, and what she'd become."

"Did your parents do that?"

"No. They didn't even take the request seriously, probably because my grandfather hinted that the woman had been a dance girl working out of a saloon."

"You mean a prostitute?"

"It sounded like it. Not only that, but she'd also had another illegitimate kid. Maybe my parents were worried she'd hit them up for support money, or try blackmailing them."

Laurie tittered. "Just the sort of nightmare every family imagines. Do you know what her name was?"

"Here's where the story gets even more embarrassing. My father said it was something like Sassy, or Shookie. Maybe even Shuckie, or Suckee.

With horrible names like those, how could she or her illegitimate daughter be respectable?"

"Like mother, like daughter?"

"Exactly. He's quite a moralist, my father, so he preferred to let the whole thing slide. My mother is worse, a total snob, and she wished my grandfather had kept his mouth shut. That's why I find the story interesting." He picked up his coffee mug, drained it.

Laurie stared at him. "Go on…"

"Go on with what? That's all I know. My father only told me the story about five years ago, in one of those embarrassing father-son male bonding moments."

"But you want to know more, right? That's why you're here?"

He grinned. "Guilty as charged. Actually, it's sort of more than just wanting to know. I'd like to find out who the illegitimate daughter is. Maybe meet her."

"I get it now." She laughed shortly. "You think this would be a good story to write. You also think a colorful past would be an interesting addition to your too-respectable family history."

"You're a very smart lady."

"Possibly. Or maybe I'm just a mind reader."

****

He asked her out to dinner. He enjoyed talking with her, and thought it might be easier to get to know her outside the family context. He knew Barry would be tending bar this evening, replacing Bob for a few hours, so he didn't feel guilty about abandoning him. "Is there any place with decent food out this way?"

She dimpled. "Within a two-hundred-mile radius?"

"Something like that."

"There's the Dew Drop Inn ten miles down the

main road. It's pretty tacky, and the food isn't inventive, but it is homemade."

It was more of a diner than a restaurant. He ordered two beers, and they went to sit in a booth along the row of windows. The lights were low enough, there was a homey atmosphere, and decent country music whined out of the old-fashioned jukebox in one corner. It was a bit like stepping back into the '50s. There was only one sour note: the waitress was none other than Elsa.

"She works here?"

"Forgot to mention that." Laurie smirked. "In fact, it even slipped my mind. My brother's the one who thinks about her nonstop, not me."

Elsa sashayed over to a table where one person sat alone, the same sly-eyed knowing man he'd seen in the Mizpah. Mike watched, fascinated, as she struck a come-hither pose, leaning on one hip, her pelvis thrust forward. The man's eyes were hot.

Mike turned back to Laurie, saw she was observing him with undisguised amusement. "You've joined Elsa's fan club?"

"No way. The lady's definitely not my style."

"But she has my brother hooked. He's had a secret crush on her ever since Elsa turned fourteen. That was when she discovered she was a beauty and decided to head for stardom. I don't think she'd give Barry the time of day if he didn't live in San Francisco."

"What sort of stardom is she aiming for?"

"She sings."

"Yes, Barry told me that. Is she any good?"

"Yes, she is, actually. Her mother is a professional singer from Russia, and she trained her well. But the problem is, Elsa's just plain lazy. If you want to get anywhere in this world, you have create your own chances. Elsa's only game is seduction. That might net her a husband, but it will probably be the wrong sort of husband."

"Like Mr. Drool over there."

"Mr. Drool?" Laurie giggled. "Exactly! But she's not the only young woman in Blake's Folly who thinks some prince will come and rescue her. Elsa's best friend Jennifer Treemont is of the same ilk. They both think physical beauty and vulgar charm can work miracles."

Elsa's shrill laughter seemed to confirm Laurie's words. Mike watched her for another minute, then shook his head. "I tried to talk to Barry about her, warn him."

"Don't waste your breath. We've all done the same thing. He's aiming for a broken heart, and there's nothing any of us can do about that."

"Words of wisdom. Okay, I'll back off. Who's the guy she's talking to?"

"Him? Barney Badger, a local con man and fast talker. I've been told that his mother was one of the many prostitutes in the town's famous brothel; his father was a drifter with a gift for the gab. Barney seems to have inherited their character traits. He pans for gold, borrows money, sells anything he can get his hands on, legally or illegally, and has a soon-to-be-ex-wife tucked away somewhere. He also claims to be a Los Angeles talent scout, which is why Elsa's over there, being coy, and not over here, taking our order."

He laughed. "So she's forgotten our existence? Let's forget hers. Tell me about you. This afternoon, all I did was complain about my work. I'd like to hear about what you're doing. Barry said you collect seeds. What for?"

"To preserve the native plant species that are at risk."

"Why?"

"Wildfire damage is one reason. Another is because increasing pollution is changing the environment. With fewer birds around to regulate the insect population, invasive weeds are smothering the natural ground cover. Let's not even get started on the developers who come in and destroy all plant life before subdividing. Out here, their projects always flop, but the damage remains, so we go in, replant."

"It sounds like interesting work." It did. And when compared to his own, highly enviable. "Remember how, just a few years ago, in the sixties, we criticized what the older generation was doing to the world? I was right there, along with everyone else, questioning materialism, consumerism, and political norms, demonstrating against the war in Vietnam, demanding equal rights for Black Americans, and gender equality for women. We all spoke up, we all challenged established authority."

"And?"

He leaned forward, trying to put order into his feeling of dissatisfaction. "But here we are, just a few years later. Sure, there's still rebellion against authority and the demand for personal freedom, but there's also a new individualism, an obsession with self."

She nodded. "And maybe with financial success. I have a professor who claims that people once studied for knowledge, but in the near future, higher education will only be used to acquire the skills necessary for making money."

He stared at her. How good it felt to be talking to someone who seemed to be on the same wavelength. Oh sure, he knew other intelligent women, but like the men around him, they seemed to be caught up in the desire to acquire social status and possessions.

"You guys ready to order?"

It was Elsa, bored, rude, standing beside their table, finally. Doing the strict minimum to keep herself in a job. Was she like this with everyone, Mike wondered, or was this special treatment because he was Barry's friend. "Laurie?"

"A grilled cheese sandwich, please."

Elsa jerked her head in his direction.

"The same. With fries." He waited until she had sashayed off. "Did you always know you wanted to study botany?"

"Pretty well." She laughed shortly. "I always felt drawn to the natural world as well as to learning. The most difficult thing was trying to convince my family that my goals were legitimate."

"They didn't want you to study?"

Her mouth twisted wryly. "They certainly didn't. They thought it was cute that I was the best student in our school, but education had to stop there. My parents were completely hostile to anything that might take me out of the stay-at-home-be-a-good-wife scheme."

"Sounds archaic."

"Dream on. Despite all the big talk and protest, American life is still family-centered. Even though women are stepping into jobs more demanding than secretarial work or teaching, they're still expected to be home when their kids get back from school, to prepare dinner, do laundry, dishes, ironing, then be ready and willing to strip off whenever hubby demands some sexual release."

He stared at her, amazed by her frankness, her honesty. Yes, this was the sort of woman he liked, the sort he wanted to be around. The sort who would rescue him? From Tracey-Ann? Or from himself.

"So despite your parents' opposition, you were determined to pursue your studies?"

"I was. I took summer jobs, I worked evenings, and I paid my way. Then, a few years ago, my father had a heart attack. My mother died two years later. To my complete and utter surprise, Bob and my big sister Ruthie said that if I needed help to continue my studies, they'd pitch in."

"They were proud of you?"

Her grin was impish. "They know you can't keep a good woman down."

****

By the time they returned, the bar of the Mizpah was as crowded, as noisy as it had been the night before. Bob was behind the bar now, and Barry was sitting up at the counter, drinking a beer. They joined him.

"How did it feel to be back in the stirrups again?" Mike knew Barry had worked the family bar every summer before moving to San Francisco and becoming an advertising man.

"Not bad. I enjoyed it. I'll keep it in mind if city life ever gets to me."

Mike gawked. "You serious?"

"Perfectly."

"Spend the rest of your life in Blake's Folly?"

"Why not? This evening, I got to talk to people I haven't seen it years. It was fun. And enlightening. Put a few things back into perspective."

"Don't you know you can't go home again," Mike scoffed. "Thomas Wolfe said it all." But he wondered what perspective Barry was referring to. Surely he wasn't planning to come back here and marry Elsa.

Barry only grinned at the literary reference. "I'm no George Webber." His grin broadened. "And you're no Thomas Wolfe. Not yet, anyway."

Annoyed at the dig that hit too close to home, Mike only grunted. Barry might be right, but who knew? Maybe he would get around to writing the classic American novel like Wolfe had done. Then Barry wouldn't look so smug.

An hour later, her shift at the Dew Drop over, Elsa joined them. Barry ordered her the usual vodka. Without thanking him, without showing the slightest interest in joining in the conversation, she stood there, her eyes roving over the men in the bar.

Surely he notices how indifferent she is, Mike thought. Surely. But he watched, fascinated, as Barry slipped his arm around Elsa's slender waist. Despite her air of complete indifference, she didn't resist. She even seemed to be leaning into him. *Who knows what's really going on behind all that mindless boredom?*

"Mike tell you he wants to find some long-lost relative of his?" Barry asked Laurie. "His grandfather's illegitimate daughter?"

"He did." She turned to Mike. "How are you intending to go about it?"

He shifted uncomfortably. He didn't really have a plan, at least not a well-organized one. It had just been an idea he'd had back in San Francisco, had used as a good excuse for getting away from his problems. Now, here in Blake's Folly, it seemed like pure whimsy. "What seems easy when you're far away doesn't look obvious once you're in place."

Barry raised his brows. "Weren't you the one who told me you wanted to question a few of the old timers?"

"Yeah, I was. But do you really think anyone knows about what happened some seventy or eighty years ago? It doesn't seem likely."

"You didn't sound negative before."

"You're right. But we're talking about an illegitimate child. Was that ever an open subject?"

"There were probably a lot of illegitimate children back in the old days. No matter what anyone says about fidelity, marriage, and the perfect family, people probably didn't act any differently back then than they do now."

"Except now everybody's more open about it."

There was a brief silence. Mike stared at Elsa. She had actually come out and said that? Normally, she never opened her mouth. She had almost sounded intelligent. Then he dismissed the thought. Wasn't she simply an expert in the field of infidelity?

"I could go with you to talk to a few people, if you'd like," Laurie offered. "They might be more open with me than with a stranger."

"Hey, I'd appreciate that."

"Old Granny Mason." It was Elsa again. "Has to be the biggest gossip in town, the old witch. Daughter Faith's the same." Something—was it mockery?—twisted her mouth into a smirk, then she reached for her vodka—her third, Mike noted—and knocked it back with one gulp.

Mike saw Barry tighten his arm around Elsa's waist, look down at her, his face pink with enthusiasm. *Like a proud parent whose dumb kid has finally said something halfway clever.*

"Yes, that's a good suggestion, Elsa." Laurie nodded. "Granny Mason might be the best place to start. She's just about the oldest resident in town."

"Oldest *living* resident," Mike added cynically. "I bet the graveyard is full of others."

Laurie met his eyes evenly although her lips were twitching. "But without a Ouija board, they'll be reluctant to give us any information."

****

The weather changed abruptly and without warning. A gusting wind pulled in a veil of high cloud, and the dry heat faded. Dust swirled on the roadway, and sun-dried scrub shivered.

"I feel as though I need a winter coat."

"Abrupt weather change is part of life here. You get used to unpredictability."

Which, to his ears, sounded strange enough. What could be more predictable than this slow local way of life, this eventless-ness?

The house they arrived at was small, wooden, well maintained, and painted a blinding white. A sour-faced blowsy creature opened the door. She certainly didn't look like someone who'd willingly impart information.

"It would be super if we could talk with your mother for a few minutes, Faith. I'll bet she has lots of stories about this town in its heyday.

"What you want to know all the old stuff for?"

"Because Mike is only out here for a few days, and he's interested in the history of Nevada's former silver-mining towns."

He had to admire her. Laurie knew the right words, had the perfect reassuring tone for an Open Sesame reaction. Then again, she'd known Faith Mason her whole life.

Begrudgingly, the woman ushered them into a tiny living room filled to overflowing with cheap furniture, ceramic vases, and fairground knickknacks—flying swans, pseudo baroque candy bowls, replicas of hoop-skirted ladies, and a tasteless clutch of pink ceramic poodles. Presiding on the sideboard and a few low tables were a stuffed owl, a stuffed baby coyote, and what looked to be a long-deceased stuffed terrier.

Granny Mason, ancient, wizened but sharp-eyed, was seated in an armchair near the window—a watch post she had probably maintained all her adult life. "All of a sudden, young folks want to know what happened way back when?"

"Things have changed radically, Mrs. Mason," he began smoothly. "I'd love to hear what you remember."

"What sorts of things have changed? You think the world's a better place these days? You think you're better than we ever were?" Her beady eyes flashed.

He had no desire to take up the argument. A verbal skirmish like this could go on for hours, and would never be satisfying. "I hope you don't think I'm rude, but I would like to know in which year you were born, Mrs. Mason."

"Why should I be ashamed of my age? God's seen fit to keep me here all these years. I was born in 1889, and I seen plenty. This town has no secrets for me, and things haven't changed, even though folks has left, either runnin' away and heading for sinful places, or else going out feet first."

"Well, Blake's Folly certainly is calm, nowadays," Laurie interjected soothingly. "But back when the silver mines were up and running, when miners and cowboys filled the town on Friday nights after receiving their pay, this must have been a mighty dangerous place. Do you remember anything about that time, Mrs. Mason?"

"You talking about the saloons? The gambling? The fancy girls? Why would I know about shameful things like that? Those immoral people, the covetous, the swindlers, why leave my house for the likes of them? My husband was a God-fearing man, and yes, he got out in the world, but believe you me, he turned a blind eye to revilers and drunkards. In this house, we never stop fighting the devil's sin and temptation. The Lord is the one who saves us."

"Mrs. Mason, we're particularly interested in finding out about an illegitimate child who was born back in the old days."

"Satan." Faith's sharp voice cut into the air. "Those led by Satan are given over to evil. They have to repent of their sins and be saved. The sacrifice on the cross is for them, and God has warned the wages of sin is death."

****

"Well, that got us far," Laurie said when they were finally back out on the street.

"I'm not surprised. Last night, when Elsa told us to go speak to those two cranks, I was certain she was making fun of us. Now, I know my suspicion was right."

"You really think so?"

"I really do," he confirmed.

"Why would Elsa do a thing like that?"

"Who knows? To make herself feel superior?"

They walked slowly through the streets. The shrouded sun had disappeared over the horizon, and without street lamps, the dark was complete. The buffeting wind had died at dusk, taken with it the earlier chill. Now, a bouquet of sandy earth hung in the air, mixed with the tang of dry vegetation, and the summer evening's softness enveloped them.

"Old bigots drive me crazy."

"They've always been around."

"They have," Laurie conceded. "They've always made everyone's life miserable with their fanaticism. Even back in the old days, when violence was rife, the bigots were the ones who demanded that women remain pure, untouched, and invisible. Imagine only being allowed out to go to church meetings, or to do good works. The only way a young girl could escape a suffocating family circle was by joining the church choir."

"Things were worse on isolated prairie farms. My grandmother Hattie told my mother that she'd once lived in a one-room hut with no glass in the windows, just buffalo skins. That's how many people lived. Imagine spending your life making candles, looking for wood, cleaning, boiling water to do laundry by hand, transporting garbage to dung heaps, cooking on an open fire, spinning your own thread, and weaving everyone's clothes. And far too often, husbands thought they had the right to dominate, be violent."

They had reached the little quadrangle of

improvised log benches, but the old timers who reigned here by day had departed. She sat. He sat down beside her. "I'm starting to doubt my own motives. What am I really doing? Just looking for gossip I can put in a story."

"Aren't you also following up on your deceased grandfather's wish?"

"I suppose so."

Her lips twitched. "Besides, an intelligent story can introduce facts, teach people something about history."

"Perhaps." He sighed. "One thing's certain, though: the twentieth century has declared independence from the past, from everything that went on before, and from history as a whole. Once upon a time, history nourished tradition. Now, we reject tradition."

"And replace defunct belief systems with others that are often very foolish."

They sat for a long time, both lost in thought. There was something comforting in being with a soul mate, he thought.

When he leaned over and kissed her, it seemed like the most natural thing to do. Her mouth, soft, warm, opened to his, and their tongues touched, played. And when the kiss ended, they looked at each other, laughed, then kissed again, just as tenderly, just as naturally.

Until, leaning back slightly, she reached up, covered his lips with steady fingers. "Come. Let's get back to the Mizpah. I'm sure everyone's wondering where we are."

****

"You looking for cowboy lore like most folks from

the city?" Raymond Flat shaded his eyes against the afternoon sun's glare, and his jowls twitched with suspicion. "Nowadays, everyone's head is filled with rubbish from television and Hollywood."

"No, I'm just curious about local history," said Mike. The alert-looking elderly couple, seen on the makeshift bench a few days earlier, had been replaced by these three cantankerous geezers. Mike was certain that talking with them would only lead to a dead end.

"Well, let me tell you, by the time this town sprung up, the open range was closing. It was a hard life, and the old-time buffalo hunters and the cowboys fought each other, killed each other, too. Towns like this one wasn't pretty places, neither. Everywhere you looked was dust, rotting garbage, and manure. And when they tried educatin' folks, ordered 'em to clean up, they just went and dumped all the rot in back courtyards, or in another part of town." Indignantly, he stabbed at the hard ground with his cane.

"And them cowboys the city gals get all romantic about? Another fairy tale," Luke Miller added. "Those men rode for hours just to get here, and when they did, they drank and turned into hyenas. Just human debris, that's what they were, and they wasn't welcome no place. Respectable town folk appointed marshals and deputies to deal with the likes of them."

"Do you know anything about the dance hall girls?" Barry asked.

"I know them ladies sure knew how to move." Randy Fletcher cackled. "Men paid a dollar a dance for the privilege, and quite a few abandoned their families for them. Lot of jealousy back then, and that ended in fist and knife fights. Shoot-outs. That's what life was like out here, and don't let no one tell you different."

"But none of you were around back then," Barry said judiciously.

"You bet we weren't. What do we look like? Around a hundred years old?"

"Way older than that," Mike muttered when he and Barry were out of earshot.

"Not very useful either," said Barry as they headed out to the outskirts of the town.

"Can't say we didn't try. I told your sister last night that this was a wild goose chase."

Barry shot him a sly look. "Did you, now. Last night?"

"Early evening. After we left the Mason harpies' den."

"I see." Barry winked. "If I weren't certain that my little sister can take care of herself, I'd have to pull out my six-shooter."

"Nothing to worry about." Although Mike couldn't help remembering the kisses, about how much he'd enjoyed them. About how he appreciated meeting a woman with a sharp mind.

The houses were behind them now, and the road had become more rutted. They climbed a little rise, and another structure came into view, large, yellow, but badly in need of a coat of paint and a few new joists.

"What's this place?"

"It's the old Treemont mansion. They owned the silver mines and were once the richest, most powerful family in the area."

"Pretty neglected now, and not much like a mansion. Looks to me like the money ran out a long time ago."

"I'm sure it did. After the silver mines closed, the family probably lived off what was left. Old Alexander Treemont was a well-known artist, but his work looks dated these days: traditional watercolors, desert landscapes. When the old man and his second wife died, his son Edward moved here from Reno, and he began selling off as many paintings as he could. He had to. He'd run up big gambling debts. Then, he racked up even more debts by half-rebuilding part of the house, adding too many badly-done heteroclite touches, then just letting everything sag. These days, he and his wife live a hand-to-mouth existence."

"How are the mighty fallen."

Barry's shout of laughter rang out in the warm dry air. "You quoting the Old Testament? Now I've heard it all. Or is just the influence of the Masons."

Mike also laughed, then stopped.

A woman had appeared. Motionlessly, she stared at them for a minute. Then, very slowly, she crossed the broad front porch, came down the steps, sauntered in their direction. Mike watched her, fascinated. Long, straight hair fell like a cape to her waist. She was tall and exceedingly slender, and that slow, languid way of moving showed she was well aware of her appeal.

"Hi, Barry. What brings you out this way?" Her voice was sexy, whispery, and her slightly slanted hazel eyes slid from Barry to him in an amused, casual way.

"Just showing Mike the town."

"Uh-huh?" She stood there, one hand on her hip, emphasizing a tiny waist and the soft curve of small breasts under an almost transparent Indian cotton shirt. Tilting her head back, she smirked. "And what does Mr. San Francisco think of little Blake's Folly? It's quite the exciting place, wouldn't you say?"

It took him a minute to find a coherent response. "San Francisco? Word travels fast."

She only laughed, a breathy sound that made the hairs on his arms stand on end.

"Don't be fooled, Mike." Barry's voice was dry. "Jennifer Treemont is Elsa's best friend."

Ah, yes. So, this was the woman Laurie had referred to the other night in the Dew Drop Inn. What had her exact words been? That both Jennifer and Elsa thought physical beauty and vulgar charm could work miracles. Maybe they could. Still, he didn't see anything that looked vulgar. The woman standing in front of him was sure of her powers and incredibly beautiful. What was vulgarity in Elsa's case was pure seduction in Jennifer's.

Her little pink tongue appeared, slid slowly across her upper lip. "How long you guys in town for?"

"Just today and tomorrow."

"Uh-huh." A sudden breeze lifted her hair, turned it into a lace fan. Reaching up, she caught a few strands with her fingertips, played with them.

Fascinated, Mike watched. Felt himself harden.

The clearly visible bulge must have betrayed him. Her eyes glinting, a secret smile playing on her lips, she turned slowly, moved back toward the house, her narrow hips swaying seductively. "Bye-bye, boys. See you around."

He stared after her, unable to move, aching for her to appear again.

Barry sniggered. "Like what you saw?"

"Who wouldn't?"

"She has dreams of becoming a model."

"Out here?"

"Is that a joke? No, she left town when she was seventeen. I don't know why she came back."

"To see her parents?"

"Hardly. From what Elsa tells me, Edward and his wife Priscilla don't approve of her. They give her a hard time."

"I can imagine why they would. She looks like trouble."

"Worse than that. She's pure poison. If you know what's good for you, stay away from her."

"Hey, kid. We're leaving the day after tomorrow." He didn't add that Elsa seemed to be of the same toxic variety. Barry would find out soon enough.

****

She was in the Mizpah that evening, standing over in the far corner with Elsa, both of them in secret conversation, laughing, their eyes never still, roving over the men in the bar. He could clearly see the braless outline of small pert breasts under her tight square-cut shirt, noted the curving slenderness of long legs revealed by the shortest miniskirt he had ever seen.

He knew he was staring at her, and he forced himself to look away, turn back to Barry, Bob, Ruthie, and Laurie, join in the conversation about the changing music scene. Then, found himself watching her again, taking in every suggestive feminine movement and feeling the reaction like a dart to his groin. Slowly she raised one arm, let her fingers caress her hair in a slow, sensual movement, let them fall, slip lightly over her breasts. Yes, she knew she'd snagged him, all right. The lazy show was for him.

He looked away again. What was everyone talking

about now? Hard rock? The subject bored him. He emptied his glass, caught Laurie's eye. She looked amused. Because she was laughing at him? Had she seen him watching Jennifer and sensed his fascination?

He felt ridiculous. Superficial. He'd mocked Barry, had felt superior, and here he was, just as stupidly besotted as his friend. Feeling guilty, too, which was ridiculous. He didn't owe Laurie anything. They'd shared a few kisses, exchanged ideas. Had she expected things to go further?

A full ten minutes passed before the two women finally came over to them. Barry ordered Elsa's usual vodka, and Jennifer's Manhattan—of course she'd order a mixed drink, never something simple. Mike saw Barry's smirk. *He doesn't like her, that's obvious.* Big deal. He didn't like Elsa either.

Abruptly, Barry changed the subject, began giving details of an account he and Mike had worked on a month ago—why the hell was he bringing that up? Weren't they on holiday? Couldn't he think of some more interesting subject than advertising? But when he saw Elsa's calculating eyes, he understood: San Francisco, the possibility of life in the fast lane, were things that might attract her, increase his appeal.

"So you two work together?" Jennifer had moved, was standing beside him. Her breathy voice was low, intimate.

"That's how Barry and I met."

"What sort of ads?"

"It all depends."

"Fashion? Or just products."

"We'll be working on the Helga Howson account in a few weeks."

"The clothes designer?"

"That's the one."

"You hire models, right?"

"Not me personally. It's up to the agency and the client. But models are also hired for other work other than fashion. We use them for product presentation— car ads, jewelry, wines, cigarettes." He forbore telling her he was a measly pen pusher, not some high roller or decision-maker in the commercial world. Why be honest? What difference did that distinction—a mere misunderstanding—make out here, in a Nevada cowboy bar at the end of the world?

"I was in San Francisco, looking around." Reaching up, she pulled her long silky hair to one side, slipped it over one shoulder to emphasize the perfection of her cheekbones. "I might start modeling."

"You'd do very well at it." She had the height, the shape. He took in her thin nose, the perfect lips, and finely drawn brows. Beauty that was wasted on a dump of a town like this one.

"I know." Her smile was arch, confident. "I'm photogenic. I already have great pictures, and I'm getting my model portfolio ready."

"Good." She was clearly as self-obsessed as many of the other beauties in the profession.

She shifted, leaned over, put her glass down on the bar, and he froze. Had her hand deliberately brushed his crotch? Surely, he was mistaken. Dreaming. He stared at her but she was looking elsewhere, and her expression was one of studied indifference. Then she leaned back, her eyes meeting his. "I hear you're asking questions about your family, about some relatives who once lived here."

He forced his voice to remain calm, as if nothing unusual had happened. "Yes, my grandparents met in Blake's Folly. I was told that my grandfather had a daughter with a dancing girl, and I want to know more. Find out what happened to both of the women."

"Secrets are hard to dig out. People only tell you things if it makes them look good."

No, he hadn't been mistaken. He felt her hand again, just barely touching his thigh, lightly, but deliberately. He tried to ignore the stiffening in his crotch, concentrate on what she was saying. "Do you know something?"

She licked her lips. She knew very well what she was doing to him. "You don't know about the room."

"What room?"

"I can show you tomorrow."

"Okay." Show him what?

"Meet me in here at eight, tomorrow night."

Her hand moved again, sliding over his hardness. Very deliberately.

"I'll be here."

She nodded. "I know you will be."

****

She was dressed in a loose white shirt and a thin, billowing cotton skirt, nothing like the seductive clothes she had worn last night. Doubting she would show, certain her game was provocation only, still he had been waiting for her for the last two hours, unable to do anything else. She'd hooked him.

He stood as she approached his table with her soft sway. "Hi."

Her eyes, beguiling yet shrewd, met his. "You ready?"

For what? "Yes, sure. Not that I know where we're going." He was trying to sound confident, cynically amused. To his own ears, his voice was high, almost squeaky.

"Upstairs."

"Upstairs?" He glanced over in the direction of the bar and saw Bob was watching them, his expression unreadable.

"Come on, then." She made her way through the saloon toward the staircase, began climbing, her hips a magnetic sway, her long hair undulating with every slow and sensual step. She wasn't going to his room, was she? Surely not. What would Bob think? What about all the others who had seen them leave together?

"Are you sure this is okay? That Bob doesn't mind?" Now he sounded like a guilty adolescent.

"He knows where we're going. I told him last night I'd show you the special place."

On the landing, she turned, passed the row of former bedrooms, turned left again, continued down a long dark passage, then stopped in front of the last door. Opened it.

They were in a room, large, musty, caught in early evening's shadow and filled with abandoned furniture: tables stacked on top of old dressers, ruined chairs lying on their sides, their legs broken, seats tattered. Floating motes, caught by the last pale streaks of a fading summer sun, glittered like fairy dust before vanishing.

"What is this place?"

She shrugged. "Now? Now, it's nothing. Just a place people dump things they don't want." She closed the door.

"Okay. Then why are we here?"

212

"You wanted to know things, that's why. You wanted to know about dancing girls, about the past. Here's your big chance."

"Tell me more."

"About?" Her eyes glowed.

She was toying with him again, that was clear. What was he supposed to say? What was she trying to tell him?

Then, shifting closer, she reached out, began undoing his belt buckle, unsnapping his jeans, pulling down the zipper. Grasping the waistband, she tugged down both pants and jockey shorts, exposing him and his erection. She laughed softly, touched the tip's sticky wetness, then let her fingers circle round and round the head, slowly, agonizingly. His groan came from far away, and her hand cupped him fully, pulling back the skin, tightening. He reached for her, and she laughed again, stepped back, releasing him, and he almost screamed with frustration. But she wasn't finished.

Smiling still, knowing her power, she slipped off her flat shoes, then reached down, lifted her skirt high above her waist. She wore no underwear, and he watched, fascinated, as, in one fluent movement, she stepped backward, slid onto the top of a large table, raised her legs, opening to him.

"Come play with me," she coaxed, her voice deep, throaty. She reached for his hand, guided his fingers, let them glide along her wetness, slipped them into her opening. He felt her buck, once, twice, again, saw her catch her lower lip with pearly teeth. Then, her face flushed, her eyes dark, she pulled at her white blouse, yanked it over her head. The rosy-tipped nipples were hard little beads, and he lowered his head, suckled.

"Come. Come inside. I want you deep inside me. Come. Come..."

It was all happening fast, too fast. The situation was unusual, unplanned. Nothing in his fantasies had prepared him for this, but she'd know that, he was certain of it. How could he possibly have guessed she would give herself like this, like a gift, a reward? For what?

He rammed into her, climaxing hard and too soon, spurting, clutching her narrow hips, screaming. She pulled him forward, using him like a dildo for her own pleasure, digging her nails into his skin until her own keening orgasm came.

Then silence.

He stood still, his head spinning, his knees weak and trembling, his legs hardly holding him up, his jeans and underpants sagging comically around his shoes. His penis, wet, soft, and useless, slipped out of her depths.

Fully recovered, she watched him, that same enigmatic smile playing over her lips. Then, cupping one smooth breast in her hand, she pulled hard on the nipple, and bending her head, licked the rosy tip, still holding his eyes. Still toying with him.

She raised her head. "Do you like this? Do you like watching?"

He could only nod, his throat tight.

She laughed, reached for the thin cotton blouse beside her. Shook it out, slipped it over her head. Met his eyes, lowered her hand, let her fingers slide between her spread legs, caress the wet slickness, the result of their coupling, open her soft folds so he could see inside her.

Then, smiling still, always smiling, she let the hand

drop, lowered her legs, and stood.

The billowing skirt dropped back into place. "Time to go back downstairs."

She went to the door, opened it, waited, obviously amused, while he jerked up his jeans, his fingers fumbling ineptly with the snap and the belt buckle, not certain if he felt relieved or crushed, if he wanted to laugh or rage at her.

Silently, they went back down the corridor, down the stairs. Only when they reached the smoke and noise of the main room, did she turn.

"We'll have fun when I get to San Francisco."

****

He sat by the window in Barry's room, smoking a cigarette, something he rarely did. What had happened earlier this evening was also very rare in his life. Perhaps it was an everyday occurrence for rock stars and movie moguls, for big shots in the advertising world—the creative directors, the photographers. But for a low-on-the-totem-pole copywriter?

Barry was lying on his bed, saying nothing, depressed, and Laurie was slumped into an armchair. It was late. The bar had closed, and the streets were empty. Out toward the west, a coyote howled, was answered by another, somewhere farther to the north.

"Okay, what happened with Elsa?" he asked Barry.

"Nothing happened with Elsa."

"Which is why you're in such a lousy mood."

Barry only grunted.

"Well, there's always Christmas in Blake's Folly," Laurie chirped.

"Go to hell."

She laughed. "Looking forward to it."

Barry propped himself on his elbows, stared at Mike. "What about Jennifer?"

"What about her?" He was hedging, feeling strangely flustered and, in Laurie's presence, almost ashamed.

"You both disappeared. Where did you go?"

"We came upstairs. She wanted to show me a room at the end of the corridor. You both must know the one I'm talking about. It's filled with old furniture."

"She would," Laurie scoffed.

"Really? Okay, clue me in. Why would she? Because when I asked her what the hell we were doing there, she only said something vague about dancing girls."

Probably just wanted to sound mysterious and interesting."

Barry shook his head. "No, there's a bit more to it than that. Wasn't her grandfather, the artist Alexander Treemont, once married to a woman who used to run a brothel?"

Laurie sniffed. "I don't think that's true. You know how everyone loves telling stories about rich men marrying showgirls and prostitutes."

"Hey, wait a minute, folks," Mike interjected. "There's something I'm missing here. What does that have to do with the room?"

"Nothing much, really."

Laurie stood, yawned. "I think the woman Barry's referring to was the owner of the Mizpah, but that was way back in the 1940s. In those days, this was a respectable roadhouse, not a brothel. So, you see how rumors fly in places like this where nothing much ever happens?"

"Tell that to Granny Mason."

She laughed. "Well, goodnight, boys. I'm headed for bed. What time are you hitting the road tomorrow?"

"Early. Eight, nine."

"Okay. See you both at breakfast. Sleep well."

****

Mike slung his bag into the trunk of the car, turned, looked at the weed-strewn road, the shacks, that hill of battered trailers and shanties. What sort of future did a place like this have? None. The past was over and done with. Who cared about the old stories? No one.

He'd failed to learn anything, and he'd probably never come back again. Even if he did, he'd only find a few more empty lots, ruins, and burnt-out buildings. Blake's Folly was nothing but a trap, and he knew all about falling into those. In a few hours, he'd be right back where he'd been five days ago. Life was shit.

****

Laurie stood with Bob on the front veranda, waving goodbye until the car turned a corner, then disappeared from view.

"You think he'll come back here with Barry?"

"I doubt it," Laurie said.

"Did he ask for your phone number?"

"He did. He said he sometimes gets to Sacramento."

"You want my advice? If he looks you up, don't get involved."

Laurie laughed, her heart light. "Don't worry. I never, not even for one single second, had the slightest intention of doing so."

V

The Room Upstairs: 2021

Of all ghosts, the ghosts of our old loves are the worst.
~Sir Arthur Conan Doyle, (1859-1930),
The Memoirs of Sherlock Holmes

Lance saw the woman doubled over in the dirt road, her legs bent backward and to each side of her in what looked to be an exceedingly painful position. Had she been hit by a car? Probably not: few enough cars passed this way. She might have had an attack of some sort. He loped toward her, thinking only of rescue and alleviating pain, because that's what a veterinarian's job is all about, and humans happen to be animals, too.

He was less than ten feet away, when she raised her head and glared at him with fury. The look, as toxic as a poison arrow, halted him in his tracks. She certainly didn't look as though she needed his help. She didn't look as though she'd ever need anyone's help.

"Um...I'm sorry. I saw you down there, in the road, and I thought..."

He saw her fury seep away, transform into visible regret. "You chased it away."

"Right."

Swinging her bent legs into a more reasonable position, she stood up without using her hands. For someone who wasn't young, she looked to be in perfect shape. Or at least she had maintained an admirable flexibility.

He knew who she was, all right. Who else had a long bushy ponytail of silvery hair? Who else had three dogs trailing after her—three dogs now sitting calmly in the shade of the abandoned laundry and watching him, wary-eyed. They knew he was one of the vets who gave them shots every year, and that meant he was no real friend.

The woman in front of him, what was her name? Lucy something…oh yes, Lucy Barnes, and she worked in Rose Badger's vintage clothing shop whenever Rose roared off to Reno. For the first time, he noticed the camera.

"Look, I thought you had fallen or…"

"Yes, I realize that's what you thought." She didn't look as though she were about to forgive him for it either.

"You were taking a photo?"

"Yup."

"Of what?"

"A *Xysticus*."

"A what?

"Oh, sorry. A ground crab spider."

"Of a ground crab spider?"

She relented slightly. "They're called crab spiders because they look and move like crabs."

"Yes," he said dryly. "I think I've worked that one out."

"Right."

"What for? Why were you taking a photo?"

"Because I like them. I like macro photography, I

219

like taking photos of spiders, and this particular spider was very pretty."

"Pretty. Got it."

She looked annoyed again. "Veterinarians don't consider arachnids worthy of notice?"

"Did I just tell you that?" he said a little too defensively because she was right: he never noticed them. Okay, he never killed them either, because he knew how useful they were, but that was as far as things went. "What was particularly pretty about that one? I mean spiders look like spiders to me. I never thought aesthetics came into it."

"Really?" She even looked surprised.

"Really." Inwardly, he sighed, regretting his attempt to maintain chatty conversation. It was always the same when you dealt with nuts, cranks, and fanatics: they couldn't understand how normal people functioned.

"Well, most crab spiders are brown and beige so they can blend into their surroundings and catch prey easily. They do have splotches though, and this one had a nice leaf marking on its *opisthosoma*." She smirked. "Sorry, that's the posterior part of the body. The front part is the—"

"*Prosoma*," he interrupted.

The smirk faded and, wordlessly, she stared at him.

It was his turn to be haughty. "Since you know I'm a veterinarian, you'll probably accept that, in this century, we do go to school. And while we're there, we manage to study a little science."

"Sorry," she said contritely.

"That's all right." He tried not to look too self-satisfied. "Go on, tell me something interesting about crab spiders."

"Hey, all spiders are interesting, but I don't think you're looking for technical information."

"How do you know? Try me."

"Have it your way." She shrugged. "What I find particularly interesting about crab spiders, is that, before mating, males tie the females up with silk—some people refer to it as the bridal veil."

He could make a snide comment about some human males doing the same thing, but he knew that, with someone like her, he might be on dangerous ground. "What for?"

"Because they deposit sperm on the veil, and it's taken up by their palp organs. Then they introduce these palps into the female's external genital structure, which is called an *epigyne*."

He stared. What a strange thing to be interested in. "It sounds very impersonal to my ears. Is that actually considered copulation?"

"Well, yes. It's sexual reproduction without an actual penis. But the male and female organs do fit together, sort of like a key in a lock."

More dangerous territory. "You're not afraid of being bitten?"

She sighed with something that sounded suspiciously like resignation. "Hey, Bud, do you worry about the dogs you treat biting you? They have big sharp teeth. If that teensy little crab spider had bitten me hundreds of times while I was photographing it, nothing would have happened. Why? Because I'm definitely not a small insect. Besides, it would only attack me if it felt threatened."

"Or if it wasn't in the mood to have its portrait

done."

She actually chuckled. Which was a relief, since most cranks usually don't have a sense of humor.

"You aren't afraid of spiders?"

All trace of amusement was replaced by disgust. "Because I'm a woman? Because every single woman on earth is idiotic? Because as soon as any of us see a spider, we have to run and grab a male who will rescue us from something smaller than a fingernail?"

Boy, oh boy. Was she always ready for a fight? "Well, okay. Right. Now that I see you're fine, that there's nothing wrong, I'll be on my way. Let you get back to spying on the sex life of small creatures and wallowing in the dust in the middle of a road." He saluted. "Have a nice day."

He turned, began walking back toward Rose Badger's shop, Second Hand Rose, but that impossible woman's heckling voice followed him: "Hey, Buster, let's not even begin to mention the sort of stuff you wallow in out at those ranches."

Damn his White Knight instinct that had shot into the picture and netted him an Amazon.

****

He made himself comfortable in the velvet plush chair, smiled at Rose. Now, she was just what he liked. Charming, gentle, her hair was a natural gold, her smile dazzled, and she was a woman who adored men.

His heart flip-flopped as it always did in her company, and that was the funny thing: he and Rose had never gone beyond friendship. He had once considered taking the relationship further, so had she, but it hadn't happened and probably never would. Which was perfect. Lance had never indulged in anything other than temporary relationships—he valued his independence too much—and a fling with Rose might have destroyed their easy camaraderie. What they did share, closeness and real affection, was more important than what a few months of passion would have brought.

"I just had a run-in with your Amazon."

Rose's large blue eyes were amused. "My Amazon?"

"She works here. Her name's Lucy Barnes, right?"

"Lucy's an Amazon? First I've heard of it."

"Okay, maybe she's only a Valkyrie."

"Whatever did you do to offend her? Lucy's a usually a pussycat."

He blinked. "You can't be serious."

"I am."

"Okay. Here was my crime: I made a spider she was photographing run away."

"Oh, I see. Yes, that's the sort of thing that might offend her. Still, her bark is worse than her bite."

"Sweetheart, pussycats don't bark."

Rose's lips twitched. "Do Valkyries?"

Lance sighed. "She's influencing you. You aren't usually this contrary."

"Well, I must admit Lucy does have a strong character." She sat down on the low chair opposite him, rested her elbows on her knees, and cupped her adorable face in both hands. "I promised her that I'd leave all spiders where they are here in the shop. That if any of them caused a problem, I was to call her, and she'd move them for me."

"That should please your customers."

"Well...I don't get very many of those out here. If

any do complain, I've learned how to explain that spiders are really useful creatures. Or I get Lucy to come and educate people. That's the best thing. Whenever I need her, Lucy is on hand."

"Where does she live?"

Rose sat up straight and stared at him for a minute, her eyes blank. "You know what? I don't have the faintest idea. She just showed up here in Blake's Folly some months ago. From someplace east—New Jersey, I think. I've always assumed she's taken up residence in an empty trailer or in one of the abandoned houses. I never even asked her. Isn't that self-centered of me?"

"I'd vote for the abandoned house. Dust, spiders, creepy crawlies, rodents, reptiles."

"Yes, sounds like the right scenario. Especially since she's good friends with Alice and the rattlesnakes."

"Alice Treemont?"

"How many people named Alice do you know out here? How many of them are herpetologists? Lucy adopted three of those stray dogs that Alice collects. I also know that Lucy and Alice go out sighting and photographing rattlers together."

"I'll bet they do." Lance sighed. "Why am I not surprised? There aren't any normal people in this community."

Rose giggled. "I'm fairly normal."

"No, you aren't. You're stunning, talented, and amusing. You have an angel's voice, and half the men in Nevada are in love with you. Not only that, you have a rescue dog named Noodle. None of that is normal. How about you and Noodle having lunch with me in the Mizpah now?"

"Promise to keep on sweet-talking me, and I'm yours."

****

The Mizpah had seen worse days. Sometimes neglected and left to sag by indifferent owners, sometimes cherished and coddled, its second-floor balcony was still in place, so were the broad sash windows. Inside, the floor was as glossy and polished as it might have been a hundred years earlier, and the brass rails gleamed. Old framed paintings hung on the walls, and an ancient wooden clock was still steadily ticking its way through the centuries. The saloon's present beauty was due to the fact that it had been taken over by the laconic Ned Stalks and his sour wife Trix. As truculent as both were, they had spent much free time in restoration work, bringing the Mizpah back to its former glory.

"Are you coming to the concert on Friday night?" Rose asked as they settled into a corner booth in the Mizpah's main room.

"Wouldn't miss it. After all, it is a benefit for the Lone Canyon Animal Shelter, and since I'm their volunteer vet, it would be an insult not to be there."

Rose dimpled. "Just checking. I suppose you're coming with Caroline."

"Yes." He didn't elaborate. Caro was one of the women he saw most frequently, and she expected to accompany him on social occasions. But was bringing her to a Blake's Folly shindig the best idea? Probably not.

Without even being asked, Ned Stalks arrived with two glasses of chardonnay. He knew his customers. "What's on the menu, Ned?"

"Depends what you're looking for," said Ned sulkily.

Inwardly, Lance groaned. This community really was chock full of oddballs. Which was what made it...well, if not easy going...interesting.

"How about a cheese plate?" Rose asked.

"Sounds good to me," Lance agreed.

Without another word, but with a scowl, Ned turned his back on them and headed for the kitchen.

"If I didn't know he's flattered when people ask for the cheese plate..." Lance shook his head.

"Yes, he's just fanatic about finding and serving excellent cheese, luckily for us."

"A smile would go a long way, too."

"You can't have it all." Rose picked up her glass, sipped, and briefly closed her eyes with contentment. Ned also managed to procure the best wines California could produce. "Did you know that I'm going to sing on Friday?"

"Where? Here? In the Mizpah?"

"Yes, I know. It's the sort of thing I swore I'd never do. Since it's for the benefit, I decided to sacrifice myself. I've been working on a few numbers with Bill Flats and Luke Miller."

"Bill Flats and Luke Miller? You have to be joking. Along with Sly Grimes, they're the worst musicians in the American West."

Rose grinned. "Believe it or not, everyone only has that impression because the music they play with the Old Boy's Band is just awful, and they rarely rehearse together. Bill is too busy raising racing snails, and Luke spends all his time with Pa Handy, trying to invent something useful with all that scrap metal in his junkyard. As musicians, though, neither Bill nor Luke are half bad when you divert their attention."

"To what?"

"Decent music. The sort of stuff my maternal grandmother used to sing over at the Red Nag."

"I heard about her. She was quite a celebrity in the area. A shame the Nag closed down all those years ago."

"It certainly is. And that's only because Elsa, my mother, inherited the Nag when my grandparents died. She hated the place, wanted nothing to do with an old saloon, so she just let it fall apart. It's a disaster, these days. Polina and Cal would have been heartbroken."

"And the building doesn't interest you?"

"How could it? It still belongs to Elsa, and she'd never in a million years let me take it over, especially if she knew I wanted it. That's why I had to buy my own place before I could open Second Hand Rose. It used to be a furniture workshop back in the 1920s."

"That's right. Before that, it was a newspaper office."

"How do you know? You don't even live here."

"Sweetheart, there are a lot of things I know about Blake's Folly. I might even share them with you one day. Right now, though, tell me what you're going to sing on Friday. Russian songs?"

"I save those for the Saturday nights with the balalaika orchestra at the Russian Club in Reno. No, I'll be doing the old piano bar songs people listened to in the casinos, the ones my grandmother sang to charm my grandfather."

"Sounds interesting. Anyway, you couldn't do a bad job on any sort of music."

"Don't be fooled. Back in my younger days, I screamed my heart out touring with a very awful rock band."

"Hard to imagine."

"Good." She laughed. "I shouldn't even have confessed that."

He chuckled, then sobered. "Hey, wait. You told me you'd never sing here in town because your mother would show up and cause a scene." Elsa Badger and her paramour, Alf Paltry, lived in a beat-up trailer on the edge of town. Elsa had a talent for making her daughter's life miserable, especially when she wanted cash for cigarettes and a good supply of vodka. Lance had never seen the woman sober, but he'd witnessed several disagreeable confrontations.

"True, she always is a major problem. But she won't be showing up here this Friday."

"How do you know?"

"Because I've bribed Alf with booze and cigarettes, that's how." Her eyes sparkled. "Yes, I know it's not ethical, but who cares?"

"Well done." He grinned back at her. And realized, as ever, how relaxed he felt in her company. Wondered, not for the first time, why he didn't feel as happy when he was with Caro.

****

Surrounded by ten dogs of indeterminate breed, Lucy Barnes and Alice Treemont sat at the huge desk in Alice's library. It was an imposing room—it hadn't changed much in well over a hundred and fifty years— with its old armchairs, gold-framed paintings, and heavy books snug in glassed-in cupboards.

"This whole house is beautiful. I love coming here.

It's like stepping into another era."

"You should have seen what a mess it was when I first came back to Blake's Folly," Alice said. "I had to plaster holes in the walls and have the roof patched up just to make it livable. My grandparents had let the place fall down over the years, and my mother stayed in California. But when I was tiny, there were exquisite oriental rugs on the floors, and every single wall was covered by my great-grandfather's watercolors."

"I remember seeing those when we were sent out here that one summer."

Alice grimaced. "Yes, there were still quite a few back then, but most were eventually sold off to pay my grandfather Edward's gambling debts. As for the best furniture and the rugs, they were pilfered when my grandparents died and the house was left empty."

"Well, you've made the place more than livable now." Lucy pushed a photo in Alice's direction. "Here, take a look. Isn't she a cutie? Look at that fuzzy brown abdomen and those cute hairy legs."

"She is splendid," Alice agreed. "What is she? A folding door spider?"

"You've got it. An *Aliatypus janus*. Unfortunately, I wasn't able to get close enough to her to catch those eight shiny eyes, one pair in the middle, and a cluster of three on each side."

"Think how much she spends on mascara."

"And liner." Lucy chuckled. "Actually, I only saw her burrow at the last minute. They're very reclusive creatures, and she hid as soon as she realized I was taking interest in her."

"They dig their own burrows, don't they?"

"Yup. Coat them with soil and saliva, then line

them with silk. The entrance is disguised by pulling together two sides of the silk rim. After that, they just wait patiently for centipedes or other creepy crawlies to come along."

"How in heaven do such reclusive females manage to find a mate?"

"Easy. After heavy rainfall, the females come out to repair the entries. That's when the males start wandering around and looking for them. When they find a female they like, they pat or stroke her with their legs to initiate mating."

"Long-term attachments?"

"Nope. Temporary. Just like some of the men around here. "

Alice laughed. "You thinking of anyone in particular?"

"Lance Potter's a pretty good example. Every time you see the guy, he has some new glamour-puss in tow, but even though he's nice to them all, he reserves his gooey-eyes for Rose Badger. Why didn't those two get together years ago?"

"Because they're both flirts. That's the way they have fun. Nothing serious, no commitment."

"Except Rose is now with Jonah Livingstone, and Lance doesn't even seem upset."

"He isn't. That's what I'm saying. It's just a game. A very safe game, because Rose and Lance know they have nothing to worry about."

"I guess so." Lucy looked doubtful.

"Lance is rather gorgeous, though. Everyone has to admit that."

"Which is why he picks and chooses amongst the beauties of this world."

Alice searched her face. "You don't like him very much, I take it."

"How can you say that? I don't even know him. To me, he's only one of the vets in a clinic that's miles away from here."

"He's really a very nice man. We've gotten quite close over the last year or two. Did you know that he sleeps here, in my house, when he has a late night in Blake's Folly and doesn't want to drive all the way back home?"

Lucy sniffed. "Well, the only time I've ever had a conversation with him was out on the road the other day. He caught me taking a photo of a spider, and he was pretty condescending. Otherwise, as far as men like Lance Potter are concerned, I'm the invisible woman. No chic, no glamour, no beauty, no style, no makeup, no resin nails, no hair dye, and no collagen lips." She leered. "No threat, either."

****

Early winter had finally arrived; nights were icy, and dark slipped in early. Perhaps that compounded his faint depression. Lance and rescuer Nate Wilson had just spent an exhausting afternoon trying to convince an abandoned dog—one that had been tied up and left to die in a house basement—that they weren't enemies. He hated cruelty, and he saw it far too often; he sometimes had to fight to believe that human kindness did exist. Thank goodness, the dog, skinny, barely able to stand but still ready to kill them both, was now safe in the animal rescue kennel. Once the poor creature was neutered, in good shape, and ready to accept that humans could also be caring, he, Nate, Alice Treemont, and the other volunteers would look for a good family to adopt him.

Instead of heading directly home, he veered off the main road and headed toward Blake's Folly. He didn't feel like spending the evening alone, but having a good dinner in charming company would certainly improve his humor. For some reason he didn't feel like analyzing at the moment, he didn't want to call Caro. No, the most congenial, diverting woman he knew was Rose Badger. If she were free, that would be excellent. And if her current lover, geologist Jonathan Livingstone, happened to be around, that would be even better: the more the merrier.

Pushing open the door to Second Hand Rose, he stepped inside. Stopped dead, his heart plummeting lower still. No, Rose wasn't here. The comforting thought of a flirtatious evening disappeared, slid outside to join the frigid desert air and glacial stars. Sitting at a small round wooden table over to the left, was the Valkyrie. She looked up from the book she was reading and stared at him with just about the same amount warmth he was feeling toward her.

"She's not here." No "hello," no preamble of any sort.

"Yes, I can see that." He tried to sound as if that didn't matter.

"She went to Reno with Jonah."

"Fine. I'll come back another time." He turned to go, return to the wintry evening, and begin the long drive home.

"Hey, wait." She was staring at him. "Why not come and sit down for a while. Make yourself comfortable. You want a coffee?"

"A coffee?" He gaped at the Valkyrie as if the

word "coffee" were a new one he hadn't yet tried out. "You're offering me a coffee?" *And hospitality?*

She lowered her head and a certain amount of amiability disappeared. "That's right, Buster. Real freshly-made coffee in a pot, no instant, no chemicals."

"My name's not Buster."

A wicked grin appeared, one made more mischievous by her slightly crooked and uneven teeth. "Okay, Bud. But the offer for coffee still holds."

"It's not Bud either."

That grin broadened. "Look, you can't get around me. I know what you call me."

"Oh, yes?"

"Yup. Just to let you know, Rose spilled the beans."

"Ah."

"I'm the Valkyrie, right?"

He took a deep breath. Then, felt amusement pushing aside the dark dreariness. "Yeah, that's right."

"But you're wrong." She got to her feet, as if preparing a devastating blow. "You wanna know why?"

Even he had started smiling now. "Why not? If I don't, you're still going to tell me, right? Because that's your style."

"You got it, Bud." Hands on her hips, she looked at him with what could only be called triumph. "Because the Valkyries were virgin warriors, and I'm way too old to be a virgin, that's why."

Impossible to suppress the chuckle bubbling up from deep in his belly, that turned into a roar of laughter. How had she managed to win him over in such a short time? *Damn.*

She was still grinning, still waiting for his answer

about the coffee. He stared at her for a minute, then forced his own broad smile into something more serious. "Look, let's forget about the coffee."

"Okay." The grin faded, and she shrugged as if she didn't care one way or the other, which was probably true. "Whatever you'd like."

"Instead of coffee, how do you feel about going out to dinner with me?"

Now she was the one who stared as if the word "dinner" were a new one. "Me?"

"At the moment, you're the only one in this room aside from some 2,000 tiny loyal spiders that probably follow you everywhere. But I'm not asking them if they're hungry because I know what the answer would be."

"As for dinner, I'm a vegetarian."

He almost felt like rolling his eyes. "You would be."

"You got something against people who refuse to kill animals for food?" She was back in Valkyrie mode.

"Absolutely nothing. Alice Treemont is more than a good friend of mine. Alice is a vegetarian. Alice is also an outstanding cook, and I love eating at her house. I'm open as far as food goes." He paused before adding, "And I'm open to new ideas, too, okay?"

Warily, she nodded.

"So are you letting me take you out to dinner or not?"

"Where?"

"Why are you making me miserable?"

The crooked grin was back. "Maybe that's my role in life."

"That's what the landscape looks like at the

moment." He sighed, but he was only pretending to be doleful. "Okay, the place I'm inviting you to is the Three Penny Inn."

Her eyes opened wide. "That's miles away. Besides, it's a flashy place."

"So?"

For the first time, all the bright bravado melted completely, and she even looked unsure. "So I've never been there. Anyway, I can't go to flashy places dressed like this, right?" Her hand waved, indicating the faded jeans, the plaid flannel shirt, and the walking boots.

"You can go change. We have time."

She was still looking uneasy. "I don't own any flashy clothes."

"Then, don't change."

"Why go there?"

"Because the food is really very good, the wine is excellent, there's no background music, people talk softly to each other, and they're polite. Sometimes, I'm in the mood for a little refinement, and tonight happens to be one of those nights. Does any of that sound good to you?" Why was it suddenly so important she accept his invitation?

"No, look…"

"Don't you dare refuse."

She scowled. "What…did…you…just…say?"

"You heard."

The scowl disappeared. There was a long silence. Then, she relaxed. "Okay, I'll do what I can. I have to go home first, shake up my cupboard, clean up a little."

"Sure. I'll take you there in my car."

"What for? It's only about eight hundred steps away."

"It is? Where do you live?"

"In the Mizpah Saloon."

Now he was staring. "In the Mizpah? Nobody lives there. Aside from Ned Stalks and his evil wife Trix. And a few mice."

"And me." She paused just long enough for the wickedness to return. "And quite a few very nice spiders."

"That, I don't doubt. You stay in one of the old hotel rooms upstairs?"

"Not exactly." She began shoving her arms into a wrecked green jacket. "I rent a room way up in the back. It was a place where they used to store old furniture, but I fixed it up. It's quite impressive now—if you like that kind of thing. Believe it or not, I even found a book on spiders in the bookshelf—an 1889 edition. That's incredible, isn't it? How many people do you meet in life who are interested in spiders?"

"Imagine that." He doubted that he sounded sincerely enthusiastic.

"And, by the way, Bud, Trix isn't really evil. Her bark is worse than her bite."

"Either I'm having a déjà vu incident, or this is a conversation I've already trudged through with Rose."

"What's that supposed to mean?"

"Oh, it's just me being a man of mystery."

****

The Three Penny Inn? Why had he invited her there? She stared mournfully at the clothes in the old wooden wardrobe. No way she could clean up enough for that place. She went to her dresser, pulled out a black sweater and a pair of black jeans: these would have to do. She even had a pair of black boots. Okay, she'd look like an undertaker, but so what? Who was she trying to impress? She knew perfectly well that if he'd had a choice, Lance Potter would never have asked her to go out to dinner. He'd been hoping that Rose was around because he was madly in love with that woman, just like all the men in the state of Nevada.

No, he'd invited her because he didn't want to be alone, she'd sensed that the instant he'd walked into the shop. He'd looked...what? Lost? Bedraggled? Miserable. And she'd come to the rescue by offering him a cup of coffee. "Idjit," she chided. She felt like kicking herself. Now, look what she'd gotten herself into. Right at this moment, he was waiting for her downstairs and was probably deeply regretting his invitation. Well, tough luck. "Except now you'll have to make polite conversation for the whole evening with someone who doesn't even like you."

Her hair. What was she supposed to do with it? Brush it, for one. Another style? What sort of other style? And why was she feeling like a teeny going on a first date? She clipped it back into its usual low ponytail, pulled at it until it fell over one shoulder, and puffed it up at the sides and the top. Okay, it looked a bit fancier that way. Sexier? No way.

She couldn't wear her old green rag of a coat, could she? No, she'd have to risk freezing to death in the jacket she wore in spring—one that was black, naturally. She grabbed it and headed back down to the bar.

He was watching her as she approached, his face unreadable. Unless that was a smug smile tugging at his lips.

"It's the black widow spider look," she said

quickly, before one single snarky word could cross his lips.

"No way. Don't black widow spiders have a red hourglass-shaped marking on their bodies?"

"Hey, good try. I'll make an arachnologist out of you yet. You're almost right. Yup, there's an hourglass marking, but it's on the underside of a widow's abdomen."

"And you…" he began.

She raised her hand to stop his words. "No way, Buster. No way I'm gonna pull up this sweater and let you take a peek."

He chuckled. "Phooey."

"You bet your booties. But you seem to be a nice guy, and you did invite me out for a flashy meal, so I won't keep you on tenterhooks: No, I don't have a red hourglass-shaped marking on my abdomen."

"A shame."

She squinted up at him. *Damn*, he was handsome. A real lady-killer. "Because you like toxic women?"

His chuckle turned into delighted laughter, but he managed to shake his head. "Hardly."

"Okay, Bud, we'll make a deal. Let's both admit I'm dressed like an *Aphonopelma mooreae*."

"Right." His grin was still broad. "And what's that when it's at home?"

"Hey, you've got a long way to go before becoming an honorary member of the Eight Legs Society. An *Aphonopelma mooreae* is a North American cobalt tarantula."

"And you told me you were a vegetarian. Don't tarantulas eat insects, caterpillars, other spiders, frogs, toads, and lizards, even small rodents and snakes?"

"Sheesh. I do have to admit you're not bad. But tarantulas happen to hunt in trees or on the ground. Since you've invited me to a restaurant, not to an open field, I'll try to behave myself."

"I doubt it."

"Did you really just say that?"

"Yup." Those very nice eyes of his twinkled. "I really did."

****

Once they got to the restaurant, she didn't look uncomfortable anymore, as if she'd accepted that chic would never be her thing, but what the hell did it matter? She was right, too. In those black pants and sweater, she was neither elegant, nor chic, but she did have a light, rangy way of moving that was amusing...and appealing, in some unusual easy-going way.

With her approval, they drank an excellent red wine, and she ordered an asparagus cream soup to start with, then roasted herbed vegetables on spiced Thai rice, and sprinkled with acajou nuts. He was amazed that the Three Penny Inn could come up with an interesting-sounding vegetarian meal at short notice. But she didn't seem in the least bit surprised.

"There are more of us around, these days. Good cooks have learned to adjust, be creative."

"Even in backwoods Nevada?"

"Good point."

"You're from New Jersey?"

"Nah. I was born and raised in San Francisco, but my first husband got a teaching post back in Paterson, and we moved there."

"How many have you had?"

"What? Husbands?"

"Yes."

"Only two. Once widowed, once divorced."

"Children?"

"A grown-up daughter. But we went our separate ways years ago."

"What sort of work did you do back there?"

"I was a librarian, but the budget was cut, and the library where I worked closed. I decided to change my life, come out here. I could do it, too, because I had a house I'd bought eons ago, and it was worth rather a lot all these years later."

"All of that must have been difficult for you."

She stared. "Difficult? How so?"

Didn't women love telling him how hard things could be? "Well, you know. It's the sort of thing that gives people heavy emotional baggage and all that."

Her cheeks puffed out with annoyance. "Ups and downs? Success and failure? That has nothing to do with baggage, Buster. It's called life. Don't try to dump me into some silly self-indulgent wimp category, okay?"

Chastised, he nodded. "It's a deal. If you promise to stop calling me Bud or Buster, I will."

She leaned back in her chair, scrunched up her eyes, and scrutinized him. "I don't know. I quite like calling you Buster and Bud. They both suit you, in some crazy sort of way."

"Have it your own way, Brunhilde."

Her jaw dropped. "Brunhilde, you said? As in Brunhilde, the Valkyrie?"

"You've got it."

"Hey, guess what, Bud? I think I'm gonna like

that." Then she doubled over, holding her stomach and guffawing heartily.

Grinning, he watched her. *Boy, oh boy. She really takes the cake.* "Good, Brunhilde. I'm getting sort of fond of being called Bud and Buster, too. Just as long as you're the only one who does it."

"We'll see about that. You know how rumors fly in a tiny place like Blake's Folly."

"I certainly do. I don't even live there. I live forty miles away, but I think every single resident knows the most intimate details of my social life."

Her eyes flashed evilly. "I can assure you, they do. But it's your own fault. You're a very good-looking bachelor, and you have a whole string of glamour-puss women that you usually show up with. Don't you think that sort of thing draws attention?"

She was right. The funny thing was, she seemed to know all about him, and he had never really noticed her...probably because she didn't fit into that glamour-puss category. Which was pretty stupid. Because he was having more fun talking to her than he'd had lately with those other women. With her, there was no pretense, no posing. And he was pretty sure she didn't expect anything from him, either.

"Tell me why you left New Jersey."

"Does there have to be a reason?"

"There usually is, when someone makes a big move like that."

"Yeah, you're right." She picked up her fork, stabbed an olive. "I guess you could say I wanted to put some distance between me and a guy named Joey."

"He was making trouble?"

Her eyebrows shot upward with surprise, and the

forked olive stayed poised in the air. "Joey? Make trouble? That would have been nice, for a change. But no, I was bored, and I couldn't explain that to him in a way he understood. I felt hemmed in, and I wanted out. He wanted us to sit around and grow old together. No way I'm ready for that stage. I probably never will be."

He had to chuckle. "I believe you. You don't mind living alone?"

"I *like* living alone," she said, annoyed again. She chewed the olive, put down her fork, and glared. "Are you one of those people who put everyone into comfortable little boxes?"

"I hope not. Sorry." Conversation with her was like dancing over a minefield on tiptoe. But he did enjoy watching her, seeing her lively reactions to everything. She could never have been pretty, but raw character certainly made up for that. "Okay. How did you get from New Jersey to Blake's Folly?"

"That's a really long story."

"Who cares? We have excellent wine to drink and good food to eat. I'll survive."

"You asked for it. It all started nine years after my parents divorced. When I was twelve, my father, Mike, decided to drum up a few gooey paternal feelings. My mother, Tracey-Ann, had decided I was a pain, so she shipped me off to him during the summer holidays. He had moved to Sacramento by then, and was living with this Jennifer bitch."

"Jennifer bitch?"

"You bet. She hated me being there, hated looking at me. She didn't like my father very much, either. The two of them spent all their time screaming at each other. The only good thing was, she had a daughter around my age, and we got along just fine. Neither one of us fit in with other kids. She was really shy; I was a tomboy. We didn't like organized group activities, or sports, or games, or dances—the sort of shit people are always telling you to go in for. But we were fascinated by everything around us, frogs, flies, flowers, snails. Especially spiders and snakes. Then, one summer..."

"Wait..." he interrupted. "I've just worked it out. The daughter you're talking about...did she happen to be Alice Treemont?"

"Got it."

"That's quite a coincidence."

"How so? There's no coincidence in this. Kids meet other kids all the time. In my father's version of the story, he met Jennifer in Blake's Folly, and they had a passionate affair. He looked her up again after he divorced my mother."

"You and Alice stayed friends over the years?"

"No way. My father and Jennifer were only together for four years. My father was a waste of time. He told everyone he was a serious author, but he never wrote anything but advertising copy. As for Jennifer, she nurtured big dreams about becoming a fashion model and screwed every man who crossed her path. After leaving my father, she ended up with some guy in L.A., doing peep shows before going on welfare."

Lance wasn't sure whether he should be laughing or commiserating. He chose being noncommittal. "Quite a pair."

She was the one who laughed. "Well suited, I'd say. Anyway, the last summer my father and Jennifer were together, they had a battle with smashed furniture, shattered plates, verbal violence, and a punching match—you know the kind of home-grown drama I'm talking about."

"Not from first-hand experience. I run before a relationship reaches that point."

"Wise decision." She nodded with approval. "Things were really bad, and they shipped us off to Alice's grandparents in Blake's Folly. That changed my life. With kids like Sly Grimes and Billy Flats, we scared ourselves silly in abandoned houses and old mines. I went out into the hills with Alice, and we snuck up on snakes and spiders, watched them for hours. It was magical, and I always knew I wanted to come back." She spread her arms. "So, I did."

"And so did Alice."

"But she's exceptional. Despite her slag of a mother, she put herself through university, did a doctorate in zoology, married a really awful Hollywood film mogul, became an actress, then gave everything up to return and work as a herpetologist."

"Why snakes and spiders? Because everyone hated them?"

"Because those creatures are outsiders, too? Maybe. But I think we both realized that, by using our minds, we could make our environment a better place. Thanks to Alice, I learned to respect western diamondbacks and sidewinders because the only thing snakes want, is to be left in peace. Like spiders, they're necessary to a healthy environment. But since humans really enjoy being ignorant, they kill both."

"As a veterinarian, I'm confronted by ignorance on a daily basis."

"I'll bet you are."

By the time they left the restaurant, a silvery frost

had covered the ground. The moonless indigo sky was sprinkled with shivering stars, and in the far distance, he heard a coyote's echoing howl. With surprise, he realized he hadn't felt quite this relaxed in a long time.

"Funny, isn't it?" he said as they drove back.

"What's funny, Buster?"

"The sort of people who are coming to live in Blake's Folly these days. Everyone expected the place to die out like any ghost town, but Jace Constant, Alice's man, is a writer from Chicago. And Jonah Livingstone, a half-Paiute geologist and amateur cellist, came here to be with Rose. And now you've come back after all these years. You think you'll stay?"

"Why wouldn't I? There are still a few cranky characters around, and I like chewing the fat with them. Everywhere else, folk have been ironed out by television and the movie industry. They want to conform, and they're proud of it."

"You don't own a television."

"Watch mediocrity?" Her voice was scathing. "Let myself be anesthetized into buying junk food, cars, perfume, and soap powder? My life isn't long enough to waste like that."

"I'd forgotten I'd invited a Valkyrie to dinner. Do you always question everything?"

"Yes," she said simply.

"I was afraid of that." He sighed but knew that laughter and admiration weren't far off. "I suppose you have to be an original to be drawn to a place like Blake's Folly. Didn't you and Alice ever play with dolls? Have doll's houses?"

"Dolls and doll houses? You really see someone like me going in for that sort of crap?"

"You have to admit, that's what little girls usually play with," he countered.

"There you go again, trying to slot me into one of society's comfortable little boxes."

"No. I'm not really. I'm just dipping my toes into unknown waters, seeing what that feels like. I've been hanging around with the little box people for far too long."

****

Just as he'd feared, it had been a big mistake bringing her out here. Caro was a lawyer, very sophisticated and savvy, and she would never relax in a place like the Mizpah, would never find cranky characters amusing: Pa Handy, who lived in a junkyard; Mick Fletcher, a tough cookie who'd lived a hundred miles from anywhere with a toothless old trapper fifty years her senior; Zeke who, whenever he'd had too much to drink, bored everyone with his story of rats that had rotted in the town's old water tank. Right now, Nate Wetly was jawing on about how he'd held off thieves with a shotgun while standing in the buff in the snow, and a tipsy Jane Grimes was extolling the talent of her son Sly, the worst singer and guitar player in the modern world.

To illustrate how true that was, Sly and the other members of the Old Boy's Band were now on stage and waging a full-scale war on old rockabilly hits.

Jonah Livingstone winced. "Even though we're two thousand miles from Tennessee, I can hear poor Elvis rotating at breakneck speed in his grave."

Lance laughed, glanced at Caro again. Her smile was tight, her eyes hard. Even the way she had dressed was wrong: suede pants, a silk blouse, and high boots—

pretend casual. Chic didn't count for much in this local world of sagging trousers, worn jogging suits, and run-down shoes, but friendliness and a smile did. Caro was acting as though someone had dumped her into a grim western, one that sentimental cowboy films and romance novels hadn't prepared her for. Inwardly, he groaned, wondered how to make the best of a bad situation. He didn't feel like leaving, but he couldn't send her all the way back to Reno in a cab, could he?

He looked around the room, hoping to find someone Caro just might find entertaining, then caught sight of the Valkyrie, way over there, sitting up on the stairs near the back of the room. Removed from the general hubbub and watching people. Another crank.

Had she felt his eyes on her? She looked his way, then her eyes shifted to Caro, and back to him again. She looked...amused? Something else, too. Mocking? As if she'd sussed out the situation, had seen how uncomfortable he felt, how condescending Caro was. Well, so what? Why did that make him uncomfortable? What did Brunhilde have to do with him? With his life?

The Old Boys gasped on. Turning so he didn't have to see Caro's displeasure, Lance started enjoying himself again. Finally, after a chord so dissonant it must have been inspired by Burg's atonal *Lyrical Suite*, Sly put down his guitar. Grabbing the microphone, he began talking in the strange and incomprehensible pseudo-southern lingo he had invented for his on-stage persona.

"Raht-ee, ny-ow foo-ohks, we haive a spayshul trit tonight. Our own Rosie Badger hays ah-greed to sing a few sayongs wiff Lu-oo-ooke on pe-yano for th' baine-fitt and Bay-ill on druhms."

Rose stepped up onto the stage, as beautiful and glowing as always. Lance had heard her perform at the Russian Club and knew how talented she was, and when her liquid sugar voice slid into a sultry "Why can't you whisper that you love me," everyone fell silent. She sang three more numbers before stepping off the stage, although the applause continued. Like everyone, he was entranced, and Caro noticed it.

"You look like you're in love with her."

Was she going to make a scene? He hoped not. But he wouldn't lie either. "It's true that, although I'm not in love with her, I certainly love her."

"Well, you'll have to explain the difference."

No, he didn't, but he couldn't blame Caro: Rose was a hard act to beat. She would stir up jealousy in any woman.

Once again, he caught the Valkyrie's eye. She was still way over there on the stairs, and she grinned at him, jerked her chin in Rose's direction, then gave a very definite thumbs-up. Well, okay, not every woman.

****

It was a grim evening of icy rain and violent wind, but here inside the shop, with its soft lamplight, deep shadows, and velvety fabrics, life was cozy. Hearing the door open, Lucy looked up from her book. Saw Lance come in, stamp his shoes on the welcome mat.

"She's not here," Lucy said before he'd even asked. Just so he didn't make himself too comfortable before being disappointed.

"I can see that."

"Right."

"And if the 'she' you're referring to is Rose, I wasn't looking for her."

"Oh. Well, if you're looking for Jonah and the others, everyone's meeting up over at the Mizpah tonight. Some sort of powwow."

"Sounds interesting, but I wasn't looking for them either."

"Then, let me guess. You're here hoping to find just the right vintage dress because you want to change your style. Go in for something soft, silky, with a little swing to the skirt."

Chuckling, he shrugged off his wet coat, hung it on the antique coat rack near the door. "As tempting as that sounds, I'll check into it another time. Tonight, the reason I'm here is to see you."

"Me?" She stared at him, lost for words. But not for long. She never did know how to keep her wise-ass mouth shut. "A real glutton for punishment, aren't you."

"Obviously." He sat down on the chair opposite hers.

"Okay, Bud. Out with it. Why me?"

"For your conversational skills."

"Give me a break." She felt strangely flattered. Not that she'd let him know it.

"I'm serious. Talk to me. I've been taking care of sick animals all day long, inspecting herds of cattle, refusing to cheat on blood tests, arguing with a dishonest rancher, and fighting the weather. I decided that the best, most enjoyable antidote to a rough day like that would be to come see you."

"And that's because?" *Damn.* He even looked like he meant it.

"Because you make me laugh."

"I'm the local clown?"

"No, Brunhilde. Because you're interesting and totally irreverent. And because conversation with you never goes the way anyone expects it to."

"Oh." She stared at him.

"Don't tell me you're lost for words."

"I am, actually."

"Impossible."

"Almost impossible, I'll give you that."

"Where are your dogs, by the way? I know you have three of them."

"I bring them to Alice's when I work here. As you've seen, they're shaggy. Very shaggy. They shed so much that all the dresses in this place would look like fur coats if I allowed them in."

"That would please customers."

"Depends on how kinky they are."

His snigger joined hers. "Okay, bad start. Let's try and find some normal topic of conversation. What about spiders. I know you have a lot to say on that subject."

"That's normal conversation?"

"Still making my life miserable?"

She winked with something that looked too much like delight. "It's fun, doing that."

"Go on, tell me more about spider mating."

"Are you serious?"

"Completely. And afterward, when you close up shop here, we can go over to the Mizpah, meet with everyone, have a drink and some dinner."

"Is than an order or an invitation?"

"Your call. In the meantime, how can you differentiate between male and female spiders?"

"I can't believe you really want to know this."

"Go on."

"Okay, then." She shrugged. "Females are usually larger. Some males are tiny, and they can climb all over the females without being considered prey. Not only that, but the males have enlarged palps so you can identify them easily."

"And males always get eaten?"

"No, that's what people always say, but it isn't true. However, spider courtship can be quite a lengthy and nerve-wracking affair because males have to convince females to mate with them and not see them as prey. Sometimes, a male will wait for days before a female considers him desirable. Some actually bring presents, a wrapped-up fly, for example. Others dance in front of desirable females, waving their legs and posing, or making drumming sounds."

"Those sound like techniques any man could use with reasonable success, although I'm not too sure about the wrapped fly. What about spider babies?"

"Some mother spiders carry egg sacs around with them. When the babies hatch, they take care of them until they leave the nest. One famous nineteenth-century entomologist, Jean-Henri Fabre, saw bereaved spiders comforted with cocoons of other spiders, or pellets of cotton wool."

"In other words, the more you know about them, the more appealing they become. Why do people hate them?"

"I suppose because some people associate spiders with the things they consider repulsive like lice, dirt, slime, and dust. Arachnophobia can also be linked to sexual problems and sexual repression. What's definitely true, is that half of all women but only ten percent of men are afraid of spiders." Her eyes glinted naughtily. "Now try and work that fact into a discussion about sexual equality."

****

When they arrived at the Mizpah, Jonah, Alice, Rose, and Jace were sitting with Sly Grimes, Mick Fletcher, and Ma Handy in the back room. Rose's dog Noodle came over to greet him with soggy enthusiasm.

"Why are you all looking so grim?" Lance asked as he scratched Noodle behind his ears.

"We're getting on in years," Jace informed him. "We're turning into old-timers, and old-timers don't like change."

"Speak for yourself, Grandpa." Alice squeezed his arm affectionately. "But we've just discovered that Big West Tours is putting Blake's Folly on the map for ghost tourism and trekking tours, and we're worried about the problems that will bring."

"The state of Nevada has some six hundred ghost towns to tempt people," Lance said. "With luck, the worst devastation might pass Blake's Folly by."

"Ghost tours are nothing more than tourist-trap circuits with gruesome murder stories told by part-time actors wearing cheap period costumes and talking in fake mobster or vampire accents."

Mick Fletcher removed the toothpick from her mouth, an act reserved for life's more portentous moments. "Because of them Big West Tours, Ned and Trix are mumbling on about renovating the upstairs bedrooms. Probably want to turn the whole place into a fern bar, so it's goodbye to the Mizpah we know and love."

"Fern bar?" Rose's mouth twitched. "Complete

with frozen daiquiris and Harvey Wallbangers? Power dressing and padded shoulders? How wonderfully retro."

"Well, I ain't drinking no beer in no fern bar."

"I believe you."

Alice repressed a smile. "I think the immediate effects are more worrying than the threat of fern bars. Out at the nature reserve, we see what tourism brings: tons of rubbish left out on the hills; damaged habitats; people churning up the countryside with four-wheel drives, dirt bikes, and ATVs; or cranks shooting down animals."

Jonah leaned forward. "Don't forget the homogenized history Big West Tours pumps out, with fake shoot-outs and invented heroes. It's not just because I'm part Paiute, but you'd think someone would occasionally mention the government-subsidized Native American genocide carried out by volunteer military companies, state militias, and federal troops. No one talks about the Native women who were raped, then sold with their children as slave labor, or the vendettas against Mexicans and Californios, or the lynched Chinese workers."

"You're absolutely right, Jonah. Can't we find some way of minimizing the damage? Turning tourism into something educational? Letting people know what really happened?"

"One thing we can do is open a library," Lucy suggested. "A place where people can get information, where we could hold lectures, debates, and conferences. As a former librarian, I could get things started. Besides, there are so many empty historic buildings we could fix up and use, and I'm sure lots of local people would be happy to participate in the project."

"Where would we get money to buy books?"

"We don't need money." Lucy flipped her hands in the air. "All we have to do is put the project on the Internet, ask for used books about the West. So many libraries are getting rid of their stock or are closing down, I bet we'll be swamped in no time."

"That's probably true." Lance loved her enthusiasm. She was certainly an original and a crank, but a very nice one.

****

On Sunday morning, when most people were still lazing in bed, Lance had been called out to Joe Lansing's ranch to help a mare with foaling problems. Now, it was ten o'clock and the free day stretched in front of him—unless another emergency cropped up. He thought of things he might enjoy doing—walking, visiting friends, letting himself be spoilt by one of his charming ladies, going home and relaxing, having lunch somewhere. Rejecting them all, he swung off the main highway and drove down into Blake's Folly.

He saw Lucy, perched on a barstool, as soon as he entered the Mizpah. "There you are."

Her eyes teased. "Why does that surprise you, Bud? I'm always here. This is where I live."

"That isn't what I meant. You could have been out in the middle of nowhere, tracking down creepy crawlies."

"Nah. It's cold out there and about to rain. I thought it would be more fun to sit inside, chew the fat with a couple of the old guys. Pa Handy was telling me how, when he was born, his father was out prospecting, and when he received word his wife had had a baby, he stole a speeder and rode it all night over the rail line, just to get to her."

"You do a lot of that, listening to stories?"

"You bet. That's why I like living in a saloon-cum-hotel. I don't believe in ghosts, but believe me, this place can be pretty spooky. Sometimes, I get the feeling the walls are watching me. I wish I knew more about the people who passed through here, how they felt, what went on in those rooms upstairs. There's no way I'll ever get that information, so to compensate, whenever someone tells me something interesting, I write it down."

He looked at her speculatively. "I was certain you'd do something like that."

"Why were you certain?"

"Just a feeling. Don't ask me where it comes from. What do you do with the things you've written down?"

She looked uncomfortable. "I try turning them into stories that I send off to magazines. Then I sit and wait for rejection slips. Occasionally—very occasionally—someone likes what I've done and publishes it. I suppose I'm just a frustrated Nell Murbarger. You know who she was?"

"The writer who did those articles about Nevada and the strange characters who lived here?"

"That's the one. Back in the 1950s, she got to meet and interview women like Josie Pale who lived alone in a junk-filled shack in the Black Rock Desert, some ninety-eight miles from the nearest town. Before that, Josie had lived in mining towns, run boarding houses, and defended her own claims at gunpoint. Nell was quite an original too, bumping down dirt tracks in an ancient car and not being afraid of anything, unlike many people today. But wait." Lucy stopped, held up her hand, palm outward. "Before I start rambling on and on about the world going to hell, tell me why you're in town this early."

"I was called out to assist a mare with placentitis."

"Ah." She looked blank.

"Today's problem was a foal born inside the fetal membrane. And since I was only fifteen miles from Blake's Folly, I thought I'd come here and look for you."

"Why?"

"To ask you if you'll have lunch with me at my house, forty miles away."

Her eyes opened wide. "You've come all the way here just to invite me to have lunch way out at your house?"

"Don't fall off your chair with surprise, Brunhilde."

"Well, you have to admit this is a bit unexpected." Then, some of her usual swagger returned. "That means I don't have to get all gussied up?"

"Exactly."

"And, if you don't mind me asking, why at your house?"

"Because I'm a good cook."

"You are?"

"How about you? Are you any good at it?"

She sniggered. "I can make a mean lettuce and tomato sandwich. I'm not bad at toast and butter, either."

"I'll bet skills like those come in right handy."

"I thought I was the one who was always supposed to be snarky."

"I'm learning how much fun snarky can be."

"Okay, then." Her brow crinkled. "I have another question: why me?"

"Because you're fun," he said simply.

"Oh." She stared at him, her face unreadable.

"Cat got your tongue?" he asked smugly.

****

She moved from room to room, inspecting everything. "I never pictured you in suburbia.

"Neither did I. I just took this place because it was close to the clinic, yet near enough to the empty plain that I love. After I settled in, it just seemed too complicated to move."

"You have a television."

"You don't approve."

"What does my approval have to do with it?"

"Okay, why are you against television?"

"Don't you know that passively watching television greatly reduces our capacity for critical thought? The images change so rapidly our brains can't process them, so we end up not thinking things through, but ready to accept any form of propaganda, buy any product, and feel miserable or diminished if we don't."

"That's pretty radical."

"Yeah. But it's true, too. Besides, nobody has to subscribe to my point of view, and I don't mind at all." She shrugged. "Okay, change of subject. What's for lunch?"

"Pot luck. I didn't plan this out, so you'll just have to take what comes."

"Which means?"

"How about if I make a homemade pizza with my own crust, with black olives that I cure myself, some excellent mozzarella, and all the vegetarian trimmings you'd like."

"You're on."

"You even get to help."

"You might regret it."

"Don't worry. I'll be watching your every move."

While he mixed the whole-wheat flour, olive oil, water and yeast for the crust, she pitted olives, chopped fresh garlic and parsley, sliced tomatoes, a green pepper, zucchini, and fresh mushrooms. He put all the vegetable ingredients in a bowl to marinate in olive oil, and spiced them with freshly ground black pepper, dried rosemary, fresh basil, salt, and a little squeezed lemon.

Lucy watched with approval. "I'm already drooling. Where did you learn to cook? Does it come with being a veterinarian?"

"No." He put the dough in a warmed oven to rise, poured out two glasses of wine, then settled on a stool opposite hers. "Cooking is an antidote to being a vet."

"What's that supposed to mean?"

"It takes me away from the stress of the job. If a veterinarian doesn't have an out, then life can seem very dreary. This is a profession with a high suicide rate, which is why we've created support groups." He shook his head, as if trying to make bad thoughts disappear, and took a sip of wine.

"Go on," she urged.

"It's not really pleasant conversation."

"So?" She sensed he needed to talk. That this was the real reason he'd invited her. "Make an exception. I'm always the one who does the blabbing. This time, it's your turn."

He looked at her. "Okay, then. Well, just as a start, we work very long hours and we have a lot of territory to cover. I can't tell you how many social engagements and invitations I miss because an emergency call comes through. Also, I love all creatures, but euthanasia is just part of the daily routine, because of neglectful owners, or owners who can't—or won't—pay for treatment, or because shelters are overcrowded. Nothing is worse than killing a healthy, hopeful animal. I can't tell you how many times I've explained to people that letting their cats and dogs have litters is a bad choice. In this country alone, some three million cats and dogs are put down every year." He looked down at the counter. "Let's not even get started on all the wild animals shot for fun, or run down and left to die slowly out in the wild."

"How did you choose to be a veterinarian?"

He smiled faintly. "I don't know if I chose anything. My father was a vet, so was my grandfather, my great-uncle, and one great-grandfather, too. It was what everyone expected me to do."

"But?"

"We're very isolated in this profession. That's good for me, because I tend to be an introvert, but dealing with people can be hell. There are the hostile owners who sue us because, quite incorrectly, they hold us responsible for a sick pet's death, or those who think we should treat their animal for free, who threaten to kill the poor creature—or us—if we don't. Others launch hate campaigns against us on the Internet. That's very common these days." He stood, went over to the stove.

"So cooking is the positive way you have of

dealing with stress?"

"Just like walking in the desert is, or meeting with everyone in the Mizpah." He took out the ball of dough, began flattening and stretching it. Looked over at her, amused. "Or just talking with you, Brunhilde. Somehow, you always manage to make me laugh, or argue about something. Or you talk about things I don't know. Best of all, you force me to think, analyze. I like that. A lot."

Trying not to show how touched she was, she tried to joke: "Which is why you always want to feed me up. Just to keep the machine going." But the words almost caught in her throat. She wished she hadn't started to really like him.

****

Deidre's apartment was spacious and designer decorated. There was a preponderance of white: white carpets, white walls, white furniture, and a white baby grand piano that she never played, although she did plan to get around to taking lessons…when she found time. The only splotches of color were the abstract paintings on the walls. How fortunate she didn't like house pets. Lucy's very shaggy dogs came to mind; the three of them probably shed enough fur in a week to build another whole dog. But why the hell was he thinking of Lucy? He was in a different world here, in Deidre's chic world. And just now, Deidre was approaching with a glass of chilled white wine, while tempting smells emanated from the kitchen.

She settled beside him. She was striking, with her chin-length dark hair, her large eyes, and her supple figure. And that silken caftan-like robe she was wearing suggested her bedroom, the one where this evening was bound to end up, as it always did when they were together.

"I don't understand what the problem is, Lance. What's wrong with ghost tours? They're fun."

"History isn't just fun." He noted how caustic he was sounding. "There might be amusing moments, strange turnabouts and historical surprises, but it should also be pertinent. Handing out ghost-detecting machines, convincing people that photos of dust are really ghosts, and recounting grisly murders aren't relevant activities. There are plenty of places where tourists get that already. They don't need it in Blake's Folly."

"So you want local history to be dry and dull, just so people are bored?"

"Why dry and dull? Knowledge can be stimulating, and learning something new is gratifying. The winning of the West has always been presented as a glorious achievement, the triumph of civilization over savagery, but it wasn't that at all. Human casualty, genocide, and environmental destruction were part of that history—a large part."

"What's the point of underlining it?"

"Because that's the only way we can change things. Look at the problems we're facing today: ecological problems, a whole new range of viruses, global warming, plastic continents forming in all the oceans—all the collateral damage of the consumer society. If we hope to do better, we can't keep on catering to pure silliness and ignorance."

Deidre's nose wrinkled. "You're sounding very radical, darling. Don't forget that people go out to places in Nevada because they want a fun excursion.

They're not going to school, and most of us hated history when it was doled out to us. We want the romantic stuff, the handsome cowboys riding to the rescue. We want brave cattle ranchers defending their territory."

"Another myth. The fight was between big powerful ranchers who formed stock-grower's associations and used violence and terror to drive out small farmers."

"Oh, Lance. Why are we even arguing about this? Come. Dinner is ready, and I've made something I know you'll love." She put her wine glass down on a crystal coaster, stood, held out her hand. "No one cares about those old battles."

"They only want the Hollywood version," he muttered as he took her hand and rose to his feet.

She made no comment as they headed into the dining room, but he saw her annoyance. He was sounding very much like Brunhilde. Being a Valkyrie, even by proxy, certainly did ruffle fur.

Where was she now? Sitting with a few locals in the Mizpah, "chewing the fat," or cozied up in that back room of hers, reading? He sat down at Deidre's elegantly set table, glanced over at the alluring lady and wondered if he could find a good excuse for leaving early.

****

"You're spending more time than ever out here in Blake's Folly," Jonah remarked. He and Lance were standing on Alice's broad veranda. The night was cold, and unhindered by the glare of city lights, billions of stars were spattered dust.

"Very true. I am." Had anyone noticed that the last

few times he had particularly sought out Lucy, aka Brunhilde. Nothing special in that. He had always maintained steady, very satisfying friendships with women. Lucy was simply his most recent friend. "I come here for the interesting and unusual company. And if you're wondering...yes, you're included in the category."

Jonah chuckled. "Good."

"Actually, I do have ties to this town. My great-grandmother lived here for all of her adult life, although her children preferred life in Carson City. However, with your Paiute genes, you have a much stronger claim to the area than I do."

"Claim?" Jonah's eyebrows rose. "My Paiute grandfather married my grandmother, who was a half-Paiute schoolteacher from Idaho. Her own father came from Sweden. As for my mother's parents, they came from Italy, so the mix is quite complete. Maybe it's the Italian genes that have influenced my musical taste—as you know, I play the baroque cello in an amateur orchestra, and the music we play originated in Italy in the 1500s. Now that I've been influenced by Rose, I'm also playing with Reno's Russian balalaika orchestra."

"Isn't that the beauty of a melting pot? Think of who we are out here—Native Americans, Latin Americans, Anglo and Afro-Americans, Asians, Europeans, and Middle-Easterners. That mixed culture is part of our history, too, but we don't hear much about that side of it."

Jonah shrugged. "So, back to square one? The importance of eliminating fake news?"

"Yes. How people love hanging on to myths. Do you remember all those stories about red-haired cannibalistic giants living in the Lovelock Cave? Despite the lack of proof and all the debunking, people still want to believe in their existence."

"And in the Sasquatch, and the Abominable Snowman, although no bodies of those creatures have ever been found, no scat, no hair samples, nothing. And the films purporting to show them were rigged."

"What about Native American myths?"

"Those were different. They were a way of understanding the earth's past, interpreting the paleontological and historical objects people saw all around them."

"Today, when people can't understand what's going on around them, or feel they've lost control over their lives, or are just plain scared about the future, they invent supernatural beings and powerful outside forces to convince themselves there's a reason for disorder."

"Whereas, there's an easier, more satisfying way to solve the problem," Jonah said, his voice solemn. "By doing something that has meaning. It doesn't have to be creating a world-shaking piece of art, or building another skyscraper. Just something that gives a sense of personal satisfaction, something small, amateur, something that doesn't involve making money. I became a career geologist because that's what I wanted to do, but I didn't foresee the frustrations I'd be faced with. I soon realized I needed a meaningful bolt-hole. That's what got me playing and interpreting music."

He's right, Lance mused. Having a bolt-hole, doing something that isn't stressful. It was an excellent idea, one that appealed to him. But what could he do? He was no musician like Jonah, no singer like Rose, no defender of snakes like Alice, no story-writer or spider fanatic like Brunhilde. His parents were genealogy buffs, but although the information they gleaned was interesting, he had no wish to chart family trees. He enjoyed cooking, but it wasn't an overwhelming craze. He did love taking care of animals and rescuing those he could, but what, outside of work, did he really feel passionate about? His affairs with women were lighthearted and uncommitted; and although he'd once sincerely enjoyed working with wood, building, repairing things, helping friends with restoration work, he hadn't done any of that for years. Why had he let the interest drop?

He stared out into the night, out to where, beyond the little rise, the uneven silhouettes of wrecked shacks lumped together on the horizon. Knocking some of those back into shape might be fun. But in a hopelessly ruined semi-ghost town like this one, where the hell would anyone begin?

****

Inside the bashed-up trailer, the air was fuggy with smoke, and the television was blasting out the bleeps, buzzes, and canned laughter of a quiz show. Elsa Badger and Alf Paltry sat on a sofa bed staring at him, drinking glasses in one hand, burning cigarettes in the other.

"Doan know what you'd want the place for. Nothin' much left," said Elsa. "All my daughter's fault, too. Rose never took care of it, just let the whole thing fall down. Jus' thinks of herself all the time, can't be bothered with me and Alf, here. Don't come to see if we need anything, just makin' money hand over fist in that second hand shop of hers and not giving a damn about me that raised her up."

265

Lance waited patiently. He'd met many people like Elsa, those who blamed everyone in the world for their dissatisfaction, who refused to accept that they alone were responsible for the wrecks they had become. He also knew that Elsa had done little to raise her daughter: Rose's two grandmothers had, thankfully, done that job.

"Why you innerested in the place allava sudden?" Elsa's little eyes set in a puffy face were hostile. She must have been a true beauty in her younger days with the sleek blonde hair, flawless skin, and large expressive eyes her lovely daughter had inherited. There was no trace of that loveliness now. Heavy drinking and chain smoking had taken their toll. "What's it to you anyways?"

"The Red Nag is a landmark. It shouldn't be allowed to fall down."

Squashing her burning cigarette in an overflowing ashtray, Elsa shook out another from the pack nestled beside her thigh, lit it with a shaking hand, took a deep drag and began coughing, a choking racking sound.

Lance waited until she caught her breath. "I'd like to restore it."

"What for? Whachya gonna do with it? Can't make money with an old saloon these days. It was a pretty flashy place when I was a little girl, with all them divorcees filling the state. That's all done with now. Coulda done something with the place if my ex hadn't run off with a slut half his age. Shoulda known better when I married a man like Barney Badger, but what do you expect? I was eighteen at the time. Said he was gonna manage my career for me, take me places."

Beside her, Alf only grunted. He was, at the very best of times, a man of no words.

Lance knew he had to be patient. If he refused to listen to the list of complaints, there would be little chance of achieving his goal.

Elsa's eyes narrowed with suspicion. "You ain't thinkin' of givin' the old place to that lousy daughter of mine?"

"There would be no reason for me to do that. I'm not rich enough to buy up buildings and give them away. No, I'd like to come live in Blake's Folly. I'm getting pretty tired of commuting."

Elsa still looked reluctant. Violently jealous of her daughter, she probably knew of his close friendship with Rose.

He was running out of persuasive arguments. "Look, I'm willing to pay your asking price, and I doubt you'll find another person who will do that. I'm sure you wouldn't mind having some money in the bank for a few luxuries." Luxuries like slot machines, booze, and cigarettes. Lance eyed the heaped clothing, crumpled paper, and straining garbage bags on the floor; the over-filled ashtrays and empty vodka bottles covering every flat surface and threatening to topple floor-ward at a sneeze.

"Yeah, I see what yer lookin' at. Cash will get me and Alf outta this wreck, into somethin' flashy." Elsa began another volley of coughing. Caught her breath and took a slug of vodka. "You got ready cash?"

"Yes, I said I have."

"You got an attorney?"

"I do."

"Okay, you got yourself a deal. I'll sell the old place to you. Just let's get this over with as fast as possible, before my daughter finds out what I'm doing."

****

She was strolling through the back streets with her three dogs when she caught sight of Lance in the distance. He waved, came toward her. She waited, her heart beating a sure and happy patter. *Damn.*

"I figured I'd find you somewhere."

"Of course you did, Buster. You know what Einstein said about matter being neither created nor destroyed."

"Here we go again, missing the boat for normal conversation." He was smiling, a good sign.

"If that's a problem…"

"No way it's a problem." He crouched down, patted all the dogs, ruffled their fur.

"Really?" Was he making fun of her? No, he didn't look like he was. His eyes were warm, and he looked happy to see her. For some silly reason, that made her feel inexplicably shy. And very good.

He stood. "You want to go on an outing with me?"

"What kind of outing?" Her voice sounded funny to her own ears, perhaps because what she really wanted to do was bounce and boing around with pure delight on the crumbly roadway.

"How about a walk?"

"I was already walking," she said, trying to sound like her usual, sarcastic self and not hopelessly besotted like the many thousands of other women draped around Lance Potter's feet.

"Yeah, I caught that. I was just wondering if you'd like to leave town for a few hours, get out into the big, wide world."

"Wow. How big and wide are we talking here?"

"About twenty miles. Do you ever get that far on

your own?"

"Sometimes. I had a car, but it died right after I arrived. I've never replaced it." Now he was looking at her as if she were a lunatic. "Yeah, I know. Don't say another word, because I can read your thoughts: if you don't own a car in this country, everyone thinks you're underdeveloped. You should hear the kind of crap I take when people find out I don't own a television."

"People out here, in Blake's Folly?"

"Nah. Come on. Alice and Jace in front of a TV? They spend their lives writing, researching, and reading. And Rose and Jonah spend all their free time practicing music together. Everyone else spends life in the Mizpah, telling tall tales, or betting on snail races. That's why I like this place."

"Without a car, what do you do when you feel like getting out?"

"This isn't the end of the world, you know. This might surprise you, but the Greyhound bus passes on the main road twice a day. I take that whenever I want to go to what crazy people call civilization." Her chin jutted defiantly. "Say what you like, but taking public transportation is also being ecologically responsible."

"Did I criticize you?"

"Not yet." She peered at him. He didn't look like he was about to begin, either. He was still looking warm and happy.

"So are you going to climb into my car, come with me out into the wild woolly world?"

"You bet, I am. What about the dogs?"

"They'll have to stay. I'm afraid they might chase away some of the wildlife." He looked as if he expected her to protest.

Why would she? "Okay, we'll take them over to Alice's."

"I have to warn you: it will be cold out where we're going."

"So what? I'm wearing gloves, and a scarf, and even if this jacket looks like hell, it's warm as toast."

His eyes took in the frayed cuffs, the worn collar, and the torn strips on the sleeves, but she didn't see disapproval. Only amusement. "Warm is what's important."

They headed out along the rutted lane, passing long-abandoned cabins and empty lots filled with waving, yellowed grasses where, once upon a time, buildings had stood and life had buzzed.

"Don't you sometimes wish you could step back in time, see how things were?"

"Often. But I don't think we'd find the experience very pleasant. Life was hard, back in the old days, and justice was rough. Rustlers and bandits were left to rot on gibbets right here, on the edge of town."

"I don't think the dog fights, dog and badger baiting, or cock fights would be tolerable sights either. Funny how priorities have changed over the last century. Once, social injustice and terrible working conditions were the main things that had to be tackled. These days, we're still confronted by those problems, plus quite a few others that nobody imagined back then: urban sprawl, contamination from old mines, from the solvents and aviation fuels on military bases, and the irreversible damage that was done out at the bomb testing ranges."

"And because of the high cost of cleanup, those issues will never be dealt with."

Beyond the low hill where prickly scrub and dry tufts scratched the sky was Alice's yellow house. "Just think. This place was home to wealthy mine owners, and they were ruthless people. I met Alice's grandparents the one summer I came to stay out here. By then, their money and status was gone, but not their pretensions."

"My great-grandmother also lived here," Lance said. "For well over thirty years."

She stopped abruptly and gaped at him.

"Don't look so surprised, Brunhilde. My great-grandmother married Alice's great-grandfather, Alexander Treemont."

"You and Alice are related?"

"No, it was Alexander's second marriage. They married very late in life and never had any children. Alexander's two sons from his first marriage—Edward, Alice's grandfather, and his brother William—never wanted to recognize their union. They even refused to come out here while my great-grandmother was alive."

"Why?"

"Because theirs was a prominent mine-owning family, and my great-grandmother was only a businesswoman. Before marrying Alexander, she'd owned a brothel."

"Isn't that interesting. And how small the world is."

"Yes, the world is incredibly small, especially in incredibly small places."

She laughed. "True."

****

He took her out to the flats near the old Spieler Mine, now a conservation area. It was a favorite place of his, and he wanted to share it with her. Why? Because he liked her company, and he didn't know any other women who would enjoy this sort of outing on a freezing cold afternoon. *Are those the only reasons?*

In the far distance, soft hills rose gently, without dramatic topography, high crests, or startling colors, were broken only by outcroppings of shale and exceptionally tall sagebrush. Following a faint trail, he led the way to a gulley, well out of the bitter wind, and they made themselves comfortable on a natural seat of slate. "This is where I like to come and observe the local residents."

"Like jackrabbits? I love watching them dart here and there through the brush."

"We might hear a few horned larks and black-throated sparrows, too. And if we're very lucky, we'll see sage grouse."

"Lucky?"

"The population is falling because of over-hunting and pollution. Environmental groups are petitioning for them to be listed as an endangered species."

"Have you ever seen coyotes or mountain lions out here?"

"I have. They come for the antelope, mule deer, and rodents."

"Alice and I spotted them closer in to Blake's Folly, but that was way back when we were in our teens. It's pretty rare to see them now."

They sat for a long while. In the air was a heady tang of dried vegetation, and the broad sky was a delicate blue. Stalks shivered, grasses rattled percussively, and distant whirlwinds curled, lingered briefly, then settled.

"Look. Over there." He pointed to the west where the white rumps of two buck antelopes flashed against the scratchy landscape.

"How nice." She even looked like she was enjoying herself.

"You're not bored, just sitting here?"

She turned to him, her eyes happy. "Why would I be bored? Do you know how many times I've sat in some desolate place with Alice, just staring at a crack under a rock? Then, after endless hours, a head will appear, then a whole huge snake slides out to warm itself in the sun. Do you know how rewarding seeing something like that is? How exciting?"

Touched, he looked away. Stared out at the yellow and beige landscape most would call monotonous. "What do you think of this sort of scenery?" He half expected the usual snide comment.

"I think it's gorgeous," she said simply.

"You mean that?"

"Why would I lie? What would be the purpose of it, Bud?"

"I suppose you could be trying to be polite."

The corners of her mouth twitched. "You caught me doing that yet?"

He had to chuckle. "Always a first time."

"Just let me know when that time comes around, okay?"

"I guess I just have to get used to being with an honest person."

"What's there to get used to?"

"Being able to count on someone." And realized how grateful he felt, for her presence, her steadiness, and her camaraderie. For the good feeling of just sitting close beside her. He wished he could slip an affectionate arm around her shoulders but wasn't certain such a gesture was right. Would she read something deeper into it? Perhaps, more importantly, he should analyze his own feelings first. Lucy Barnes was very different from the women he'd always known, had always been with. She was a world away from his usual light-hearted affairs.

Pushing aside his confusion, he took a deep breath. "Out here, I feel perfectly happy, as if the world is at my fingertips. Friends and colleagues always ask why I don't go back to Carson City where I grew up, or move to Reno and stick with small animal practice—you can make a hell of a lot more money treating house pets in a city. But I want to spend as much time as possible in places like this." He laughed wryly. "That's why I'm often in Blake's Folly."

She furrowed her brow. "I don't see the connection."

"Don't you? That's where I find people who see the value in preserving what we have, who are willing to live simply. They're out here because they also need this wide open space, or because, despite the vagaries of history, they've hung on."

"Amen."

****

In Alice Treemont's kitchen, the walls had a yellowish hue that only time could bring. A chaotic assortment of ancient wood-burning stoves vied for space with heavy wooden tables, rustic chairs, vast cupboards, shelves lined with old glass bottles, and green plants. And just outside the frame windows, a stark desert night quivered in the moonlight.

"I might have come up with one good idea," said Jace. He, Lance, Rose, Jonah, and Lucy had just finished a delicious dinner of mushrooms and herbs simmered in red wine, and served over smoky hunks of polenta cooked in one of Alice's wood-burning ovens.

Lucy glanced over at Lance, saw he was relaxed, happy, and her heart warmed. She loved seeing him like that. Even though he did more listening than talking at these gatherings, she realized how important they were to him. To her, too, and she wondered how she had managed to live in other places for all those years. Without these people now sitting around the table. *Without knowing someone like Lance.*

Yes, she and Lance were no more than friends, but that sort of friendship was worth a great deal. What if, eventually, he fell in love with someone else, with one of those many women in his life? That was bound to happen one day, and when it did, it would be heartbreaking. Yet, the eventuality had to be faced.

Despite herself, and quite against her better judgment, he had worked his way into her heart. *A big mistake.* She had to make certain he never discovered how she felt. If he did, that would ruin everything, she was certain of it. He wouldn't feel comfortable with her anymore. He would feel in some way responsible for her emotional state. Besides, it was only a childish crush, wasn't it? She'd recover from it quickly enough. Inwardly, she shook herself. No, it wasn't a crush. It was far more than that. Something quite wild and secret.

Jace leaned forward, resting his arms on the table. "Once, many years ago, when I was covering the old silver and gold mining towns in Canada, I ended up in the town of Cobalt. It's not exactly jumping with activity, and most of the buildings are recent and definitely lacking in style. But back in 1906, silver was so plentiful that trains called *The Millionaire Express* and *The Cobalt Special* arrived daily with rich investors. Immigrants from the Balkans, Russia, Poland, Scotland, Romania, Wales, and Ireland worked in the mines for low wages because they dreamt of having a stake in the luxury and wealth. The silver soon ran out, but the finest buildings—grand hotels, an opera house—were still standing in the 1970s. Until two fires completely destroyed the town. It's not beautiful now, but to show what the place used to be like, there are panels on all the streets with old photographs and information about the town's history. Perhaps we could do something similar."

"I think that's a brilliant idea," Alice said. "We could include data about local wildlife, and explain why the ecological balance has to be kept."

"And add in a few juicy stories about local people," Lucy said. "They'd make Blake's Folly seem more real."

"Dr. Laura Waterton, one of the trustees at the Conservation Area, grew up here. I bet she'd tell us a few tales. Her family once ran the Mizpah."

Lance nodded with enthusiasm. "And, Alice, you still have quite a few of your great-grandfather's paintings of the old mines. We could photograph them, use them to illustrate what went on here. Besides, he was quite famous in his day, and people still know his name."

"Thanks to Susanna Lacey, your great-grandmother." Alice turned to the others. "Susanna was

Alexander's second wife. She once owned the very flashy, high-class brothel here in Blake's Folly, but after marrying Alexander, she sold up and became his agent. She's the one who made him famous."

"Interesting," said Jonah. "I've heard about the town's famous brothel, but I never knew Alexander's wife had been the madam."

"Their marriage caused quite a scandal, not only because of her profession and the difference in social standing, although that was shocking enough, but they were both around sixty years old. Back then, that was considered old age, too old to marry and have an exciting life."

"My paternal grandmother was one of the prostitutes who worked in Susanna's brothel before marrying my grandfather and becoming respectable," Rose added. "She described what it was like, the rooms, the clients, the atmosphere, the luxury."

"You're lucky. I wish I'd been around to hear my great-grandmother's stories," Lance said. "Susanna was a very old lady when my parents first came out here to meet her, but her memory was intact. Her daughter, my grandmother Margaret, never told my father that Susanna was still alive and well in Blake's Folly."

"How annoying. Why not?" Lucy asked.

"Because Susanna was a real rule-breaker, an unconventional lady with a scandalous past." Lance chuckled. "She told my parents that, before becoming a madam, she had been a prostitute in the Red Nag Saloon, then a dance hall girl in the Mizpah. She'd also had two out-of-wedlock children—a son, and a daughter—with two different men. Her daughter Margaret, a very priggish housewife, was ashamed of being illegitimate, and she didn't want anyone to know. Unfortunately for her, both my parents are genealogy fanatics and amateur historians, and they made my grandmother's life a misery until she'd agreed to spill the beans about Susanna's whereabouts."

"Lance?" Lucy moved to the edge of her seat. "Hold on a minute…"

The corners of his mouth twitched. "Are you having trouble with this, Brunhilde?"

"Do you know when Susanna's children were born?"

"I do. Her son Clarence was born in around 1885, and he became a veterinarian in Carson City. My grandmother Margaret was born in January 1890. She married Thomas Potter, her half brother's partner, in 1910." He raised a quizzical eyebrow. "What part of the story is so shocking to you? You look like you've seen a ghost."

"You couldn't be closer to the truth." Her voice sounded weak and flabby. Everyone around the table was watching her now. "Okay, listen. You know my father, Mike, came out here to Blake's Folly in the 1970s. The reason he came, was to clear up a mystery. Of course, he didn't clear up anything. He got side-tracked, screwed Alice's mother, then ran home to my mother who was pregnant."

"What fun," said Rose. "So what was the mystery?"

"It had to do with my great-grandfather. Way back in the 1880s, he had been one of the journalists working for the local paper."

"*The Morning Sun.*"

"That's right." Lucy nodded. "And while he was

278

here in Blake's Folly, he met my great-grandmother Hattie. They got married, headed for the Yukon. Eventually they settled in San Francisco where my grandmother, Arabella, was born. One day, during the First World War, an old friend showed up in my great-grandfather's office, told him he had another child, also a girl, and that she'd been born in 1890, just months after he'd left town with Hattie."

"That must have been a bombshell. Who was the mother?"

"A dance hall girl."

Jace guffawed. "Your great-grandmother must have been pleased by that bit of news."

"She never found out. My great-grandfather never dared mention it—probably because Hattie was one of those hard-nosed domineering pioneer women, and she ruled the roost. By the time Hattie died, my great-grandfather was a sick old man. But, because he wanted to know what happened to his former lover and their daughter, he told my grandparents the story and asked them to investigate."

"Did they?"

"No, they didn't want to get involved. After my great-grandfather mentioned that the woman had also had another illegitimate child, my grandparents decided she was bawdy, immoral, and would ruin the family name."

"Why didn't your great-grandfather contact his old friend again, ask him for information?" Rose asked.

"He couldn't. The friend had shipped out and become a volunteer ambulance driver on the front line. He was killed at Passchendaele."

"Strange...I heard that my great-grandfather's

brother also died there," said Rose.

Lance was grinning from ear to ear. "And now, Brunhilde, you're about to announce that your great-grandfather's name was Westley Cranston, right?"

She stared at him. "Right. Yes, it was. And you know that because…"

"Because Westley Cranston also happens to be *my* great-grandfather."

"I did realize that was a possibility. When you mentioned that your great-grandmother was a former prostitute and dance hall girl, when you told us your grandmother Margaret was born in 1890…" Lucy's hands flapped, a meaningless gesture. "You see what I mean about seeing a ghost?"

"If you'd mentioned Westley's name and told me the story, I'd have filled you in a while back."

"You're absolutely certain Westley Cranston was your great-grandfather?"

"Of course, I am. I said that Susanna was quite unconventional. She never hid who the fathers of her children were, although, back then, quite a few other women with illegitimate children didn't either. Because they couldn't legitimately use the father's last names, they often added them to the child's legal name. Susanna named her son Clarence Bally Lacey because his father was a man named Jim Bally. My grandmother was Margaret Cranston Lacey."

"Incredible." Lucy sank back in her chair. "Your grandmother was the person my father was looking for when he came to Blake's Folly."

"Since we were living in Carson City, not Blake's Folly, he never would have found us."

She scratched her head, still strangely dazed. "This

is an awful lot to take in."

"Didn't your father ever mention Susanna Lacey's name?"

"Only that she was known as Sassy Shuckie, or something else quite vulgar."

"That's close enough," Lance confirmed. "Her professional name was Sassy Sookie."

Lucy let out her breath. "Actually, it's quite a sad story. My great-grandfather never forgot her. He told my grandfather that he'd always loved her, but he died in the 1950s without ever seeing her again."

"That's a shame, because he could have. Susanna was still alive and in good health, back then."

"A story of lost chances?"

"Yes." Lance's voice was unusually gentle. "Lost chances."

"Lovers never meeting again. Missed opportunities."

"You know what's really crazy?" Alice said. "Susanna married Alexander, my great-grandfather, but no one in my family ever talked about her. She was a taboo subject."

"But you know the story?" Jonah asked.

"That Susanna had been a prostitute and had had two children? Yes, but only thanks to Lance who told me about her a few days ago. My mother, Jennifer, once hinted at it, although I wonder how much she really knew. Probably not a lot. Still…Jennifer did briefly live with Mike, Lucy's father. Mike wanted to know who the mysterious missing mother and daughter were, but obviously my mother never bothered telling him anything."

"Incredible." Lucy goggled. "Jennifer was certainly

no goody-goody, so why would she hide something like that?"

Alice laughed. "Because she pretended to be a very classy lady. I once heard her claim she was a Bavarian duchess, a direct descendant of the Wittelsbach dynasty. A grandfather who had married a former prostitute, dance girl, and brothel owner with two illegitimate children wouldn't fit into the pretty picture."

Lucy turned to Lance. "Hey, Bud?"

"Yes, Brunhilde?" His eyes were twinkling again.

"This means we're related, right?"

"We are. But only very distantly."

"Nothing original in that," Rose chirped. "In a town like this, everyone married everyone's cousin, half brother, or half sister, or uncle, aunt, or great something-or-other. That's why there's such a collection of crackpots all in one place."

****

Early the next morning, Lance parked his car in front of the Mizpah. Lucy was waiting for him, a thick woolly scarf around her neck, and her raggedy jacket zipped up tight.

"Okay, Brunhilde. You ready?"

"Bright eyed and bushy tailed. Don't you want to come inside, have a coffee first? It's only seven o'clock."

"No time."

"What's going on, Bud? Why did you ask me to meet you this early?"

"Because I have to drive out to a ranch that's sixty miles away. Then, I have to return to the clinic, which is another forty-five miles in the opposite direction. If I manage to get back to Blake's Folly this evening, it will be very late, and that's only if another emergency doesn't crop up. In other words, this is the only time of day that I'm free."

She tried not to feel disappointed that he wasn't staying. "Free for what?" she asked as they headed down the street.

"Free to show you something. I'd like to get your opinion before I sign my soul away at four o'clock this afternoon."

"Yes, Doctor Faustus."

His brow furrowed.

She laughed. "Don't worry. It's just librarian stuff, selling your soul to the devil and all that. I'll fill you in sometime."

"You do that."

"How far are we going?"

"Only two streets over."

"Good, because it's freezing out here."

The sky was hazy, the air crisp, and winter's pale sun turned frozen ruts into glimmer. There wasn't a soul about this early, but even at the best of times, wandering folk were rare in Blake's Folly. They passed buildings long abandoned, their windows boarded up, their signs faded, and their clapboard weathered rusty brown: the old laundry, the general mercantile, the bicycle shop, an ancient gas station. At the former barbershop, the striped pole hung at a crazy angle.

Lance came to an abrupt halt. Looked down at her. "Okay, here she is."

"She?"

"The Red Nag."

"And so? I know perfectly well this is the Nag, the

saloon that belonged to Rose's grandfather. That still does belong to her mother."

"Maybe not for long."

"What does that mean?"

"Because…" He paused, and a slow grin worked its way across his mouth. "Because I'm going to buy it. Rose's mother has agreed to sell. Finally."

"What? This place?" She stared up at the building. It was a wreck. Most of the glass in the windows had disappeared, and the wooden sidewalk had more holes than excellent blue cheese. She didn't dare think about the condition of the roof. Still, she knew enough to keep her mouth shut; after all, he hadn't asked for her opinion. Not yet, anyway.

"Come. I'll show you the inside."

"You have the key?"

"I do."

They stepped into what had been the saloon's main room. It was completely empty.

"Unfortunately, Rose's mother sold off the furniture as well as the paintings and the mirror that once hung over the bar."

Lucy went to the middle of the room and looked around. Yes, it was pleasingly proportioned and did have potential, but the whole place needed a hell of a lot of work. "Okay, tell me why you want to buy what's left of a ruin."

"For several reasons. The first is because I'm a sentimental guy, and I like the idea of coming back to a place once inhabited by my great-grandmother. The second is because I like the idea of moving to Blake's Folly. My friends are here. This is the countryside I love. I also really like working with my hands, doing carpentry, so I'll enjoy fixing the Nag up and restoring it to its former glory. I've spoken to Jace—he worked on Alice's house and knows a lot about old wood—and he said he'd be happy to help me. And, finally, I suppose I just like having a project, creating something."

Yes, she could understand that, but fixing up this place was like starting from scratch.

He came over to where she was standing. "Well, what do you think?"

"Not much left." Which was a nice way of saying there was almost nothing left.

"There are a few old tables and chairs in the back. And an ancient rusted-out washing machine that must have been incredibly modern in the 1940s."

"That's certainly a plus," she said in her usual smug way. Then she ordered herself to cool down, stop being the crusty old dame, for once. This place represented something to him, something important. That was why he had asked her to come and see it. "The floor is beautiful—or will look beautiful once those planks get a good coating of linseed oil."

He quirked an eyebrow. "How do you know?"

"Because I've worked on old houses. I restored my own house back East, and I know that old wood loves warmed linseed oil mixed with turpentine."

"I never pictured you knowing stuff like that."

"There you go again. Slipping me into a comfortable little box."

His brow furrowed. "You wouldn't fit even if I did try."

She couldn't stop herself from reaching over, taking his hand, squeezing gently. "Nah. Don't worry.

It's just me, my big mouth, and my usual know-it-all self-defensive act." Reluctantly, she pulled her hand away. Damn, but it felt nice touching him. His skin was warm, amazingly soft for a man who often worked out in the open. She tried to regain her composure. "Look, if you're really set on buying this place and fixing it up, you can count one hundred percent on my help, too, okay?"

"Sure. That would be fantastic." He smiled, but she noticed how he was staring at her, his eyes flickering with something very much like uncertainty. The silence stretched out endlessly. When he finally spoke, his voice was strangely hushed. "Well, go on."

What the hell was happening here? "Go on with what?" She took a deep breath. "What were we talking about?"

"About restoration, I think."

"Oh, yes. Right."

He was thinking hard, she could see that. About what? Then he closed his eyes, reached up and rubbed his forehead with his fist. Dropped his hand.

"Lance? Is there something wrong?"

There was another brief silence. When he opened his eyes, the confident, jocular gaze was back. So was the sexy lazy smile. "What's with the Lance bit? I thought I was Bud. Or Buster."

"Yeah." She relaxed. "It's just that you looked incredibly odd for a minute, and you had me worried."

"That's the problem."

"What's the problem?"

"The way we read each other. The way we get along. The way I like being with you and looking at that extraordinary face of yours." He hesitated, but only for

286

seconds. "The way I keep watching out for you all the time, wanting to see you. Do things with you."

She took a deep breath, told her heart to stop pounding so wildly. "Where are you going with this?"

"Then you reached over, squeezed my hand."

She crossed her arms and prepared for war. "That bother you, Bud?"

"Stop scowling, Brunhilde. Yeah, it bothered me, all right. I liked it. A lot. Didn't you?"

Cautiously, she nodded.

"And when we were at Alice's, your words 'lost chances' clued me in, told me that something's missing. Let me know there were a few things we had to work out. Finally."

"Work out?" Then she saw the intensity in his face, saw it mix with something like wonderment. And tenderness.

"That's right. Accepting the way I feel. Finding out what your feelings are. Questioning where we stand, the two of us, you and me. Where this should go."

"Ah." Her throat closed; her knees wobbled.

He stepped closer, reached out, ran his fingers along her cheek, let his thumb caress her lower lip. "Look, lady, I would love to continue this conversation, but I have to get into my car and hit the road. Could we meet up this evening? I'll try and get here as early as possible, but since I have to work with animals, I might be tied up. Is that okay with you?"

"Sure it is." She tried to sound as cool and impersonal as she usually did. Then she melted completely. "I'll walk back to your car with you, but only if you'll let me link my arm through yours. Just to see how that feels."

"Pretty forward, aren't you?" But he was laughing, a low rich sound.

"That's what being a Valkyrie is all about."

"It is."

They stepped outside into the luminous icy morning, and he took a deep breath, let it out slowly. Catching her arm, he tucked it through the crook of his and pulled her more tightly against him. "How's this for starters."

Excitement skittered along her nerves. "There really is more to come?"

"If we're lucky."

She saw his eyes were astoundingly clear, and her heart swelled. "I'm willing to bet that we are."

He gazed down at her. "So am I." Then bending his head, he took her mouth in a kiss that began with gentleness and deepened into pure joy.

****

He was late getting to the Mizpah. The room was crowded, Sly and the Old Boys were finishing their last set, and the noise level was almost intolerable after the drive through the dark silent night. Alice, Rose, Jace, and Jonah were sitting at their usual corner booth, but Lucy wasn't with them, and a wave of disappointment rolled over him. Perhaps she was in her room. He could always go upstairs, knock on her door, and ask her to join him down here.

Which was when he saw her, sitting on the stairs. As usual. Yes, that's where she'd be. Keeping out of the general hubbub, removing herself from the crush, the chaos, but still participating. He made his way through the throng, wanting to be beside her, to get there as quickly as possible, a needle drawn by a hefty magnet.

She grinned at him with that crooked wicked grin he'd become quite addicted to, and he settled one step lower down. Why was he feeling shy? Hadn't seduction been his modus operandi with women since adolescence? "You don't like mixing with the crowd, do you?"

"It's more that I prefer small groups where conversations go somewhere. In a crowd, you have to shout to be heard. If you have to do that, you know the discussion isn't going to be interesting. It probably gives some people the feeling of not being alone, of being in the center of things where life is happening, but it's not my thing."

"Not mine either."

"I figured that was it."

He was amused. "How did you figure it?"

"Because you like being alone. Because you like doing things alone. Because you like people, but you don't say much in a group. You prefer listening. I also noticed how you like being with animals, stroking them, talking to them, being perfectly satisfied with them nuzzling you and not answering. It's very cute. And touching." Then she pushed at his knee with one hand. "Hey, I don't want to get all sentimental and lovey-dovey on you, Buster."

"Don't mind if you do." He reached out, ran his hand slowly down her thigh. "Because I think it's time for us to get used to being in that stage. We've done the best chums bit for long enough, don't you think?"

She gawped at him wordlessly for a minute. Then her lips quirked into a sweet smile. "For starters, you can keep on caressing my thigh like that. It feels mighty nice."

"It feels mighty nice to me, too," he said, touched by the unexpected sultry note in her voice. Reaching for her hand, he raised it to his lips, kissed it, folded her fingers through his, and kept them there. "You feel like continuing this discussion in a place that's a little more private?"

"Where did you have in mind, Buster?"

"You ever going to show me that room of yours?"

Her eyes were amused. "Getting straight to the point?"

"If I want something badly enough, that's the sort of thing I do."

"Good to hear." Her voice softened. "I happen to be one of the things you want badly?"

"Very definitely. I want to hold you in my arms. I want to kiss you. I'd really like to make love with you, but that sort of wanting has to be mutual."

"For sure, it does." There was a faint flush on her cheeks. "I can guarantee it is mutual. It has been for a while now."

"Really?"

"Really. I just didn't think it was going to happen."

"It's taken me by surprise, I have to admit that. Isn't it nice we've finally come this far?"

"It certainly is. I have to warn you, though: it's pretty damn cold up there."

"We'll see."

"Uh-uh." She stood. "We won't see anything. I *know* it's cold. *You're* about to experience it."

His heart full, he followed her upstairs and down a long corridor, a place of deep shadow, lit only by one weak bulb at the far end. The noise of the crowd could barely be heard up here, and the air had a strange unfamiliar quality to it, as if it held secrets. The closed doors of former bedrooms only added to the mysterious feeling. Was this the place where his great-grandmother had stayed? Had one of those rooms been hers? He'd never know, for the saloon must surely have changed considerably since those days, and renovation vanquishes ghosts thoroughly.

Lucy stopped when they reached a small landing. "There's no light beyond here. Just keep holding my hand. I can do this blindfolded." She led him down another passageway, almost completely dark, pushed open a door at its end.

He found himself standing on the threshold of a large square room lit by a table lamp, but deep with shadow. In one dim corner, Lucy's dogs dozed beside a heavy wooden desk. Beyond, were shelves of old books, a few armoires, and two tattered leather armchairs—the sort of things people left behind when moving into new decades. A broad window looked out onto a silent courtyard with lean-tos once housing exhausted beasts, long-vanished carters' and cowboys' nags. Yes, he could understand Lucy's fascination with this place. It was a room filled with phantoms and stories, where the very air, although perfectly still, gave the strange feeling of movement. Unless he was letting his imagination run away with him, letting turbulent feelings override common sense.

"Do you like it?" She was waiting for his answer, and hoping it would be a positive one, he could see that.

"Oh, I do. But I'd probably like it even more in summer. Right now, the place is freezing."

"I warned you. And if you think this place is cold,

wait till you spend a night in the Red Nag."

"I'm not crazy. I'll be putting in a few comforts before I become a full-time resident there."

"Just putting in a few window panes will be ten out of ten on the comfort scale," she scoffed.

"Okay, there's no heat up here. Is there plumbing?"

Her crooked thumb pointed back out into the corridor. "Out near the landing and dating from the 1950s. That room is really tiny, with a minuscule window up near the ceiling—the sort of place they might have put the hired help in. Of course, there were no baths and toilets at all when this place was first built."

"How do you sleep in a place this cold?"

"Beds are warm."

"Is that an invitation? Because that's the way I'd like to take it." He closed the distance between them, reached out and cupped her shoulders.

"It is."

"More good news. There's also something else."

"What's that, then?"

"What you told me. About not being a real Valkyrie because…"

"Oh yeah. That…" She started laughing again. "The bit about not being a virgin?"

"I'd like to find out for myself." But even he noticed how gritty his voice had become. And how her laughter ceased. Pulling her into his arms, he found her lips, feathering them gently at first, getting used to their shape, their warmth, the feel of her mouth against his, before deepening the kiss and pulling her closer still. She folded herself against him, opening to him, curling her arms around his neck.

He pulled away, just slightly, loving the softness of her gaze, the sweetness he read in her face. "That was even nicer than this morning."

"Wasn't it just."

"How about if we take this a step further. Do the negotiating in a warm bed. You did mention something like that, didn't you?"

She laughed. "Sure I have a bed. It's right over there, in that little nook just behind the curtain. But it's not a warm bed. At the moment it's as cold as this room is."

"Climbing into it is going to be hell." But he was already reaching under her sweater, pulling it up over her head.

"Only for a little while. Then things will probably warm up quickly." She reached for the buckle of his belt, undid it, and began unbuttoning his jeans.

"Now, who's moving fast?"

"Come on, Buster. Let's not waste time or we'll die of exposure. Let's get naked as fast as possible, then run to the bed."

"Good idea."

The sheets were as icy as she'd said they would be. He pulled her close, seeking her warmth, running his hands over her smooth skin, caressing the softness of her breasts, loving the feel of her, the scent of her skin, the rich odor of her thick hair, the way she curled her leg over his hip and arched into him, moving closer still, until their intimacy touched. Lovingly, she returned his caresses, exploring him, meeting his kisses with returning passion, opening to him with a soft whimper as he moved between her legs and delighted in her wet warmth. He paused for only a moment. Looked down at her face caught in the feeble light.

"Are you okay?"

Reaching up, she cupped his cheek tenderly. "Very much so. This feels strangely right, doesn't it?"

"Oh yes, that it does." Then, certain of her feelings, of his own, he forgot about words and entered her deeply, savoring her response, her movement, her breath, the joy of them finally coming together. As if, in some strange uncanny way, fate had brought about this very moment.

****

He looked around the room, took pleasure in dust motes floating like slow-moving stars on the cold air, in early sunbeams dancing across the old wooden furniture. Here, in bed, things were warm, toasty, and the redolence of sex was heady, enticing, conjuring up the night's passion, and the tenderness. Still, one glance told him Lucy was thinking hard. *Typical*. "Okay, what's going through your head now?"

"I think I've just been hit by a realization—either that, or I'm just mixing things up. But this situation suddenly seems very strange."

"Being here in bed with me?"

She smiled, kissed his shoulder. "No, that isn't strange. It's very nice."

"Only nice?"

"Stop fishing, Bud. But okay, it's wonderful."

"Exactly what I was thinking. So what's the problem? What's strange?"

"You're the great-grandson of Susanna Lacey and Westley Cranston, right?"

"Right. We did work that out two nights ago, as I recall."

"And I'm Westley Cranston's great-granddaughter."

"Right again. So what's strange?"

"What if we're completing a love story that didn't work out a hundred and thirty years ago?"

"We'll never know."

"True." Her brow furrowed. "What if, right at this very moment, we're in the same room they were in together? What if this is the same bed?"

"It's possible, I suppose. But those are other things we'll never know for sure."

"By the way," she said, trailing lazy fingers over his shoulder, "do you know what the word Mizpah means?"

"No, but I'm sure you do." He caught her fingers, kissed them one by one, nipping the soft skin gently.

"Stop trying to distract me. Why are you sure?"

"That you know the answer? Because you wouldn't have asked me if you didn't. Also because you're the librarian. Looking things up comes with the mentality."

"Maybe, but listen. This is important. The word mizpah has changed meaning a lot over the centuries, but it now stands for the strong emotional bond between people who are separated either physically or by death. Don't you think that's interesting? It could refer to Westley Cranston and Susanna Lacey."

"It could. But we're making up for it."

"Also true…" Then suddenly, she pulled herself out of his arms and sat up abruptly. "Hey, wait a minute. If all this is true about our ancestry, if we really do have the same great-grandfather, Westley Cranston, that means this is incest."

He had started laughing.

"What's so funny?" she challenged.

"Only yesterday, I was pretty sure you'd bring that up."

"What?" She stared down at him. "How could you know I'd bring it up? How could you have known yesterday, that we'd end up in the same bed last night?"

He grinned archly. "Instinct."

"Well, well." She cocked an eyebrow. "Aren't you proud of yourself."

"Yup." He pulled her back down under the covers and into his arms. "So I knew I had to do some looking up, for a change. I wanted to know what constitutes incest, because you have to argue about everything, and I had to be armed for the attack."

"Attack," she scoffed.

"Listen to me. If we shared the same grandparent, we'd be cousins, not what's called kissing cousins. However, we go back one generation more. Therefore, we're kissing cousins. Even if we were going to make babies—which we're not, since we're pretty well past that age—we can do exactly what we want."

"Well, since we've already done it…"

"Several times, as I recall."

"That's certainly true."

"And we did it very well, don't you think?"

She only laughed, but he saw her cheeks turn pink, and he caressed the line of her stubborn-looking jaw, again taking pleasure in seeing her, touching her, in the strange feeling that this was exactly the right place to be. That he would always feel that way with this woman. He took a deep breath. "Okay, Brunhilde. Time for some serious stuff."

"Such as?"

"Discussing what the next step is. For example, are we going to keep on doing this sort of thing?"

"Is that what you want?" Her voice held a new note, uncertain, doubting.

"You bet it is. And you?"

She squeezed her eyes shut. "Well, I know I won't interest you for very long. I'm not your sort of person."

"Really? What's my sort of person?"

She still hadn't opened her eyes. "You know. Painted toenails, perfume, hair dye, Botox, appointments at a tanning studio, that sort of thing."

"You're sure that's what I like?"

She opened her eyes. Finally. "Well, isn't it? I mean just from observing."

"Then, what am I doing here with you?"

"Maybe you're out for a little *nostalgie de la boue*."

"Okay, literary lady, want to tell me what that is?"

"An attraction to low-life culture. To lying around in the mud for a while."

He looked surprised. "That's how you see yourself?"

"Of course not. But it might be how you see me…in some subconscious way."

"And this, from the very woman who insists she isn't complicated. Who doesn't believe in emotional baggage, or in being slotted into some self-indulgent wimp category." He sighed. Then rolled on top of her, imprisoning her under him, catching her wrists in his hands, leaning on his elbows and looking down at her. "Okay, Brunhilde. Here's the question in full. Are we going to stay together or not? Because the long haul is what I want. The only problem is, you need two people wanting the same thing if being a couple is going to work."

She managed to extricate her feet, hook them around the backs of his legs. "Well, if that's what you'd like…"

"It is. And you?"

"It's very certainly what I'd like, no doubt about that."

"Good to hear," he said, his voice husky.

"So guess what?"

"What?"

She grinned. "That means we're on, Buster."

VI

Watercolors: 2022

"This must be the wood," she said thoughtfully to herself, "where things have no names. I wonder what will become of my name when I go in?"
~Lewis Carroll, (1832-1898),
Through the Looking-Glass

On the afternoon Alice Treemont climbed into her attic, a blustery wind made old house eaves ache, and the sky was dense with ominous cloud. She'd come up here hundreds of times over the years, to this world of rejected objects: abandoned toys, canes and umbrellas, worn boots, broken chairs, and old steamer trunks from the early days of travel. In one corner, she'd even stored her own suitcases, those filled with clothes from the past, from her frivolous younger days as an actress. How many times had she vowed to give everything away, or to sell the flashiest garments in Rose Badger's second hand shop?

Today, she hoped to discover what might have been overlooked—a diary, old letters, photographs—for her curiosity had been piqued. She might even find more of her great-grandfather's watercolors, ones that Edward, her profligate grandfather, hadn't sold off to pay for his superficial life of overindulgence. She remembered Edward as a droll man, one who had never grown up or accepted responsibility. At least, he had left this big yellow house to her, and that was an exceptional gift. But the paintings?

When she was a young child, Alexander's work had hung in every room; and each year when she returned for the holidays, she'd seen how much had disappeared. Those walls with their empty spaces seemed as sad as a mouth of missing teeth. How she'd cherished them, the scenes of the bleak desert, the ruins of worked-out mines, the abandoned shanties where people had once laughed, and the shaley plain with its beautifully drawn snakes and lizards. Perhaps it had been Alexander's delicate touch that had sparked her own interest in reptiles, her decision to become a herpetologist. But by the time the thriftless Edward had died, few of those paintings remained.

She knew Alexander's work had been highly valued, that his personal touch and technical excellence had made him a favorite with collectors. People had also told her that he had been a generous, open-minded, liberal man, and she now knew that must be true: hadn't he ignored his sons' censure, defied convention and married the infamous Susanna? But what sort of life had he led? Where had he gone? What had he seen? What had excited him? *There must be much more to the story. How time erases memory so completely!*

Here were old chairs, an ancient trunk filled with forgotten rolls of wallpaper, a commode that could surely be polished up and brought back to its former glory, a clock long out of repair, an ancient typewriter. This rocking chair—who had sat in it? When had it been banished to this place of chill and gloom? In one dusty coffer, she found tiny carvings in wood: animals, real and imaginary, and skillfully defined male figurines. Where had these come from? Who had made them? Here, too, were crates of elaborate plateware, hand-painted tureens, and gravy boats, all relics from boomtown days, when large dinner parties had been given, when the town's wealthy elite had never doubted their own immutability.

Just as the rain's sharp spatters hit the old tin roof, she found a wooden box under the joists. Inside, a stiff brown folder held thick sheaves of paper—not diaries, or letters, but sketches and watercolors. Why had they been pushed out of sight? Had they been forgotten, or not been considered marketable? Alice's hands trembled as she lifted each one, held it to the frail light of the attic's window.

Yes, here was Alexander's sure touch, his unique artistic vision, but these were no desert scenes. Some had been drawn in foreign places—Rome? Moscow? France, perhaps Germany. Dusky street scenes, small shops, portraits of people long gone, their compelling stories shining through deep shadowing. And a woman, always the same one, far from young, with a heavy cloud of silvery white hair, a proud arching torso, and a gentle mouth made for laughter. Wearing the stylish clothes of eighty and ninety years ago, she sat in cafés, in restaurants, lingered in a corridor's penumbra, or posed, graceful and sensual, beside the open windows of this house. In one particularly poignant watercolor, her unbuttoned white blouse and loosened hair suggested all, but revealed nothing. Was it the tilt of her head, or the expression in her eyes that spoke of erotic passion? Perhaps it came from the artist's desire, his deep love.

Clear to see why these works had been pushed up here. Although too valuable to destroy, they were too personal. They showed, without shame or reticence, the lusty, human side of Alexander's life that her grandparents had preferred to reject, to banish.

Surely this woman he'd painted so often was Susanna Lacey. It couldn't be anyone else.

What had she been like? How had she felt? What had she seen? Where had she come from? What was her story? Alice shook her head. *I'll probably never know.*

A word about the author...

Writer, photographer, social critical artist, and occasional actress, J. Arlene Culiner was born in New York and raised in Toronto. She has crossed much of Europe on foot, has lived in a Hungarian mud house, a Bavarian castle, a Turkish cave-dwelling, on a Dutch canal, and in a haunted house on the English moors.

She now resides in a 400-year-old former inn in a French village of no interest where, much to local dismay, she protects all creatures, especially spiders and snakes. She enjoys incorporating into mysteries, narrative non-fiction books, and romances her experiences in out-of-the-way communities and her conversations with strange characters.

Web site: http://www.j-arleneculiner.com

Blog: http://j-arleneculiner.over-blog.com

Storytelling Podcast:

    https://soundcloud.com/j-arlene-culiner

The support of readers in getting the word out is essential to authors. If you've enjoyed this book, please leave a review, and thank you for your contribution.

Thank you for purchasing
this publication of The Wild Rose Press, Inc.

For questions or more information
contact us at
info@thewildrosepress.com.

The Wild Rose Press, Inc.
www.thewildrosepress.com

www.ingramcontent.com/pod-product-compliance
Lightning Source LLC
Chambersburg PA
CBHW070050030726
47506CB00002B/421